The Red Badge of Courage

Stephen Crane

THE EMC MASTERPIECE SERIES

Access Editions

SERIES EDITOR

Laurie Skiba

EMC/Paradigm Publishing
St. Paul, Minnesota

Staff Credits:
for **EMC/Paradigm Publishing**, St. Paul, Minnesota

Laurie Skiba
Editor

Paul Spencer
Art and Photo Researcher

Lori Coleman
Associate Editor

Chris Nelson
Editorial Assistant

Brenda Owens
Associate Editor

Kristin Melendez
Copy Editor

Jennifer Anderson
Assistant Editor

Sara Hyry
Contributing Writer

Gia Garbinsky
Assistant Editor

Christina Kolb
Contributing Writer

for **SYP Design & Production**, Wenham, Massachusetts

Sara Day
Partner

Charles Bent
Partner

All photos courtesy of Library of Congress.

Library of Congress Cataloging-in-Publication Data

Crane, Stephen, 1871–1900.
  The red badge of courage / Stephen Crane.
    p.   cm. -- (The EMC masterpiece series access editions)
  Summary: During his service in the Civil War a young Union soldier
matures to manhood and finds peace of mind as he comes to grips with his
conflicting emotions about war.
    ISBN 0-8219-1981-4
    1. Chancellorsville (Va.), Battle of, 1863 Juvenile fiction.
[1. Chancellorsville (Va.), Battle of, 1863 Fiction. 2. United States--History--
Civil War, 1861–1865 Fiction.] I. Title. II. Series.
PZ7.C852Re 199b
[Fic]--dc21   99-36549
                                                                                CIP

ISBN 0-8219-1981-4

Published by EMC/Paradigm Publishing
875 Montreal Way
St. Paul, Minnesota 55102
800-328-1452
www.emcp.com
E-mail: educate@emcp.com

Printed in the United States of America.
        11 12 13 14 15 xxx 17 16 15 14

Table of Contents

Stephen Crane

Stephen Crane (1871–1900) lived only twenty-eight years. In that time, he earned a reputation as a great American novelist, poet, and short-story writer; was a forerunner of literary movements that flourished long after his death; and became a respected war reporter. Crane met the most noted literary figures of his day; he lived through a shipwreck and near-death at sea; and he became one of America's most notorious literary rebels, even angering a future president. Despite so much action packed into so few years, Crane did have a regret—that he never became a major league baseball player. While we can never be sure what the loss to baseball was, Crane's chosen profession as a writer helped to spark a revolutionary change in American literature.

Stephen Crane

Stephen Crane was born in 1871, in Newark, New Jersey, the youngest of fourteen children. He had six brothers and two sisters who survived into early adulthood. Stephen Crane's father was a Methodist minister who was already over fifty when Crane was born. His mother was also a devout Methodist who wrote for Methodist journals and papers, often in support of the temperance movement (a movement that advocated a sober lifestyle and sought to ban the sale of alcohol). The Crane family moved frequently to different towns in New Jersey and New York, as Stephen's father, the Reverend Crane, moved from church to church.

The Reverend Crane died in 1880, when Stephen was only eight years old. Stephen's mother took on more writing projects, but the family was poor and continued to move frequently, most likely to escape debt. Stephen had a love of adventure as a child that sometimes drew him close to danger. When he was very young, he almost drowned when he tried to join older boys swimming in a river. Stephen also gained more first-hand experiences with death. In a town in New Jersey, he witnessed a woman being stabbed to death by her romantic partner. One of Stephen's sisters, who encouraged his love of reading, died when he was thirteen. A few years later, one of his brothers died in a gruesome railroad accident.

Despite these experiences, Stephen maintained his high spirits and was determined to live life as he saw fit. Stephen attended a number of boarding schools, one of them a military school. Although bright, he was never an excellent student. He spent his time reading books other than those assigned and playing baseball. He was a gifted catcher and

shortstop who could catch the ball barehanded. In 1890, he entered Lafayette College to study engineering, but quickly dropped out. The next year, he entered Syracuse University, where he followed his passion for reading and writing. He also continued to play baseball and dreamed of joining the major leagues despite his poor health. He excelled in English, but as he enjoyed reading everything but what was assigned for his classes, the rest of his marks were poor. The summer after his first year at Syracuse University, Stephen decided not to go back and to try writing full time.

Crane began writing as a reporter in New York City. Soon after he launched his career as a reporter his mother died. Crane was fascinated by the life in the Bowery, one of the City's notorious slums. There he drew inspiration for his first novel, *Maggie: A Girl of the Streets,* a grim, Naturalistic novel about an impoverished woman in a desperate situation. Crane's novel was too shocking for most publishers. Impoverished himself, Crane borrowed money against the small inheritance his mother had left him to publish the novel himself. Although the novel won the respect of a few American writers, it earned little critical praise and sold poorly.

Discouraged, but not willing to give up on his talent, Crane began reading widely about the Civil War. By 1894, he had finished *The Red Badge of Courage*, his best known novel about a soldier's experiences in the Union Army during the Civil War. He sold the novel for ninety dollars to be published serially (a few chapters at a time) in a number of newspapers. *The Red Badge of Courage* was published in its entirety in a book in 1895. It immediately became a best-seller and won Crane great critical acclaim. Most people, however, were stunned to learn that the young man who had written such a compelling account of war had never seen one. The same year he published his first book of poetry, *The Black Riders.*

Crane's fame startled him, in part because people began to criticize the way he lived. In 1896, he defended a chorus girl who was arrested for immoral behavior. Because Crane testified against police officers, he became a somewhat scandalous figure. The police commissioner of the City, Theodore Roosevelt, who would later become president of the United States, was among Crane's critics.

Crane escaped his growing notoriety in America and satisfied his fascination with war by becoming an overseas war correspondent, reporting on the revolution in Cuba. On his way to Cuba from Florida, he met and fell in love with Cora Taylor, a woman with a questionable reputation who had been married twice before (which was considered to be scandalous in Crane's day). On December 31, 1896, Crane set off for Cuba in the steamship *Commodore*. Two days later the ship began to sink. Crane, the captain, and ten other sailors were lowered into the sea in a small lifeboat. After a day in the lifeboat, they sighted land but the sea was too treacherous for them to make their way to safety. The boat capsized, and Crane and the other men struggled to stay alive in the cold, stormy sea. After someone on land spotted them, the crew was rescued. On land, Crane read his own obituary. Crane later immortalized his experiences at sea in the short story, "The Open Boat."

On his return, Stephen Crane and Cora Taylor left for Greece to report on the Greco-Turkish War. They married, and after the war moved to England, where Crane was befriended by fellow-American writer Henry James and British writers H. G. Wells and Joseph Conrad.

In 1898, the Spanish-American war erupted, and Stephen and Cora returned to the United States. Stephen tried to enlist in the Navy, but was rejected because of his poor health. Again, Crane became a war reporter, serving in both Cuba and Puerto Rico. After the war, Crane stayed in Havana, Cuba, to begin to write *Active Service*, a novel about the Greco-Turkish War. Apparently he contacted neither his wife nor his brothers, who began to launch official searches for him. Late in the year 1898, Crane returned to New York to visit with his family before rejoining Cora in England.

In England, Crane completed and published both *Active Service* and another book of poetry, *War Is Kind*. He also began an Irish novel, *The O'Ruddy*, wrote some tales about the American West, and published *The Monster and Other Studies*. Stephen and Cora were spending far beyond their means and socializing too much for Stephen's poor health.

To celebrate the end of the nineteenth century, Stephen and Cora organized a three-day New Year's party at a manor they rented. Some of the most noted literary figures of the day attended, including H. G. Wells, Joseph Conrad, Henry James, George Gissing, and Rider Haggard. They put on a play, played games, and celebrated late into the night. On New Year's morning one of the guests found Crane, who had collapsed with a hemorrhaging lung due to tuberculosis, a chronic and often fatal disease of the lungs.

In 1900, Crane grew stronger, but soon his health deteriorated again. He went to a health resort in the Black Forest of Germany to heal. He died there on June 5, 1900, not yet twenty-nine years old.

Time Line of Stephen Crane's Life

1871 On November 1, Stephen Crane is born in Newark, New Jersey, to Reverend Jonathan Townley Crane and Mary Helen Peck Crane. He is the last of fourteen children, eight of whom survived into young adulthood, including his sisters Mary Helen and Agnes Elizabeth and his brothers George Peck, Jonathan Townley, William Howe, Edmund Brian, Wilbure Fiske, and Luther Peck.

1874 The Crane family moves to Bloomington, New Jersey, to the Reverend Crane's new ministry.

1876 The Crane family moves to Paterson, New Jersey, when the Reverend Crane is appointed pastor of a church there.

1878 The Crane family moves once again to Port Jervis, New York, again following Reverend Crane to his new pastorate. Crane enters school for the first time in September.

1880 The Reverend Crane, Stephen's father, dies on February 16. To earn money for her family, Mary Helen Peck Crane writes for newspapers and Methodist journals.

1883 Mary Helen Peck Crane returns to New Jersey with her younger children, including Stephen.

1884 Stephen's sister Agnes Elizabeth, who encouraged his interest in literature, dies.

1885 Stephen enrolls in Pennington Seminary, a boarding school, where his father had served as principal.

1886 Stephen's brother Luther Peck is killed when he is crushed between two rail cars while working for a railroad company.

1888 Stephen transfers to a military boarding school. In the summer, Stephen writes for a local news bureau run by his brother Jonathan Townley.

1890 Stephen Crane enters Lafayette College in Easton, Pennsylvania, to study engineering. He leaves midway through the year due to poor grades.

1891 Stephen enters Syracuse University. During the summer, Stephen decides to write rather than return to college. He lives with his brother Edmund Brian, in Lakeview, New York, frequently visits artistic friends in New York City, and begins writing for newspapers. Stephen begins writing his first novel *Maggie: A Girl of the Streets*. Stephen's mother dies on December 7.

1892 Stephen Crane works as a freelance writer and publishes sketches with the *New York Tribune*. Unable to find a publisher for his first novel, Crane borrows money against the inheritance left him by his mother to publish *Maggie: A Girl of the Streets* on his own.

1893 Stephen Crane publishes *Maggie: A Girl of the Streets* using the pseudonym, or pen name, Johnston Smith. Crane reads Civil War literature and begins writing *The Red Badge of Courage*.

Crane continues to write, beginning *George's Mother*. He finds a publisher for a book of his poetry, and searches for a publisher for *The Red Badge of Courage*. Crane finally sells *The Red Badge of Courage* for ninety dollars. It is published serially (a few chapters at a time) in a number of newspapers. D. Appleton and Company then agrees to publish the entire novel.

1894

Crane travels throughout the West and in Mexico, working as a reporter. He returns home to live at the homes of his brothers in New Jersey in the summer. Crane's book of poetry *The Black Riders* is published. *The Red Badge of Courage* is published on October 5 and becomes a best-seller. The novel wins Crane critical acclaim.

1895

A revised version of *Maggie: A Girl of the Streets* is published by D. Appleton and Company, and Edward Arnold, a British publisher, publishes *George's Mother*. Also published is *The Little Regiment and Other Episodes of the American Civil War*. Crane agrees to write war stories for the McClure group of publishers and goes to Cuba to witness and report on the revolution taking place there. He meets Cora Taylor in Florida. On December 31, Crane heads for Cuba on the steamship *Commodore* that carries weapons for Cuban rebels.

1896

On January 2, the *Commodore* sinks. Crane later turns this experience into his story about shipwreck, "The Open Boat." Crane returns to Florida and Cora. Crane heads to Greece to cover the Greco-Turkish war, and Cora, who has been hired by the *New York Journal* as a war reporter, meets him there. Cora and Stephen Crane marry and go to London.

1897

Crane returns to New York, where he tries to enlist in the Navy to fight in the Spanish-American War. Crane agrees to write for Joseph Pulitzer's *World* as a correspondent reporting on the fighting in Cuba. In Cuba, Crane falls ill with fever and returns to the United States where he recuperates. Crane is fired by Pulitzer but hired by William Randolph Hearst's *Journal* to report on the fighting in Puerto Rico. At the end of the war, Crane goes alone to Havana, Cuba, where he begins a novel about the Greco-Turkish War, *Active Service*. Toward the end of the year, Crane returns to New York to visit with family before heading to England again.

1898

Stephen Crane and Cora rent a manor in England. Crane completes *Active Service*, which is published later that year, and begins to write an Irish romance called *The O'Ruddy*. He writes some short stories set in the American West, and publishes a book of poems, *War Is Kind. The Monster and Other Stories* is published toward the end of the year. The Cranes celebrate the end of the century with a three-day party. As the party ends, Stephen Crane collapses with a hemorrhaged lung and tuberculosis.

1899

Crane continues to write, working on *The O'Ruddy,* but grows more sick and more worried about deadlines and debt. Stephen Crane completes his will and goes to a sanitarium in the Black Forest of Germany, where he dies on June 5, only twenty-eight years old. Cora Crane returns with her husband's body to the United States, where he is buried at Hillside, New Jersey.

1900

The Red Badge of Courage

The Civil War

Born six years after the Civil War ended, Stephen Crane drew the inspiration for his best-known and most widely read novel, *The Red Badge of Courage,* from this terrible conflict. Sometimes called the War Between the States, the Civil War was just that—Americans were divided into two groups roughly along geographic lines. Eleven Southern states announced that they were officially seceding, breaking away from the United States to form their own government, called the Confederate States of America. The North, composed of twenty-three Northern and Western states, challenged the Southern states' right to do so and wanted to keep the nation intact. The Northern and Southern states clashed in one of the most bloody wars the United States has ever experienced.

In the decades before war broke out, the Northern and Southern states were in conflict over political, economic, social, and moral issues. In the North, the Industrial Revolution was in full swing; trade in manufactured goods was the focus of the Northern economy. In the agricultural South, cash crops like cotton, tobacco, and sugar were the economic focus. The South also relied on a labor pool of more than four million enslaved African Americans. While many Northerners found the institution of slavery reprehensible and sought to prevent new states from being admitted as slave states, the war was not fought over the issue of slavery alone. Increasingly, Southern states were finding themselves outvoted on issues such as tariffs that favored the economic interests of Northern states. Southerners were also enraged when many Northern states passed laws freeing any slaves who managed to escape to the North. The last straw for the South was a split in the Democratic party that practically guaranteed the election of Abraham Lincoln, a Republican who opposed the spread of slavery and supported acts that would strengthen the Federal government, boost the economy in the North, and help to expand the West. Soon after Lincoln's election in 1860, Southern states announced their secession. The first shots of the Civil War were fired on April 12, 1861, at Fort Sumter, South Carolina.

Both sides had certain advantages and disadvantages. The

North had a larger population—22 million compared to the South's 9 million, of which 4 million were slaves who were not eager to support the Southern cause. Some of these slaves fled to the North to claim their freedom and fight for the Union. The North was able to enlist 2 million soldiers, including almost 200,000 African Americans, while the South gathered only 900,000 soldiers. The North also had much greater manufacturing abilities, and so was able to produce more weapons, more ammunition, more uniforms, more medicine, and more shoes for its soldiers. The South, however, had an advantage in defending land it knew well; the North had to invade and crush the South into surrender, but the South merely had to defend its land until the invaders left. The South also had a proud military heritage with arguably more skilled officers than the North.

The war ended on April 9, 1865, when General Robert E. Lee, leader of the Confederate forces, surrendered to U.S. General Ulysses S. Grant. The war brought an end to the institution of slavery, and emancipated, or freed, four million African Americans. It also left the South in ruins: its land burned and pillaged, its economic system shattered, and its people demoralized. Out of a nation of about 35 million people, 620,000 men were killed in the war. More Americans died in the Civil War than in any war since, including World Wars I and II.

The Battle of Chancellorsville

Crane never calls the two days of battle he chronicles in *The Red Badge of Courage* by a specific historical name. Based on certain details in the story, however, many people believe that Crane was describing the Battle of Chancellorsville. In this battle General Joseph "Fighting Joe" Hooker led 130,000 Union soldiers against General Robert E. Lee and 60,000 Confederate soldiers. The battle took place on May 2–4, 1862, in Chancellorsville, Virginia, which lies near the Potomac River and the Rappahannock River, which is mentioned in the novel. The land around Chancellorsville was covered with thick forest, making it difficult for soldiers to maneuver. Crane portrays the wooded setting and the difficulties it presents vividly in *The Red Badge of Courage*. Although Hooker's men outnumbered Lee's, so many Union soldiers were killed that the Union soldiers retreated. They left behind, however, many dead Confederate soldiers as well, including one of the most renowned Confederate generals, Stonewall Jackson.

Life as a Civil War Soldier

Henry Fleming, the main character in this novel, discovers that war is not like the romantic, daring battles that he has imagined in dreams. Most Americans came to this realization during the Civil War. At first, men rushed to enlist and bought fancy uniforms, modeled on various European nations' uniforms. Photography was a new invention, and soldiers posed in their uniforms for portraits before heading off to war. Outside Washington, D.C., wealthy people gathered on hillsides to picnic and watch the battles unfold. This casual attitude toward war did not last long. Soon people experienced, or saw in some of the first photographs of war, the terrible death and destruction that was taking place.

Life as a Civil War soldier was not romantic. Heavy artillery, or large cannons, fired explosive shells on soldiers in battle. Bullets were shaped differently than those today, and were made to shatter bone and flesh. Medicine was less advanced then, and doctors faced with a soldier shot in the arm or leg could usually only amputate the limb, not heal it. Antibiotics were not widely used, so injured men became infected. Illnesses doctors could not treat also swept through military encampments. One out of every five Northern soldiers and one out of every four Southern soldiers died during the Civil War. In some towns, a whole generation of young men seemed simply to disappear. Many of these soldiers were very young, some only fourteen or fifteen years old.

Even when they were not fighting each other or fighting illness, soldiers still faced difficulties. The soldiers lived in crude camps in extreme weather conditions. They often fell short of food, and the food they did have was terrible—some of it was military rations left from the Mexican War two decades before, and soldiers complained that it was rotten and filled with vermin. Often soldiers plundered farms for food to eat. Romantic military uniforms quickly became tattered in war. The South, with its lack of manufacturing capability, was especially hard-pressed for uniforms. By the end of the war, many Southern soldiers fought barefoot and in little more than rags. The Union soldiers were only a little better off.

Literary Movements of the Late Nineteenth Century

Stephen Crane rebelled against Romanticism, a form of literature that dominated much of the nineteenth century. American Romantic writers wrote scholarly and often moralistic works. Their writing was sentimental, nostalgic, idealistic, and designed to inspire lofty emotions. Crane, on the other hand, wanted to present his readers with as realistic a vision of life as possible. In the late nineteenth century, a movement called Realism was gathering more and more followers, and Crane's *The Red Badge of Courage* is an example of this type of writing.

Crane's first novel *Maggie: A Girl of the Streets* was an early example of another literary movement that became popular toward the turn of the twentieth century—Naturalism. Naturalists believed that actions and events resulted from biological or natural forces or from forces in the environment. They presented characters who had little or no choices; their decisions were predetermined by their environment, their biological makeup, or both. *The Red Badge of Courage* shows certain Naturalistic tendencies as well.

A final movement that was barely beginning at the time of Crane's death, and that would later be associated with the early twentieth century, was Modernism. Modernist writers sought to express the uncertainty of the modern individuals who had lost connection to the beliefs and values of the past. Modernist writing is often fragmented, and themes are often left ambiguous, creating a sense of uncertainty in the reader. Modernist writers explored the subconscious mind through techniques like stream-of-consciousness. Stream-of-consciousness writing is literary work that attempts to render the flow of feelings, thoughts, and impressions within the minds of characters. Other Modernists, called Imagists, presented clear snapshots of a moment in time without telling the reader how to feel about the picture or image but relying on the image itself to produce emotion in the reader. Other Modernist writers, known as Surrealists, strove to heighten awareness by placing together seemingly unrelated images and forcing the reader or viewer to look for possible connections. Although *The Red Badge of Courage* predates most Modernist works, it does use some Modernist techniques.

Understanding the Text

While *The Red Badge of Courage* is not a long novel, it presents some challenges to the reader. The novel was written more than a hundred years ago and is set in an even earlier time. Ideas that may have been common in the 1860s are less common today. Here are some tips that might make passages in the novel easier for you to understand.

Heroism and honor in war: Behaving with honor in war and becoming a war hero were dreams commonly held by young men in the nineteenth century. Many parents and communities expected young men to go off to war and fight; it was something a young man did as part of growing up. Far more young men than today attended military school to train in the art of war. Soldiers also attached great importance to their regiment's flag. It was always carried at the front of the regiment in battle, and carrying it was a great honor even though doing so often meant death.

Desertion: While deserting the field of battle is still considered a very serious crime for a soldier to commit, many people today may be unaware of how serious a crime it was during the Civil War. Soldiers were in short supply; every man was needed. Soldiers who deserted the field of battle and were caught were punished in a number of ways. Some were publicly humiliated to teach them a lesson. Other were less fortunate and were branded with a letter on their faces that would mark them all their lives. Some deserters paid for their crime with their lives.

Military terms: The weapons of war and military strategy were different in the 1860s. Soldiers fought in tight ranks, shoulder to shoulder. Their weapons were mostly non-repeating rifles. This means that after every shot, soldiers would have to stop and reload their weapons. Their rifles were also very inaccurate, making it difficult to hit men who were charging toward them. Rifles, also known as muskets, were fitted with sharp blades at the end called bayonets. Often when cavalry or horsemen charged, the men would steady their rifles so that the horsemen would fall on the blades. Soldiers also used the bayonets in hand-to-hand combat, especially because their rifles were so inaccurate. Rather than bombs, large heavy guns, called artillery, were pulled in wagons by horses and used to launch exploding shells.

Throughout the novel, many military terms are footnoted. If you have difficulty understanding the action because of military terms, ask your teacher for recommendations about films set in the Civil War. Seeing such films might help you to envision the military action of the book.

Proper names: The author chose not to refer to his characters by their given names very often. If you become confused about the identity of a character, refer to the list of characters at the beginning of this book.

Dialect: The novel is filled with dialect, writing that imitates the language spoken by the people of a particular place and time. This dialect appears in dialogue, or when the characters are speaking to each other. Crane uses many contractions and different spellings of words that capture how they were spoken, rather than how you usually see them written. Some of this dialect is footnoted. If you have trouble understanding the dialect, try sounding it out aloud. If you still have difficulty, skim these passages and use the Guided Reading Questions as clues to get the general sense of a passage that gives you trouble.

Vocabulary: Crane's choice of words is sometimes challenging for younger readers. Many difficult terms appear as Words for Everyday Use, at the bottoms of pages and in a Glossary at the end of this book. If a word you are having trouble understanding does not appear in these places, try using the context of the sentence to make a reasonable guess about the word's meaning. If the context of the sentence still does not help you, read on to see if you understand the sense of the passage as a whole. If you feel that you still do not understand the passage, look up the word in a dictionary or ask your teacher for help in understanding the passage.

Characters in
The Red Badge of Courage

Major Characters

Henry Fleming (also called "the youth"). Henry is the main character, and the novel is told from his perspective. He enlists in the Union Army dreaming of battle as something glorious and romantic. His character and how it changes over the course of the battle is the focus of the novel.

Wilson (also called "the loud soldier" and, later in the novel, "the youth's friend"). Wilson is a soldier in the same regiment as Henry, the 304th. His outlook toward the world, and especially toward battle, changes over the course of the novel. He and Henry become good friends.

Jim Conklin (also called "the tall soldier" and, later in the novel, "the spectral soldier"). Jim is another soldier in the 304th regiment. He is the soldier who spreads the news that the regiment will soon see action. He is less confident about his abilities than Wilson.

The tattered soldier. The tattered soldier is one of the wounded soldiers whom Henry meets. He is eager to become Henry's friend.

Henry's mother. While Henry's mother does not take part in the action of the story, Henry thinks about her in the beginning of the novel. She is not eager to see her son go to war, but when he enlists she gives him advice.

Minor Characters

Lieutenant Hasbrouck (usually called "the lieutenant"). The lieutenant seems always eager to face battle. At first, Henry does not like him much, but later comes to respect him more. The lieutenant is mostly characterized by his swearing oaths.

Colonel MacChesney (usually called "the colonel"). The colonel helps to care for Henry after he is injured.

The general. The general always appears on horseback. He orders the men to perform actions and seems not to care about the fate of individual men. Later in the book, he orders the 304th regiment to perform a dangerous action.

The officer. One character, called only "the officer," insults the 304th regiment, making Henry very angry.

The veterans. The veteran soldiers as a group are far more bold and confident than the recruits. They seem to know what to do in every situation and often mock the more inexperienced men.

Echoes:

Letters Home—The Voices of Civil War Soldiers

Note: These excerpts from letters written by Civil War soldiers appear as they were written, including misspellings and other errors.

Indeed Dear Miss . . . there is thousands of Poor Soldiers that will see Home & Friends no more in this World If you was in Keokuk & See the number of Sick & Disabled Soldiers it would make your Heart Ache. they are Dieing . . . Every Day.

—Newton Scott, a Union soldier, October 24, 1862

Well I am here, as you might say, in the swamps of Louisiana. Am well, but don't see any prospect of getting home very soon. I have had the satisfaction, if it be any, of being shot at by the Rebs. One shell struck within ten feet of where I stood. Others were lying near me. If it had exploded, it probably would have sent some of us to our final home. I tell you, I had very queer feelings, till after the second shot. By that time I became quite cool and saw the other shots without a tremor.

—Samuel S. Dunton, a Union soldier, February 23, 1863

Whilst we were on our retreat two of our men were carrying [a fellow soldier named] Sayer who was severely wounded, one of them was struck by a musket ball stunning him, and letting the wounded man fall on the ground, his bowels comming out, the other putting them back as best he could. Then one of the Rhode Island boys took hold with me and helped. While we were carrying him the R-I-boys arm was shot away by a cannon ball. A surgeon passing by looked at Sayer & told us it was no use trying to take him any further as he could not live, so we left him there.

—Henry F. Ritter, a Union soldier, July 23, 1861

Here we made a stand, & here our company fought absolutely alone . . our men were subjected to a raking fire. I was the first who fell. I had put on my spectacles, taken good aim & fired my first shot. As I was in the act of re-loading, a rifle-ball struck me in the head, a little above the forehead; & the violence of the concussion felled me to, the earth immediately. I drew off my s[p]ectacles & flung them aside; & not believing my wound a bad one, as it was not painful, I attempted to reload. But the blood was gushing over my face & blinding my eyes; & I found it impossible to do so. I knew pretty well the extent of my wound, as I had probed it with my finger as I fell; & as the gash seemed to be a deep one, I feared faintness would ensue from loss of blood, especially as there was a large puddle of it where I first lay. So, I put aside my gun for a while, & put my white handkerchief inside my hat upon the wound & tied my silk one around the hat. By the time I had finished these precautions, the company were in retreat; & with Jones & a few others I made my way to the clump of trees.

—C. Woodward Hutson, a Confederate soldier, July 22, 1861

We have had hard times ever since we came to the vally but still harder while we was in pennsylvania. We was in Penn something the rise of three weeks, during that time we was not allowed to unsaddle our horse or sleep with our shoes off. . . . Penn is the pretiest country I ever seen or ever expect to see. . . . We had one big battle that was at Gettysburg, Penn. This was said to be the hardest fight that has been during the war and Great slaughter on both sides. The ground lay covered with the dead & wounded for miles.

—Isaac V. Reynolds, a Confederate soldier, July 20, 1863

Portrait of Private Edwin Francis Jemison, 2nd Louisiana Regiment, Confederate States of America.

Portrait of Private Robert Patterson, Company D, 12th
Tennessee Infantry, Confederate States of America.

Portrait of an
unidentified
Union soldier
from New York.

Portrait of an
unidentified
Union soldier.

Portrait of "Drummer" Jackson, 79th U. S. Colored Troops.

Questions for Critical Viewing

- Do the soldiers in these pictures look as if they are new to the war or as if they have already experienced battle? Explain your answer.
- What differences do you see between the soldiers in the Union Army and the soldiers in the Confederate Army? What similiarities do you see?
- Which of these soldiers most resembles your impression of Henry Fleming? Jim Conklin? George Wilson? Why?

Chapter 1

The cold passed reluctantly from the earth, and the retiring fogs revealed an army stretched out on the hills, resting. As the landscape changed from brown to green, the army awakened, and began to tremble with eagerness at the noise of rumors. It cast its eyes upon the roads, which were growing from long <u>troughs</u> of liquid mud to proper <u>thoroughfares</u>. A river, amber-tinted in the shadow of its banks, <u>purled</u> at the army's feet; and at night, when the stream had become of a sorrowful blackness, one could see across it the red, eye-like gleam of hostile campfires set in the low brows of distant hills.

◄ What does the fog reveal as it lifts? What is this group of people doing?

Once a certain tall soldier developed virtues and went resolutely to wash a shirt. He came flying back from a brook waving his garment bannerlike. He was swelled with a tale he had heard from a reliable friend, who had heard it from a truthful cavalryman,[1] who had heard it from his trustworthy brother, one of the orderlies[2] at division headquarters. He adopted the important air of a herald[3] in red and gold.

◄ What can one see at night across the river?

"We're goin' t' move t' morrah[4]—sure," he said <u>pompously</u> to a group in the company street. "We're goin' 'way up the river, cut across, an' come around in behint 'em."

To his attentive audience he drew a loud and elaborate plan of a very brilliant campaign. When he had finished, the blue-clothed[5] men scattered into small arguing groups between the rows of squat brown huts. A negro teamster[6] who had been dancing upon a cracker box[7] with the hilarious encouragement of twoscore[8] soldiers was deserted. He sat

◄ In what way do the men react to the tall soldier's news?

---

1. **cavalryman.** Soldier mounted on horseback
2. **orderlies.** Soldier assigned to perform various services for a superior officer
3. **herald.** Officer with the status of an ambassador who serves as a messenger between opposing forces in a war
4. **t'morrah.** Tomorrow
5. **blue-clothed.** During the Civil War, the Union forces wore blue.
6. **negro teamster.** *Negro*—term for an African American used in the nineteenth century, but generally considered to be offensive today; *teamster*—person who drives a team or truck as an occupation; here, probably a person who helps to supply the troops with necessities such as food, weaponry, and clothing
7. **cracker box.** Boxes were typically made of wood and so were more durable than the cardboard boxes most food products are shipped in today.
8. **twoscore.** Forty; a score is twenty

Words For Everyday Use

trough (trôf) *n.*, conduit, drain, or channel for water

thor • ough • fare (thər´ō far) *n.*, way or place for passage

purl (pərl) *vi.*, eddy, swirl

pomp • ous • ly (päm´pəs lē) *adv.*, arrogantly; in a self-important manner

mournfully down. Smoke drifted lazily from a multitude of quaint chimneys.

"It's a lie! that's all it is—a thunderin' lie!" said another private loudly. His smooth face was flushed, and his hands were thrust sulkily into his trousers' pockets. He took the matter as an affront to him. "I don't believe the derned old army's ever going to move. We're set. I've got ready to move eight times in the last two weeks, and we ain't moved yet."

The tall soldier felt called upon to defend the truth of a rumor he himself had introduced. He and the loud one came near to fighting over it.

A corporal began to swear before the assemblage. He had just put a costly board floor in his house, he said. During the early spring he had refrained from adding extensively to the comfort of his environment because he had felt that the army might start on the march at any moment. Of late, however, he had been impressed[9] that they were in a sort of eternal camp.

Many of the men engaged in a spirited debate. One outlined in a peculiarly <u>lucid</u> manner all the plans of the commanding general. He was opposed by men who advocated that there were other plans of campaign. They clamored at each other, numbers making futile bids for the popular attention. Meanwhile, the soldier who had fetched the rumor bustled about with much importance. He was continually <u>assailed</u> by questions.

"What's up, Jim?"

"Th' army's goin' t' move."

"Ah, what yeh talkin' about? How yeh know it is?"

"Well, yeh kin b'lieve me er not, jest as yeh like. I don't care a hang."[10]

There was much food for thought in the manner in which he replied. He came near to convincing them by <u>disdaining</u> to produce proofs. They grew much excited over it.

There was a youthful private who listened with eager ears to the words of the tall soldier and to the varied comments of his comrades. After receiving a fill of discussions concerning marches and attacks, he went to his hut and crawled

► What is the name of the tall soldier who spreads the rumor that the army is going to move?

► What does one "youthful private" do on hearing the news? Why does he want to be alone?

---

9. **had been impressed.** Had been of the impression
10. **care a hang.** Care a bit

Words
For
Everyday
Use

lu•cid (lōō´səd) *adj.,* clear to the understanding

as • sail (ə sāl´) *vt.,* attack violently with blows or words

dis • dain (dis dān´) *vt.,* refuse or abstain from because of scorn

through an <u>intricate</u> hole that served it as a door. He wished to be alone with some new thoughts that had lately come to him.

He lay down on a wide bunk that stretched across the end of the room. In the other end, cracker boxes were made to serve as furniture. They were grouped about the fireplace. A picture from an illustrated weekly[11] was upon the log walls, and three rifles were paralleled[12] on pegs. Equipments hung on handy projections, and some tin dishes lay upon a small pile of firewood. A folded tent was serving as a room. The sunlight, without, beating upon it, made it glow a light yellow shade. A small window shot an <u>oblique</u> square of whiter light upon the cluttered floor. The smoke from the fire at times neglected the clay chimney and wreathed into the room, and this flimsy chimney of clay and sticks made endless threats to set ablaze the whole establishment.

The youth was in a little trance of astonishment. So they were at last going to fight. On the morrow, perhaps, there would be a battle, and he would be in it. For a time he was obliged to labor to make himself believe. He could not accept with assurance an omen that he was about to mingle in one of those great affairs of the earth.

◄ What does the youth have a hard time believing?

He had, of course, dreamed of battles all his life—of vague and bloody conflicts that had thrilled him with their sweep and fire. In visions he had seen himself in many struggles. He had imagined peoples secure in the shadow of his eagle-eyed <u>prowess</u>. But awake he had regarded battles as crimson blotches on the pages of the past. He had put them as things of the bygone with his thought-images of heavy crowns and high castles. There was a portion of the world's history which he had regarded as the time of wars, but it, he thought, had been long gone over the horizon and had disappeared forever.

◄ In what way does the youth dream of battles? What does he picture himself doing? Do his visions seem realistic?

◄ What does the youth think about war when he is awake?

From his home his youthful eyes had looked upon the war in his own country with distrust. It must be some sort of a play affair. He had long despaired of witnessing a Greeklike struggle. Such would be no more, he had said. Men were bet-

◄ Why is the youth skeptical of the war taking place now?

---

11. **illustrated weekly.** Weekly periodical with illustrations, such as a magazine
12. **paralleled.** Hung in parallel, or facing in the same direction with equal space between them

---

Words For Everyday Use

in • tri • cate (in´tri kət) *adj.*, having many complexly interrelating parts or elements

o • blique (ō blēk´) *adj.*, neither perpendicular nor parallel

prow • ess (prau´əs) *n.*, distinguished bravery; especially military valor and skill

ter, or more timid. <u>Secular</u> and religious education had <u>effaced</u> the throat-grappling instinct, or else firm finance held in check the passions.

He had burned several times to enlist. Tales of great movements shook the land. They might not be distinctly Homeric,[13] but there seemed to be much glory in them. He had read of marches, sieges, conflicts, and he had longed to see it all. His busy mind had drawn for him large pictures extravagant in color, lurid[14] with breathless deeds.

► Who discouraged the youth from joining the army? According to this person, where was the youth needed more?

But his mother had discouraged him. She had affected to look with some contempt upon the quality of his war <u>ardor</u> and patriotism. She could calmly seat herself and with no apparent difficulty give him many hundreds of reasons why he was of vastly more importance on the farm than on the field of battle. She had had certain ways of expression that told him that her statements on the subject came from a deep conviction. Moreover, on her side, was his belief that her ethical motive in the argument was <u>impregnable</u>.

At last, however, he had made firm rebellion against this yellow light thrown upon the color of his ambitions. The newspapers, the gossip of the village, his own picturings, had aroused him to an uncheckable degree. They were in truth fighting finely down there. Almost every day the newspapers printed accounts of a decisive victory.

► According to the newspapers, how is the war progressing for the youth's side, the Union?

One night, as he lay in bed, the winds had carried to him the clangoring of the church bell as some enthusiast jerked the rope frantically to tell the twisted news of a great battle. This voice of the people rejoicing in the night had made him shiver in a prolonged ecstasy of excitement. Later, he had gone down to his mother's room and had spoken thus: "Ma, I'm going to enlist."

"Henry, don't you be a fool," his mother had replied. She had then covered her face with the quilt. There was an end to the matter for that night.

► What is the youth's name? What is his mother's response when he expresses a desire to enlist in the Union army?

Nevertheless, the next morning he had gone to a town that was near his mother's farm and had enlisted in a company that was forming there. When he had returned home his mother was milking the brindle cow.[15] Four others stood

---

13. **Homeric.** Like the ancient Greek poet's epic about the Trojan War, the *Iliad*. The descriptions of battle in this work are lofty.
14. **lurid.** Sensational
15. **brindle cow.** Cow with dark streaks or spots on its skin

Words For Everyday Use

sec • u • lar (se´kyə lər) *adj.*, not overtly or specifically religious

ef • face (e fās´) *vt.*, cause to vanish

ar • dor (är´dər) *n.*, extreme vigor or energy; zeal

im • preg • na • ble (im preg´nə bəl) *adj.*, incapable of being taken by assault; unconquerable

waiting. "Ma, I've enlisted," he had said to her diffidently. There was a short silence. "The Lord's will be done, Henry," she had finally replied, and had then continued to milk the brindle cow.

When he had stood in the doorway with his soldier's clothes on his back, and with the light of excitement and expectancy in his eyes almost defeating the glow of regret for the home bonds, he had seen two tears leaving their trails on his mother's scarred cheeks.

Still, she had disappointed him by saying nothing whatever about returning with his shield or on it.[16] He had privately <u>primed</u> himself for a beautiful scene. He had prepared certain sentences which he thought could be used with touching effect. But her words destroyed his plans. She had <u>doggedly</u> peeled potatoes and addressed him as follows: "You watch out, Henry, an' take good care of yerself in this here fighting business—you watch out, an' take good care of yerself. Don't go a-thinkin' you can lick the hull[17] rebel army at the start, because yeh can't. Yer jest one little feller amongst a hull lot of others, and yeh've got to keep quiet an' do what they tell yeh. I know how you are, Henry.

"I've knet[18] yeh eight pair of socks, Henry, and I've put in all yer best shirts, because I want my boy to be jest as warm and comf'able as anybody in the army. Whenever they get holes in 'em, I want yeh to send 'em right-away back to me, so's I kin dern[19] 'em.

"An' allus be careful an' choose yer comp'ny. There's lots of bad men in the army, Henry. The army makes 'em wild, and they like nothing better than the job of leading off a young feller like you, as ain't never been away from home much and has allus had a mother, an' a-learning 'im to drink and swear. Keep clear of them folks, Henry. I don't want yeh to ever do anything, Henry, that yeh would be 'shamed to let me know about. Jest think as if I was a-watchin' yeh. If yeh keep that in yer mind allus, I guess yeh'll come out about right.

◀ What is the mother's reaction when Henry tells her he has enlisted?

◀ What reveals that Henry's decision has an emotional effect on his mother?

◀ What advice does Henry's mother give him? What type of scene had Henry pictured instead?

---

16. **returning with his shield or on it.** In Greek literature, soldiers going off to war were advised to return alive (with shield) or dead (carried on the shield).
17. **Lick the hull.** *Lick*—beat in a fight; *hull*—whole
18. **knet.** Knit
19. **dern.** Darn; repair the holes in

Words For Everyday Use

prime (prīm) *vt.*, instruct beforehand; coach

dog • ged • ly (dô´gəd lē) *adv.*, in a manner marked by stubborn determination

"Yeh must allus remember yer father, too, child, an' remember he never drunk a drop of licker[20] in his life, and seldom swore a cross oath.

"I don't know what else to tell yeh, Henry, excepting that yeh must never do no <u>shirking</u>, child, on my account. If so be a time comes when yeh have to be kilt or do a mean thing, why, Henry, don't think of anything 'cept what's right, because there's many a woman has to bear up 'ginst sech things these times, and the Lord 'll take keer[21] of us all.

"Don't forgit about the socks and the shirts, child; and I've put a cup of blackberry jam with yer bundle, because I know yeh like it above all things. Good-by, Henry. Watch out, and be a good boy."

He had, of course, been impatient under the ordeal of this speech. It had not been quite what he expected, and he had borne it with an air of irritation. He departed feeling vague relief.

▶ What makes Henry ashamed?

Still, when he had looked back from the gate, he had seen his mother kneeling among the potato parings. Her brown face, upraised, was stained with tears, and her <u>spare</u> form was quivering. He bowed his head and went on, feeling suddenly ashamed of his purposes.

▶ How do Henry's classmates react to his decision to join the army? How does this make Henry and the other new recruits feel?

From his home he had gone to the seminary[22] to bid adieu[23] to many schoolmates. They had <u>thronged</u> about him with wonder and admiration. He had felt the gulf now between them and had swelled with calm pride. He and some of his fellows who had donned[24] blue were quite overwhelmed with privileges for all of one afternoon, and it had been a very delicious thing. They had strutted.

▶ What does Henry often think of?

A certain light-haired girl had made vivacious fun at his martial spirit, but there was another and darker girl whom he had gazed at steadfastly, and he thought she grew <u>demure</u> and sad at sight of his blue and brass. As he had walked down the path between the rows of oaks, he had turned his head and detected her at a window watching his departure. As he perceived her, she had immediately begun to stare up through the high tree branches at the sky. He had seen a

---

20. **licker.** Liquor
21. **keer.** Care
22. **seminary.** Local school
23. **adieu.** Goodbye
24. **donned.** Put on (an article of clothing)

| **Words For Everyday Use** | **shirk** (shʉrk) *vi.*, evade the performance of an obligation
 spare (spār) *adj.*, healthily lean | **throng** (thrôŋ) *vi.*, crowd together in great numbers
 de • mure (di myur´) *adj.*, reserved, modest, serious |

good deal of flurry and haste in her movement as she changed her attitude. He often thought of it.

On the way to Washington his spirit had soared. The regiment[25] was fed and caressed at station after station until the youth had believed that he must be a hero. There was a lavish expenditure of bread and cold meats, coffee, and pickles and cheese. As he basked in the smiles of the girls and was patted and complimented by the old men, he had felt growing within him the strength to do mighty deeds of arms.

◀ What makes Henry think of himself as a hero?

After complicated journeyings with many pauses, there had come months of monotonous life in a camp. He had had the belief that real war was a series of death struggles with small time in between for sleep and meals; but since his regiment had come to the field the army had done little but sit still and try to keep warm.

◀ What surprises Henry about army life thus far?

He was brought then gradually back to his old ideas. Greeklike struggles would be no more. Men were better, or more timid. Secular and religious education had effaced the throat-grappling instinct, or else firm finance held in check the passions.

He had grown to regard himself merely as a part of a vast blue demonstration. His province was to look out, as far as he could, for his personal comfort. For recreation he could twiddle his thumbs and speculate on the thoughts which must agitate the minds of the generals. Also, he was drilled and drilled and reviewed,[26] and drilled and drilled and reviewed.

The only foes he had seen were some pickets[27] along the river bank. They were a sun-tanned, philosophical lot, who sometimes shot reflectively[28] at the blue pickets. When reproached for this afterward, they usually expressed sorrow, and swore by their gods that the guns had exploded without their permission. The youth, on guard duty one night, conversed across the stream with one of them. He was a slightly ragged man, who spat skillfully between his

◀ What is Henry's attitude toward what he has seen of the enemy so far?

---

25. **regiment.** Military unit consisting of a number of troops
26. **drilled and reviewed.** *Drill*—Train military maneuvers again and again; *reviewed*—undergo formal military inspections
27. **pickets.** Sentries, or soldiers who stand guard over a point of passage
28. **reflectively.** In an unhurried, contemplative way

Words For Everyday Use

lav • ish (laʹvish) *adj.*, spending or giving generously
ex • pen • di • ture (ek spenʹdi chər) *n.*, act or process of expending; outlay

mo • not • o • nous (mə näʹt'n əs) *adj.*, tediously uniform or unvarying
prov • ince (proʹvints) *n.*, proper or appropriate function or scope; department of knowledge or activity

shoes and possessed a great fund of bland and <u>infantile</u> assurance. The youth liked him personally.

"Yank,"[29] the other had informed him, "yer a right dum good feller." This sentiment, floating to him upon the still air, had made him temporarily regret war.

Various veterans had told him tales. Some talked of gray, bewhiskered <u>hordes</u> who were advancing with relentless curses and chewing tobacco with unspeakable valor; tremendous bodies of fierce soldiery who were sweeping along like the Huns.[30] Others spoke of tattered and eternally hungry men who fired <u>despondent</u> powders. "They'll charge through hell's fire an' brimstone t' git a holt on a haversack,[31] an' sech stomachs ain't a-lastin' long," he was told. From the stories, the youth imagined the red, live bones sticking out through slits in the faded uniforms.

▶ Why doesn't Henry believe the veterans' stories about fierce and hungry members of the opposing forces?

Still, he could not put a whole faith in veterans' tales, for recruits were their prey. They talked much of smoke, fire, and blood, but he could not tell how much might be lies. They persistently yelled "Fresh fish!" at him, and were in no wise to be trusted.

However, he perceived now that it did not greatly matter what kind of soldiers he was going to fight, so long as they fought, which fact no one disputed. There was a more serious problem. He lay in his bunk pondering upon it. He tried to mathematically prove to himself that he would not run from a battle.

▶ What serious problem concerns Henry?

Previously he had never felt obliged to wrestle too seriously with this question. In his life he had taken certain things for granted, never challenging his belief in ultimate success, and bothering little about means and roads. But here he was confronted with a thing of moment. It had suddenly appeared to him that perhaps in a battle he might run. He was forced to admit that as far as war was concerned he knew nothing of himself.

A sufficient time before he would have allowed the problem to kick its heels at the outer <u>portals</u> of his mind, but now he felt compelled to give serious attention to it.

---

29. **Yank.** Yankee, native of New England
30. **Huns.** Members of a nomadic central Asian people who gained control of a large part of central and eastern Europe under Attila the Hun around AD 450. The Huns were considered very destructive.
31. **haversack.** Bag similar to a knapsack worn over one shoulder

| Words For Everyday Use | in • fan • tile (in´fən tīl) *adj.,* suitable to or characteristic of an infant; very immature

 horde (hōrd) *n.,* crowd or throng | de • spon • dent (di spən´dənt) *adj.,* feeling or showing extreme discouragement, dejection, or depression

 por • tal (pōr´təl,) *n.,* door, entrance |

A little panic-fear grew in his mind. As his imagination went forward to a fight, he saw hideous possibilities. He contemplated the lurking menaces of the future, and failed in an effort to see himself standing <u>stoutly</u> in the midst of them. He recalled his visions of broken-bladed glory, but in the shadow of the impending tumult he suspected them to be impossible pictures.

He sprang from the bunk and began to pace nervously to and fro. "Good Lord, what's th' matter with me?" he said aloud.

He felt that in this crisis his laws of life were useless. Whatever he had learned of himself was here of no avail. He was an unknown quantity. He saw that he would again be obliged to experiment as he had in early youth. He must accumulate information of himself, and meanwhile he resolved to remain close upon his guard lest those qualities of which he knew nothing should everlastingly disgrace him. "Good Lord!" he repeated in dismay.

After a time the tall soldier slid <u>dexterously</u> through the hole. The loud private followed. They were wrangling.[32]

"That's all right," said the tall soldier as he entered. He waved his hand expressively. "You can believe me or not, jest as you like. All you got to do is to sit down and wait as quiet as you can. Then pretty soon you'll find out I was right."

His comrade grunted stubbornly. For a moment he seemed to be searching for a <u>formidable</u> reply. Finally he said: "Well, you don't know everything in the world, do you?"

"Didn't say I knew everything in the world," retorted the other sharply. He began to <u>stow</u> various articles snugly into his knapsack.

The youth, pausing in his nervous walk, looked down at the busy figure. "Going to be a battle, sure, is there, Jim?" he asked.

"Of course there is," replied the tall soldier. "Of course there is. You jest wait 'til to-morrow, and you'll see one of the biggest battles ever was. You jest wait."

"Thunder!" said the youth.

"Oh, you'll see fighting this time, my boy, what'll be regular out-and-out fighting," added the tall soldier, with the air

32. **wrangling.** Arguing

◄ What is Henry beginning to feel? Why does he feel this way?

◄ Why can't Henry tell how he will react in battle?

◄ What attitude does Jim, the tall soldier, seem to have toward the idea of fighting in battle?

of a man who is about to exhibit a battle for the benefit of his friends.

"Huh!" said the loud one from a corner.

"Well," remarked the youth, "like as not this story'll turn out jest like them others did."

"Not much it won't," replied the tall soldier, <u>exasperated</u>. "Not much it won't. Didn't the cavalry all start this morning?" He glared about him. No one denied his statement. "The cavalry started this morning," he continued. "They say there ain't hardly any cavalry left in camp. They're going to Richmond,[33] or some place, while we fight all the Johnnies.[34] It's some dodge like that. The regiment's got orders, too. A feller what seen 'em go to headquarters told me a little while ago. And they're raising blazes all over camp—anybody can see that."

"Shucks!" said the loud one.

The youth remained silent for a time. At last he spoke to the tall soldier. "Jim!"

"What?"

"How do you think the reg'ment 'll do?"

"Oh, they'll fight all right, I guess, after they once get into it," said the other with cold judgment. He made a fine use of the third person. "There's been heaps of fun poked at 'em because they're new, of course, and all that; but they'll fight all right, I guess."

"Think any of the boys 'll run?" persisted the youth.

"Oh, there may be a few of 'em run, but there's them kind in every regiment, 'specially when they first goes under fire," said the other in a tolerant way. "Of course it might happen that the hull kit-and-boodle[35] might start and run, if some big fighting came first-off, and then again they might stay and fight like fun. But you can't bet on nothing. Of course they ain't never been under fire[36] yet, and it ain't likely they'll lick the hull rebel army all-to-oncet[37] the first time; but I think they'll fight better than some, if worse than oth-

▶ What evidence does Jim point out to support the rumor that their group will see fighting soon?

▶ What is Jim's opinion about how the new soldiers will do in battle?

---

33. **Richmond.** City in Virginia
34. **Johnnies.** "Johnny Rebs" was the nickname Union troops gave to Confederate soldiers.
35. **kit-and-boodle.** Kit and caboodle, meaning a group of persons or things
36. **under fire.** Under attack
37. **all-to-oncet.** All at once

Words
For
Everyday
Use

ex • as • per • at • ed (eg zas´pə rāt əd) *adj.,* irritated, annoyed

ers. That's the way I figger. They call the reg'ment 'Fresh fish' and everything; but the boys come of good stock, and most of 'em 'll fight like sin after they oncet git shootin'," he added, with a mighty emphasis on the last four words.

"Oh, you think you know—" began the loud soldier with scorn.

The other turned savagely upon him. They had a rapid <u>altercation</u>, in which they fastened upon each other various strange <u>epithets</u>.

The youth at last interrupted them. "Did you ever think you might run yourself, Jim?" he asked. On concluding the sentence he laughed as if he had meant to aim a joke. The loud soldier also giggled.

◀ What does Henry ask Jim? What is Jim's response? Why do you think Henry asks this question?

The tall private waved his hand. "Well," said he profoundly, "I've thought it might get too hot for Jim Conklin in some of them <u>scrimmages</u>, and if a whole lot of boys started and run, why, I s'pose I'd start and run. And if I once started to run, I'd run like the devil, and no mistake. But if everybody was a-standing and a-fighting, why, I'd stand and fight. Be jiminey,[38] I would. I'll bet on it."

"Huh!" said the loud one.

The youth of this tale felt gratitude for these words of his comrade. He had feared that all of the untried men possessed a great and correct confidence. He now was in a measure reassured.

---

38. **Be jiminey.** An exclamation

Words For Everyday Use	**al • ter • ca • tion** (äl tər kā´shən) n., noisy heated angry dispute **ep • i • thet** (e´pə thet) n., disparaging or abusive word or phrase	**scrim • mage** (skri´mij) n., minor battle; confused fight

Chapter 2

The next morning the youth discovered that his tall comrade had been the fast-flying messenger of a mistake. There was much <u>scoffing</u> at the latter by those who had yesterday been firm <u>adherents</u> of his views, and there was even a little sneering by men who had never believed the rumor. The tall one fought with a man from Chatfield Corners and beat him severely.

The youth felt, however, that his problem was in no wise[1] lifted from him. There was, on the contrary, an irritating prolongation. The tale had created in him a great concern for himself. Now, with the newborn question in mind, he was compelled to sink back into his old place as part of a blue demonstration.

▶ *What is the only way the youth can prove himself? What is he eager to do?*

For days he made ceaseless calculations, but they were all wondrously unsatisfactory. He found that he could establish nothing. He finally concluded that the only way to prove himself was to go into the blaze, and then figuratively to watch his legs to discover their merits and faults. He reluctantly admitted that he could not sit still and with a mental slate and pencil derive an answer. To gain it, he must have blaze, blood, and danger, even as a chemist requires this, that, and the other. So he <u>fretted</u> for an opportunity.

Meanwhile he continually tried to measure himself by his comrades. The tall soldier, for one, gave him some assurance. This man's serene unconcern dealt him a measure of confidence, for he had known him since childhood, and from his intimate knowledge he did not see how he could be capable of anything that was beyond him, the youth. Still, he thought that his comrade might be mistaken about himself. Or, on the other hand, he might be a man heretofore doomed to peace and obscurity, but, in reality, made to shine in war.

▶ *To what type of person does the youth long to talk?*

The youth would have liked to have discovered another who suspected himself. A sympathetic comparison of mental notes would have been a joy to him.

He occasionally tried to <u>fathom</u> a comrade with seductive

---

1. **wise.** Manner, way

Words For Everyday Use	**scoff** (skôf) *vt.*, show contempt; mock **ad • her • ent** (ad hir′ənt) *n.*, believer in, especially of a particular idea or church; follower	**fret** (fret) *vi.*, become vexed or worried **fath • om** (fa′thəm) *vt.*, penetrate and come to understand

sentences. He looked about to find men in the proper mood. All attempts failed to bring forth any statement which looked in any way like a confession to those doubts which he privately acknowledged in himself. He was afraid to make an open declaration of his concern, because he dreaded to place some <u>unscrupulous</u> confidant upon the high plane of the unconfessed from which elevation he could be derided.

◀ Why doesn't he openly acknowledge his fear?

In regard to his companions his mind wavered between two opinions, according to his mood. Sometimes he inclined to believing them all heroes. In fact, he usually admitted in secret the superior development of the higher qualities in others. He could conceive of men going very insignificantly about the world bearing a load of courage unseen, and although he had known many of his comrades through boyhood, he began to fear that his judgment of them had been blind. Then, in other moments, he <u>flouted</u> these theories, and assured himself that his fellows were all privately wondering and quaking.

◀ What two opinions does he have about his fellow soldiers?

His emotions made him feel strange in the presence of men who talked excitedly of a <u>prospective</u> battle as of a drama they were about to witness, with nothing but eagerness and curiosity apparent in their faces. It was often that he suspected them to be liars.

◀ When does the youth suspect that the other soldiers are liars?

He did not pass such thoughts without severe condemnation of himself. He dinned[2] reproaches at times. He was convicted by himself of many shameful crimes against the gods of traditions.

In his great anxiety his heart was continually <u>clamoring</u> at what he considered the intolerable slowness of the generals. They seemed content to perch tranquilly on the river bank, and leave him bowed down by the weight of a great problem. He wanted it settled forthwith. He could not long bear such a load, he said. Sometimes his anger at the commanders reached an acute stage, and he grumbled about the camp like a veteran.

One morning, however, he found himself in the ranks of his prepared regiment. The men were whispering speculations and recounting the old rumors. In the gloom before the break of the day their uniforms glowed a deep purple

---

2. **dinned.** Impress by constant repetition

Words For Everyday Use	**un • scru • pu • lous** (un skro͞o´pyə ləs) *adj.*, unethical, dishonest **flout** (flout) *vt.*, treat with contemptuous disregard; scorn	**pro • spec • tive** (prə spek´tiv) *adj.*, likely to come about; expected **clam • or** (kla´mər) *vi.*, become loudly insistent

hue. From across the river the red eyes were still peering. In the eastern sky there was a yellow patch like a rug laid for the feet of the coming sun; and against it, black and patternlike, loomed the gigantic figure of the colonel on a gigantic horse.

From off in the darkness came the trampling of feet. The youth could occasionally see dark shadows that moved like monsters. The regiment stood at rest for what seemed a long time. The youth grew impatient. It was unendurable the way these affairs were managed. He wondered how long they were to be kept waiting.

▶ What does the youth expect to see and hear "at any moment"?

As he looked all about him and pondered upon the mystic gloom, he began to believe that at any moment the <u>ominous</u> distance might be aflare, and the rolling crashes of an engagement come to his ears. Staring once at the red eyes across the river, he conceived them to be growing larger, as the <u>orbs</u> of a row of dragons advancing. He turned toward the colonel and saw him lift his gigantic arm and calmly stroke his mustache.

▶ What emotions do the approaching horseman and his conversation with the colonel create in the youth and the other soldiers?

At last he heard from along the road at the foot of the hill the clatter of a horse's galloping hoofs. It must be the coming of orders. He bent forward, scarce breathing. The exciting clickety-click, as it grew louder and louder, seemed to be beating upon his soul. Presently a horseman with jangling equipment drew rein before the colonel of the regiment. The two held a short, sharp-worded conversation. The men in the foremost ranks craned their necks.

▶ What is revealed of the colonel and the horseman's discussion?

As the horseman wheeled his animal and galloped away he turned to shout over his shoulder, "Don't forget that box of cigars!" The colonel mumbled in reply. The youth wondered what a box of cigars had to do with war.

▶ What does the regiment finally begin to do?

A moment later the regiment went swinging off into the darkness. It was now like one of those moving monsters <u>wending</u> with many feet. The air was heavy, and cold with dew. A mass of wet grass, marched upon, rustled like silk.

There was an occasional flash and glimmer of steel from the backs of all these huge crawling reptiles. From the road came creakings and grumblings as some <u>surly</u> guns were dragged away.

▶ In what way is one man injured?

The men stumbled along still muttering speculations. There was a <u>subdued</u> debate. Once a man fell down, and as he reached for his rifle a comrade, unseeing, trod upon his

---

Words For Everyday Use

om • i • nous (ô′mə nəs) *adj.*, foreboding or foreshadowing something, usually evil

orb (ôrb) *n.*, eye

wend (wend) *vi.*, travel

sur • ly (sər′lē) *adj.*, menacing or threatening in appearance

sub • dued (səb do͞od′) *adj.*, lacking in vitality, intensity, or strength

hand. He of the injured fingers swore bitterly and aloud. A low, tittering laugh went among his fellows.

Presently they passed into a roadway and marched forward with easy strides. A dark regiment moved before them, and from behind also came the tinkle of equipments on the bodies of marching men.

The rushing yellow of the developing day went on behind their backs. When the sunrays at last struck full and mellowingly upon the earth, the youth saw that the landscape was streaked with two long, thin, black columns which disappeared on the brow of a hill in front and rearward vanished in a wood. They were like two serpents crawling from the cavern of the night.

◀ What do the columns of men look like?

The river was not in view. The tall soldier burst into praises of what he thought to be his powers of perception.

Some of the tall one's companions cried with emphasis that they, too, had evolved the same thing, and they congratulated themselves upon it. But there were others who said that the tall one's plan was not the true one at all. They persisted with other theories. There was a vigorous discussion.

The youth took no part in them. As he walked along in careless line he was engaged with his own eternal debate. He could not hinder himself from dwelling upon it. He was despondent and sullen, and threw shifting glances about him. He looked ahead, often expecting to hear from the advance the rattle of firing.

But the long serpents crawled slowly from hill to hill without <u>bluster</u> of smoke. A <u>dun</u>-colored cloud of dust floated away to the right. The sky overhead was of a fairy blue.

The youth studied the faces of his companions, ever on the watch to detect kindred emotions. He suffered disappointment. Some ardor of the air which was causing the veteran commands to move with glee—almost with song—had infected the new regiment. The men began to speak of victory as of a thing they knew. Also, the tall soldier received his vindication. They were certainly going to come around in behind the enemy. They expressed <u>commiseration</u> for that part of the army which had been left upon the river bank, <u>felicitating</u> themselves upon being a part of a blasting host.

◀ In what way is the tall soldier "vindicated"?

The youth, considering himself as separated from the

Words For Everyday Use	blus • ter (blusʹtər) *n.*, violent commotion dun (dun) *adj.*, having a dull grayish yellow color	com • mis • er • a • tion (kə mi zə rāʹshən) *n.*, sympathy; compassion fe • lic • i • tate (fi liʹsə tāt) *vt.*, offer congratulations to

► *Why do you think the youth considers himself to be separated from the others?*

others, was saddened by the <u>blithe</u> and merry speeches that went from rank to rank. The company wags[3] all made their best endeavors. The regiment tramped to the tune of laughter.

The loud soldier often convulsed whole files by his biting sarcasms[4] aimed at the tall one.

And it was not long before all the men seemed to forget their mission. Whole brigades[5] grinned in unison, and regiments laughed.

► *What do the soldiers watch to entertain themselves?*

A rather fat soldier attempted to <u>pilfer</u> a horse from a dooryard. He planned to load his knapsack upon it. He was escaping with his prize when a young girl rushed from the house and grabbed the animal's mane. There followed a wrangle. The young girl, with pink cheeks and shining eyes, stood like a <u>dauntless</u> statue.

The observant regiment, standing at rest in the roadway, whooped at once, and entered whole-souled upon the side of the maiden. The men became so <u>engrossed</u> in this affair that they entirely ceased to remember their own large war. They jeered the piratical private, and called attention to various defects in his personal appearance; and they were wildly enthusiastic in support of the young girl.

► *Whom do the soldiers support in this confrontation?*

To her, from some distance, came bold advice. "Hit him with a stick."

There were crows and catcalls[6] showered upon him when he retreated without the horse. The regiment rejoiced at his downfall. Loud and <u>vociferous</u> congratulations were showered upon the maiden, who stood panting and regarding the troops with defiance.

At nightfall the column broke into regimental pieces, and the fragments went into the fields to camp. Tents sprang up like strange plants. Camp fires, like red, peculiar blossoms, dotted the night.

The youth kept from intercourse with his companions as much as circumstances would allow him. In the evening he

---

3. **wags.** Young men, usually jokers
4. **convulsed . . . sarcasms.** The loud soldier makes the lines of soldiers laugh by his mocking remarks of the tall soldier.
5. **brigades.** Large bodies of troops
6. **crows and catcalls.** *Crow*—sound made to rejoice over another person's distress; *catcalls*—loud cry to express disapproval

---

Words For Everyday Use

blithe (blīth) *adj.,* lighthearted; merry
pil • fer (pil´fər) *vt.,* steal
daunt • less (dônt´ləs) *adj.,* fearless

en • grossed (en grōsd´) *adj.,* completely occupied, engaged, or involved
vo • cif • er • ous (vō si´fər us) *adj.,* noisy, loud

wandered a few paces into the gloom. From this little distance the many fires, with the black forms of men passing to and fro before the crimson rays, made weird and satanic effects.

He lay down in the grass. The blades pressed tenderly against his cheek. The moon had been lighted and was hung in a treetop. The liquid stillness of the night enveloping him made him feel vast pity for himself. There was a caress in the soft winds; and the whole mood of the darkness, he thought, was one of sympathy for himself in his distress.

He wished, without reserve, that he was at home again making the endless rounds from the house to the barn, from the barn to the fields, from the fields to the barn, from the barn to the house. He remembered he had often cursed the brindle cow and her mates, and had sometimes flung milking stools. But, from his present point of view, there was a halo of happiness about each of their heads, and he would have sacrificed all the brass buttons[7] on the continent to have been enabled to return to them. He told himself that he was not formed for a soldier. And he mused seriously upon the radical differences between himself and those men who were dodging implike around the fires.

◄ Where does the youth wish he were again? What does he tell himself?

As he <u>mused</u> thus he heard the rustle of grass, and, upon turning his head, discovered the loud soldier. He called out, "Oh, Wilson!"

◄ What is the loud soldier's name?

The latter approached and looked down.

"Why, hello, Henry; is it you? What you doing here?"

"Oh, thinking," said the youth.

The other sat down and carefully lighted his pipe. "You're getting blue, my boy. You're looking thundering peeked.[8] What the dickens is wrong with you?"

"Oh, nothing," said the youth.

The loud soldier launched then into the subject of the anticipated fight. "Oh, we've got 'em now!" As he spoke his boyish face was wreathed in a gleeful smile, and his voice had an <u>exultant</u> ring. "We've got 'em now. At last, by the eternal thunders, we'll lick 'em good!"

◄ How does the loud soldier, Wilson, feel about his regiment's chances in the upcoming battle? How have previous battles gone for their side?

---

7. **brass buttons.** Symbol of rank on a military uniform
8. **peeked.** Peaked, or sickly

| Words For Everyday Use | **muse** (myo͞oz) *vt.*, become absorbed in thought |
| | **ex • ul • tant** (eg zul´tənt) *adj.*, joyful, triumphant |

"If the truth was known," he added, more soberly, "*they've* licked *us* about every clip[9] up to now; but this time—this time—we'll lick 'em good!

"I thought you was objecting to this march a little while ago," said the youth coldly.

"Oh, it wasn't that," explained the other. "I don't mind marching, if there's going to be fighting at the end of it. What I hate is this getting moved here and moved there, with no good coming of it, as far as I can see, excepting sore feet and damned short rations."[10]

"Well, Jim Conklin says we'll get a plenty of fighting this time."

"He's right for once, I guess, though I can't see how it come. This time we're in for a big battle, and we've got the best end of it, certain sure. Gee rod! how we will thump 'em!"

He arose and began to pace to and fro excitedly. The thrill of his enthusiasm made him walk with an elastic step. He was sprightly, vigorous, fiery in his belief in success. He looked into the future with clear, proud eye, and he swore with the air of an old soldier.

The youth watched him for a moment in silence. When he finally spoke his voice was as bitter as dregs.[11] "Oh, you're going to do great things, I s'pose!"

The loud soldier blew a thoughtful cloud of smoke from his pipe. "Oh, I don't know," he remarked with dignity; "I don't know. I s'pose I'll do as well as the rest. I'm going to try like thunder." He evidently complimented himself upon the modesty of this statement.

"How do you know you won't run when the time comes?" asked the youth.

"Run?" said the loud one; "run?—of course not!" He laughed.

"Well," continued the youth, "lots of good-a'-nough men have thought they was going to do great things before the fight, but when the time come they skedaddled."[12]

"Oh, that's true, I s'pose," replied the other; "but I'm not going to skedaddle. The man that bets on my running will lose his money, that's all." He nodded confidently.

"Oh, shucks!" said the youth. "You ain't the bravest man in the world, are you?"

► *How does Wilson feel about his own position in the upcoming battle? What words would you use to describe Wilson?*

---

9. **clip.** Fight
10. **rations.** Food
11. **dregs.** The most undesirable part of something, especially a beverage
12. **skedaddled.** Fled in a panic

"No, I ain't," exclaimed the loud soldier <u>indignantly</u>; "and I didn't say I was the bravest man in the world, neither. I said I was going to do my share of fighting—that's what I said. And I am, too. Who are you, anyhow? You talk as if you thought you was Napoleon Bonaparte."[13] He glared at the youth for a moment, and then strode away.

The youth called in a savage voice after his comrade: "Well, you needn't git mad about it!" But the other continued on his way and made no reply.

He felt alone in space when his injured comrade had disappeared. His failure to discover any mite[14] of resemblance in their view points made him more miserable than before. No one seemed to be wrestling with such a terrific personal problem. He was a mental outcast.

◄ *What makes the youth miserable?*

He went slowly to his tent and stretched himself on a blanket by the side of the snoring tall soldier. In the darkness he saw visions of a thousand-tongued fear that would babble at his back and cause him to flee, while others were going coolly about their country's business. He admitted that he would not be able to cope with this monster. He felt that every nerve in his body would be an ear to hear the voices, while other men would remain <u>stolid</u> and deaf.

◄ *What are the youth's perceptions about himself? About the other soldiers?*

And as he sweated with the pain of these thoughts, he could hear low, serene sentences. "I'll bid five." "Make it six." "Seven." "Seven goes."

He stared at the red, shivering reflection of a fire on the white wall of his tent until, exhausted and ill from the monotony of his suffering, he fell asleep.

---

13. **Napoleon Bonaparte.** Napoleon Bonaparte (1769–1821) was one of France's greatest military strategists; he was emperor of France from 1804 to 1815.
14. **mite.** Very little bit

| Words For Everyday Use | **in • dig • nant • ly** (in dig´nənt lē) *adv.*, in a righteously angry, or displeased, manner |
| | **stol • id** (stô´ləd) *adj.*, having or expressing little or no sensibility; unemotional |

Chapter 3

When another night came the columns, changed to purple streaks, filed across two pontoon bridges.[1] A glaring fire wine-tinted the waters of the river. Its rays, shining upon the moving masses of troops, brought forth here and there sudden gleams of silver or gold. Upon the other shore a dark and mysterious range of hills was curved against the sky. The insect voices of the night sang solemnly.

After this crossing the youth assured himself that at any moment they might be suddenly and fearfully assaulted from the caves of the lowering[2] woods. He kept his eyes watchfully upon the darkness.

But his regiment went unmolested to a camping place, and its soldiers slept the brave sleep of wearied men. In the morning they were routed out with early energy, and hustled along a narrow road that led deep into the forest.

It was during this rapid march that the regiment lost many of the marks of a new command.

► In what ways do the men become more like veterans as they march onward?

The men had begun to count the miles upon their fingers, and they grew tired. "Sore feet an' damned short rations, that's all," said the loud soldier. There was perspiration and grumblings. After a time they began to shed their knapsacks. Some tossed them unconcernedly down; others hid them carefully, asserting their plans to return for them at some convenient time. Men <u>extricated</u> themselves from thick shirts. Presently few carried anything but their necessary clothing, blankets, haversacks, canteens, and arms and ammunition.[3] "You can now eat and shoot," said the tall soldier to the youth. "That's all you want to do."

There was sudden change from the ponderous infantry[4] of theory to the light and speedy infantry of practice. The regiment, relieved of a burden, received a new <u>impetus</u>. But there was much loss of valuable knapsacks, and, on the whole, very good shirts.

But the regiment was not yet veteranlike in appearance.

---

1. **pontoon bridges.** Temporary bridge made from portable floats
2. **lowering.** Be or become dark, gloomy, and threatening
3. **canteens, and arms and ammunition.** *Canteens*—flasks or containers for carrying water; *arms and ammunitions*—guns and bullets
4. **ponderous infantry.** *Ponderous*—slow-moving; *infantry*—foot soldiers

| Words For Everyday Use | **ex • tri • cate** (ek´strə kāt) *vt.*, free or remove from an entanglement or difficulty |
| | **im • pe • tus** (im´pə təs) *n.*, driving force; stimulus |

Veteran regiments in the army were likely to be very small <u>aggregations</u> of men. Once, when the command had first come to the field, some <u>preambulating</u> veterans, noting the length of their column, had <u>accosted</u> them thus: "Hey, fellers, what brigade is that?" And when the men had replied that they formed a regiment and not a brigade,[5] the older soldiers had laughed, and said, "O Gawd!"

Also, there was too great a similarity in the hats. The hats of a regiment should properly represent the history of head-gear for a period of years. And, moreover, there were no let-ters of faded gold speaking from the colors. They were new and beautiful, and the color bearer habitually oiled the pole.[6]

Presently the army again sat down to think. The odor of the peaceful pines was in the men's nostrils. The sound of monotonous axe blows rang through the forest, and the insects, nodding upon their perches, crooned like old women. The youth returned to his theory of a blue demon-stration.

One gray dawn, however, he was kicked in the leg by the tall soldier, and then, before he was entirely awake, he found himself running down a wood road in the midst of men who were panting from the first effects of speed. His canteen banged rhythmically upon his thigh, and his haversack bobbed softly. His musket bounced a trifle from his shoulder at each stride and made his cap feel uncertain upon his head.

He could hear the men whisper jerky sentences: "Say—what's all this—about?" "What th' thunder—we—skedad-dlin' this way fer?" "Billie—keep off m' feet. Yeh run—like a cow." And the loud soldier's shrill voice could be heard: "What th' devil they in sich a hurry for?"

The youth thought the damp fog of early morning moved from the rush of a great body of troops. From the distance came a sudden spatter of firing.

He was bewildered. As he ran with his comrades he stren-uously tried to think, but all he knew was that if he fell down

◀ In what ways are the body of soldiers unlike a veteran regiment?

◀ How is the youth awoken one morning? What do he and the other soldiers do?

◀ What does the youth hear?

---

5. **regiment and not a brigade**. A brigade is a large military unit composed of a number of smaller units called regiments. The veterans mistake the regiment for a brigade because it is full of new recruits; the suggestion is that veteran regi-ments were much smaller because so many soldiers had died.

6. **color . . . pole**. Person who carried the flag, known as the colors, of a mili-tary unit; the color bearer polishes the wooden pole of the flag with oil

Words For Everyday Use	ag • gre • ga • tion (a gri gā´shən) n., group, body, or mass composed of many distinct parts or individuals	per • am • bu • late (pər am´byoo lāt) vt., travel on foot; stroll
		ac • cost (ə kôst´) vt., approach and speak in a challenging or aggressive way

those coming behind would tread upon him. All his faculties seemed to be needed to guide him over and past obstructions. He felt carried along by a mob.

The sun spread <u>disclosing</u> rays, and, one by one, regiments burst into view like armed men just born of the earth. The youth perceived that the time had come. He was about to be measured. For a moment he felt in the face of his great trial like a babe, and the flesh over his heart seemed very thin. He seized time to look about him calculatingly.

But he instantly saw that it would be impossible for him to escape from the regiment. It inclosed him. And there were iron laws of tradition and law on four sides. He was in a moving box.

As he perceived this fact it occurred to him that he had never wished to come to the war. He had not enlisted of his free will. He had been dragged by the merciless government. And now they were taking him out to be slaughtered.

The regiment slid down a bank and <u>wallowed</u> across a little stream. The mournful current moved slowly on, and from the water, shaded black, some white bubble eyes looked at the men.

As they climbed the hill on the farther side artillery[7] began to boom. Here the youth forgot many things as he felt a sudden impulse of curiosity. He scrambled up the bank with a speed that could not be exceeded by a bloodthirsty man.

He expected a battle scene.

There were some little fields <u>girted</u> and squeezed by a forest. Spread over the grass and in among the tree trunks, he could see knots and waving lines of skirmishers[8] who were running hither and thither and firing at the landscape. A dark battle line lay upon a sunstruck clearing that gleamed orange color. A flag fluttered.

Other regiments <u>floundered</u> up the bank. The brigade was formed in line of battle, and after a pause started slowly through the woods in the rear of the receding skirmishers, who were continually melting into the scene to appear again farther on. They were always busy as bees, deeply absorbed in their little combats.

---

7. **artillery.** Large guns worked by a crew of men
8. **skirmishers.** Persons who engage in fight, as in a war

> ► What does the youth think when he realizes that he will soon have to fight? Why might he think this?

> ► How does the youth feel about his decision to join the army now?

> ► What does the youth expect to see? What does he actually see?

Words For Everyday Use

dis • clos • ing (dis klōz´iŋ) *adj.*, exposing to view; revealing

wal • low (wô´lō) *vi.*, roll oneself about in an lazy or clumsy manner

gird (gərd) *vt.*, encircle; surround

floun • der (floun´dər) *vi.*, struggle to move or obtain footing; thrash about wildly

The youth tried to observe everything. He did not use care to avoid trees and branches, and his forgotten feet were constantly knocking against stones or getting entangled in briers. He was aware that these battalions with their commotions were woven red and startling into the gentle fabric of softened greens and browns. It looked to be a wrong place for a battle field.

The skirmishers in advance fascinated him. Their shots into thickets and at distant and prominent trees spoke to him of tragedies—hidden, mysterious, solemn.

Once the line encountered the body of a dead soldier. He lay upon his back staring at the sky. He was dressed in an awkward suit of yellowish brown. The youth could see that the soles of his shoes had been worn to the thinness of writing paper, and from a great <u>rent</u> in one the dead foot projected piteously. And it was as if fate had betrayed the soldier. In death it exposed to his enemies that poverty which in life he had perhaps concealed from his friends.

◀ What do the soldiers encounter? What do they note about this person? In what way has fate betrayed him?

The ranks opened <u>covertly</u> to avoid the corpse. The invulnerable dead man forced a way for himself. The youth looked keenly at the <u>ashen</u> face. The wind raised the tawny beard. It moved as if a hand were stroking it. He vaguely desired to walk around and around the body and stare; the impulse of the living to try to read in dead eyes the answer to the Question.

◀ What does the youth wish to do? What question do you think the youth has in mind?

During the march the ardor which the youth had acquired when out of view of the field rapidly faded to nothing. His curiosity was quite easily satisfied. If an intense scene had caught him with its wild swing as he came to the top of the bank, he might have gone roaring on. This advance upon Nature was too calm. He had opportunity to reflect. He had time in which to wonder about himself and to attempt to probe his sensations.

◀ Why does the setting make the youth less excited and eager to begin fighting?

Absurd ideas took hold upon him. He thought that he did not relish the landscape. It threatened him. A coldness swept over his back, and it is true that his trousers felt to him that they were no fit for his legs at all.

A house standing placidly in distant fields had to him an ominous look. The shadows of the woods were <u>formidable</u>. He was certain that in this vista there lurked fierce-eyed hosts. The swift thought came to him that the generals did

◀ What is the youth feeling about his surroundings? his commanding officers?

| Words For Everyday Use | **rent** (rent) *n.*, rip, tear
 co • vert • ly (kō´vərt lē) *adv.*, not openly; secretly | **ash • en** (a´shən) *adj.*, resembling ashes (as in color); deadly pale
 for • mi • da • ble (fōr´mə də bəl) *adj.*, causing fear, dread, or apprehension |

not know what they were about. It was all a trap. Suddenly those close forests would bristle with rifle barrels. Ironlike brigades would appear in the rear. They were all going to be sacrificed. The generals were stupids. The enemy would presently swallow the whole command. He glared about him, expecting to see the stealthy approach of his death.

► What does the youth feel an urge to do?

He thought that he must break from the ranks and <u>harangue</u> his comrades. They must not all be killed like pigs; and he was sure it would come to pass unless they were informed of these dangers. The generals were idiots to send them marching into a regular pen. There was but one pair of eyes in the corps. He would step forth and make a speech. Shrill and passionate words came to his lips.

The line, broken into moving fragments by the ground, went calmly on through fields and woods. The youth looked at the men nearest him, and saw, for the most part, expressions of deep interest, as if they were investigating something that had fascinated them. One or two stepped with overvaliant airs as if they were already plunged into war. Others walked as upon thin ice. The greater part of the untested men appeared quiet and absorbed. They were going to look at war, the red animal—war, the blood-swollen god. And they were deeply engrossed in this march.

► Why doesn't the youth speak his mind to the other soldiers?

As he looked the youth gripped his outcry at his throat. He saw that even if the men were tottering with fear they would laugh at his warning. They would jeer him, and, if practicable, pelt him with missiles. Admitting that he might be wrong, a frenzied <u>declamation</u> of the kind would turn him into a worm.

He assumed, then, the demeanor of one who knows that he is doomed alone to unwritten responsibilities. He <u>lagged</u>, with tragic glances at the sky.

He was surprised presently by the young lieutenant of his company, who began heartily to beat him with a sword, calling out in a loud and <u>insolent</u> voice: "Come, young man, get up into ranks there. No skulking'll do here." He mended his pace with suitable haste. And he hated the lieutenant, who had no appreciation of fine minds. He was a mere brute.

► How does the youth feel about the lieutenant?

After a time the brigade was halted in the cathedral light of a forest. The busy skirmishers were still popping. Through the aisles of the wood could be seen the floating smoke from

---

Words
For
Everyday
Use

ha • rangue (hə raŋ´) *vi.*, make a ranting speech

dec • la • ma • tion (de klə mā´shən) *n.*, behavior toward others; outward manner

lag (lag) *vi.*, stay or fall behind

in • so • lent (in´sə lənt) *adj.*, insultingly contemptuous in speech or conduct

their rifles. Sometimes it went up in little balls, white and compact.

During this halt many men in the regiment began erecting tiny hills in front of them. They used stones, sticks, earth, and anything they thought might turn a bullet. Some built comparatively large ones, while others seemed content with little ones.

◀ What do the soldiers do once they stop marching?

This procedure caused a discussion among the men. Some wished to fight like duelists, believing it to be correct to stand erect and be, from their feet to their foreheads, a mark. They said they scorned the devices of the cautious. But the others scoffed in reply, and pointed to the veterans on the flanks who were digging at the ground like terriers.[9] In a short time there was quite a <u>barricade</u> along the regimental fronts. Directly, however, they were ordered to withdraw from that place.

◀ How do some of the new recruits think they should fight? What type of soldiers are digging the most eagerly?

This astounded the youth. He forgot his stewing[10] over the advance movement. "Well, then, what did they march us out here for?" he demanded of the tall soldier. The latter with calm faith began a heavy explanation, although he had been compelled to leave a little protection of stones and dirt to which he had devoted much care and skill.

When the regiment was aligned in another position each man's regard for his safety caused another line of small intrenchments.[11] They ate their noon meal behind a third one. They were moved from this one also. They were marched from place to place with apparent aimlessness.

The youth had been taught that a man became another thing in a battle. He saw his salvation in such a change. Hence this waiting was an ordeal to him. He was in a fever of impatience. He considered that there was <u>denoted</u> a lack of purpose on the part of the generals. He began to complain to the tall soldier. "I can't stand this much longer," he cried. "I don't see what good it does to make us wear out our legs for nothin'." He wished to return to camp, knowing that this affair was a blue demonstration; or else to go into a battle

---

9. **terriers.** Type of small dog originally used by hunters to dig for small game animals
10. **stewing.** Worrying
11. **intrenchments.** Entrenchments, long cuts in the ground used for protection from bullets and the like in war

---

Words
For
Everyday
Use

bar • ri • cade (bar´ə kād) *n.*, barrier thrown up across a way or passage to check the advance of the enemy

de • note (di nōt´) *vt.*, make known

and discover that he had been a fool in his doubts, and was, in truth, a man of traditional courage. The strain of present circumstances he felt to be intolerable.

The philosophical tall soldier measured a sandwich of cracker and pork and swallowed it in a <u>nonchalant</u> manner. "Oh, I suppose we must go <u>reconnoitering</u> around the country jest to keep 'em from getting too close, or to develop 'em, or something."

"Huh!" said the loud soldier.

"Well," cried the youth, still fidgeting, "I'd rather do anything 'most than go tramping 'round the country all day doing no good to nobody and jest tiring ourselves out."

"So would I," said the loud soldier. "It ain't right. I tell you if anybody with any sense was a-runnin' this army it—"

"Oh, shut up!" roared the tall private. "You little fool. You little damn' cuss. You ain't had that there coat and them pants on for six months, and yet you talk as if—"

"Well, I wanta do some fighting anyway," interrupted the other. "I didn't come here to walk. I could 'ave walked to home—'round an' 'round the barn, if I jest wanted to walk."

The tall one, red-faced, swallowed another sandwich as if taking poison in despair.

But gradually, as he chewed, his face became again quiet and contented. He could not rage in fierce argument in the presence of such sandwiches. During his meals he always wore an air of blissful contemplation of the food he had swallowed. His spirit seemed then to be communing with the <u>viands</u>.

He accepted new environment and circumstance with great coolness, eating from his haversack at every opportunity. On the march he went along with the stride of a hunter, objecting to neither <u>gait</u> nor distance. And he had not raised his voice when he had been ordered away from three little protective piles of earth and stone, each of which had been an engineering feat worthy of being made sacred to the name of his grandmother.

In the afternoon the regiment went out over the same ground it had taken in the morning. The landscape then ceased to threaten the youth. He had been close to it and become familiar with it.

▶ What do the youth and the loud soldier complain about? What is the tall soldier's reaction to their complaints?

▶ What does the tall soldier do to make himself feel less angry with his companions?

▶ In what ways does the tall soldier react to the various difficulties the soldiers have experienced?

Words For Everyday Use

non • cha • lant (nôn shə länt´) *adj.*, having an air of easy unconcern or indifference

re • con • noi • ter (rē kə nôi´tər) *vi.*, engage in observation or inspection

vi • and (vī´ənd) *n.*, item of food, especially a choice or tasty dish

gait (gāt) *n.*, manner of walking or moving on foot

When, however, they began to pass into a new region, his old fears of stupidity and incompetence reassailed him, but this time he doggedly let them babble. He was occupied with his problem, and in his desperation he concluded that the stupidity did not greatly matter.

Once he thought he had concluded that it would be better to get killed directly and end his troubles. Regarding death thus out of the corner of his eye, he conceived it to be nothing but rest, and he was filled with a momentary astonishment that he should have made an extraordinary <u>commotion</u> over the mere matter of getting killed. He would die; he would go to some place where he would be understood. It was useless to expect appreciation of his profound and fine senses from such men as the lieutenant. He must look to the grave for comprehension.

◀ What does the youth decide would be better than experiencing his current troubles?

The skirmish fire increased to a long clattering sound. With it was mingled far-away cheering. A battery spoke.[12]

Directly the youth could see the skirmishers running. They were pursued by the sound of musketry fire. After a time the hot, dangerous flashes of the rifles were visible. Smoke clouds went slowly and insolently across the fields like observant phantoms. The din became <u>crescendo</u>, like the roar of an oncoming train.

◀ What happens to the youth's "plan" as soon as he sees and hears the violence of battle?

A brigade ahead of them and on the right went into action with a rending roar. It was as if it had exploded. And thereafter it lay stretched in the distance behind a long gray wall, that one was obliged to look twice at to make sure that it was smoke.

The youth, forgetting his neat plan of getting killed, gazed spell bound. His eyes grew wide and busy with the action of the scene. His mouth was a little ways open.

Of a sudden he felt a heavy and sad hand laid upon his shoulder. Awakening from his trance of observation he turned and beheld the loud soldier.

"It's my first and last battle, old boy," said the latter, with intense gloom. He was quite pale and his girlish lip was trembling.

"Eh?" murmured the youth in great astonishment.

◀ What does the loud soldier tell the youth? What does he give to him?

---

12. **battery spoke.** Group of large guns sounded

Words For Everyday Use	**com • mo • tion** (kə mō′shən) *n.*, excitement or confusion
	cre • scen • do (krə shen′dō) *n.*, a gradual increase, especially in reference to music

"It's my first and last battle, old boy," continued the loud soldier. "Something tells me—"

"What?"

"I'm a gone coon this first time and—and I w-want you to take these here things—to—my—folks." He ended in a <u>quavering</u> sob of pity for himself. He handed the youth a little packet done up in a yellow envelope.

"Why, what the devil—" began the youth again.

But the other gave him a glance as from the depths of a tomb, and raised his limp hand in a <u>prophetic</u> manner and turned away.

Words For Everyday Use

qua • ver • ing (kwā´və riŋ) *adj.*, trembling
pro • phet • ic (prə fe´tik) *adj.*, foretelling events; predictive

Respond to the Selection

What do you imagine war is like? If you were in Henry Fleming's (the youth's) position, how would you feel about the battle about to take place?

Investigate, Inquire, and Imagine

Recall: GATHERING FACTS

1a. In Chapter 1, what dreams did Henry Fleming (the youth) once have about war? To what time period did he see war as belonging when he is awake? What was Henry's mother's attitude toward the idea of him enlisting?

2a. In Chapter 1, what rumor does Jim Conklin (the tall soldier) spread? What worries does Henry have about battle? What is Jim's opinion about how the new regiment will do in battle and whether he would run? In Chapter 2, what is Wilson's (the loud soldier's) opinion about how the regiment will do? What is his opinion about whether he would run?

3a. In Chapter 3, when the regiment finally marches toward a battle, what do Henry and the other soldiers encounter for the first time, and what do they notice about this thing? What does Henry begin to think about the army's commanders? What does Wilson (the loud soldier) tell Henry once the regiment sees the battle? What does Wilson give to Henry?

Interpret: FINDING MEANING

→ 1b. Why does Henry view war differently depending on if he is dreaming or awake? Given his dreams, why does his mother's reaction disappoint him? Explain whether Henry is justified in forming this opinion of war based on his experiences so far.

→ 2b. Why does Henry ask these two soldiers these questions? What similarities and differences between Jim and Wilson do their answers reveal? What type of person is Henry hoping to discover and why? Explain what the author means when he calls Henry an "unknown quantity."

→ 3b. What do Henry's thoughts about the commanders reveal about his feelings toward the battle? What do Wilson's words and actions at the end of Chapter 3 reveal about his earlier words about battle? How do you think Wilson's words at the end of Chapter 3 make Henry feel?

Analyze: TAKING THINGS APART

4a. Identify Henry's feelings about war, death, and his own potential in the upcoming battle. How have Henry's feelings about these things changed from the beginning of Chapter 1 to the end of Chapter 3?

Synthesize: BRINGING THINGS TOGETHER

→ 4b. Based on what you have learned about Henry so far, predict how Henry will react in the upcoming battle. Support your answer with evidence you have gathered in your response to question 4a.

Evaluate: MAKING JUDGMENTS

5a. The saying, "Hindsight is always 20/20," means that if people were given the opportunity to change past actions, knowing what they know now, they would often make different, better choices. What do you think of Henry's mother's advice about war? Was her advice better or worse than the advice ancient warriors' parents gave them to "return with your shield [alive], or on it [dead]"?

Extend: CONNECTING IDEAS

➤ 5b. If you were Henry, what would you say to Wilson before he turns away at the end of Chapter 3? What would you plan to do in the upcoming battle? How might you prepare yourself physically, mentally, or emotionally, for what you plan to do?

Understanding Literature

Narrator and Point of View. A **narrator** is a person or character who tells a story. Works of fiction almost always have a narrator, even if that person is just an observer who does not take part in the action of the story. **Point of view** is the vantage point from which a story is told. Stories can be told from the *first-person point of view,* in which the narrator uses words such as *I* and *we,* or from a *third-person point of view*, in which the narrator uses words such as *he, she, it,* and *they.* In some stories, the narrator's point of view is *limited.* In such stories the narrator can reveal his or her own private, internal thoughts or those of a single character. In other stories, the narrator's point of view is *omniscient,* or all-knowing, meaning that the narrator can reveal the private, internal thoughts of any character. Who is the narrator of *The Red Badge of Courage?* From what point of view is the story told? Whose private, internal thoughts are revealed?

Characterization. Characterization is the act of creating or describing a character. Writers use three major techniques to create a character: direct description, portrayal of the character's behavior, and presenting the thoughts and emotions of a character. In Chapters 1–3, what techniques does Crane use to create the following characters? Summarize what you have learned about each character in a sentence.

· Henry Fleming (the youth)   · Wilson (the loud soldier)
· Jim Conklin (the tall soldier)   · Mrs. Fleming (Henry's mother)

Conflict and Protagonist. A **conflict** is a struggle between two people or things in a literary work. A conflict can be *external,* meaning that it takes place between a character and some outside force, such as another character, nature, or society. A conflict can also be *internal,* meaning that it takes place within a person. A **protagonist** is the main character in a story. The protagonist faces a struggle or conflict. Who appears to be the protagonist in this story? What external conflict does the protagonist experience? What internal conflict does the protagonist experience?

Chapter 4

The brigade was halted in the <u>fringe</u> of a <u>grove</u>. The men crouched among the trees and pointed their restless guns out at the fields. They tried to look beyond the smoke.

Out of this haze they could see running men. Some shouted information and gestured as they hurried.

The men of the new regiment watched and listened eagerly, while their tongues ran on in gossip of the battle. They mouthed rumors that had flown like birds out of the unknown.

◄ What do the men do as they wait and watch the battle?

"They say Perry has been driven in with big loss."

"Yes, Carrott went t' th' hospital. He said he was sick. That smart lieutenant is commanding 'G' Company. Th' boys say they won't be under Carrott no more if they all have t' desert. They allus knew he was a—"

"Hannises' batt'ry is took."

"It ain't either. I saw Hannises' batt'ry off on th' left not more'n fifteen minutes ago."

"Well—"

"Th' general, he ses he is goin' t' take th' hull command of th' 304th when we go inteh action, an' then he ses we'll do sech fightin' as never another one reg'ment done."

"They say we're catchin' it over on th' left. They say th' enemy driv' our line inteh a devil of a swamp an' took Hannises' batt'ry."

"No sech thing. Hannises' batt'ry was 'long here 'bout a minute ago."

"That young Hasbrouck, he makes a good off'cer. He ain't afraid 'a nothin'."

"I met one of th' 148th Maine boys an' he ses his brigade fit th' hull rebel army fer four hours over on th' turnpike road an' killed about five thousand of 'em. He ses one more sech fight as that an' th' war 'll be over."

"Bill wasn't scared either. No, sir! It wasn't that. Bill ain't a-gittin' scared easy. He was jest mad, that's what he was. When that feller trod on his hand, he up an' sed that he was willin' t' give his hand t' his country, but he be dumbed if he was goin' t' have every dumb bushwhacker[1] in th' kentry

◄ What happened to the man whose hand was stepped upon?

---

1. **bushwhacker.** Person who takes part in an ambush

Words For Everyday Use	**fringe** (frinj) *n.,* edge **grove** (grōv) *n.,* small wood without underbrush

walkin' 'round on it. So he went t' th' hospital disregardless of th' fight. Three fingers was crunched. Th' dern doctor wanted t' amputate[2] 'm, an' Bill, he raised a heluva row, I hear. He's a funny feller."

The din in front swelled to a tremendous chorus. The youth and his fellows were frozen to silence. They could see a flag that tossed in the smoke angrily. Near it were the blurred and agitated forms of troops. There came a <u>turbulent</u> stream of men across the fields. A battery changing position at a frantic gallop scattered the stragglers right and left.

▶ What events put an end to the gossip and force the men to become involved in the battle?

A shell[3] screaming like a storm banshee[4] went over the huddled heads of the reserves.[5] It landed in the grove, and exploding redly flung the brown earth. There was a little shower of pine needles.

Bullets began to whistle among the branches and <u>nip</u> at the trees. Twigs and leaves came sailing down. It was as if a thousand axes, wee[6] and invisible, were being wielded. Many of the men were constantly dodging and ducking their heads.

▶ What happens to the lieutenant?

The lieutenant of the youth's company was shot in the hand. He began to swear so wondrously that a nervous laugh went along the regimental line. The officer's profanity sounded <u>conventional</u>. It relieved the tightened senses of the new men. It was as if he had hit his fingers with a tack hammer at home.

He held the wounded member carefully away from his side so that the blood would not drip upon his trousers.

The captain of the company, tucking his sword under his arm, produced a handkerchief and began to bind with it the lieutenant's wound. And they disputed as to how the binding should be done.

The battle flag in the distance jerked about madly. It seemed to be struggling to free itself from an agony. The <u>billowing</u> smoke was filled with horizontal flashes.

---

2. **amputate.** Medicine was not as advanced as today during the Civil War; unable to fight infections in torn or broken limbs, Civil War doctors often amputated them.
3. **shell.** Projectile from a cannon that explodes
4. **banshee.** According to traditional Irish folklore, a female spirit who wails and shrieks; supposedly when a banshee appeared, the death of someone present was imminent.
5. **reserves.** Military force withheld from action for later use
6. **wee.** Very small, tiny

Words For Everyday Use

tur • bu • lent (tər´byoo lənt) *adj.*, causing unrest, violence, or disturbance
nip (nip) *vt.*, pinch, bite

con • ven • tion • al (kôn ven´shən əl) *adj.*, ordinary, commonplace
bil • low • ing (bi´lō iŋ) *adj.*, rising or rolling in waves

Men running swiftly emerged from it. They grew in numbers until it was seen that the whole command was fleeing. The flag suddenly sank down as if dying. Its motion as it fell was a gesture of despair.

◀ Who comes running from the smoke-filled battle?

Wild yells came from behind the walls of smoke. A sketch in gray and red dissolved into a moblike body of men who galloped like wild horses.

The veteran regiments on the right and left of the 304th immediately began to jeer. With the passionate song of the bullets and the banshee shrieks of shells were mingled loud catcalls and bits of <u>facetious</u> advice concerning places of safety.

◀ What is the veterans' reaction to the fleeing soldiers? What is the new troop's reaction?

But the new regiment was breathless with horror. "Gawd! Saunders's got crushed!" whispered the man at the youth's elbow. They shrank back and crouched as if compelled to await a flood.

The youth shot a swift glance along the blue ranks of the regiment. The profiles were motionless, carven; and afterward he remembered that the color sergeant was standing with his legs apart, as if he expected to be pushed to the ground.

The bellowing <u>throng</u> went whirling around the flank.[7] Here and there were officers carried along on the stream like <u>exasperated</u> chips. They were striking about them with their swords and with their left fists, punching every head they could reach. They cursed like highwaymen.[8]

A mounted officer displayed the furious anger of a spoiled child. He raged with his head, his arms, and his legs.

Another, the commander of the brigade, was galloping about <u>bawling</u>. His hat was gone and his clothes were awry. He resembled a man who has come from bed to go to a fire. The hoofs of his horse often threatened the heads of the running men, but they scampered with singular fortune.[9] In this rush they were apparently all deaf and blind. They heeded not the largest and longest of the oaths that were thrown at them from all directions.

Frequently over this tumult could be heard the grim jokes

---

7. **flank.** The right or left of a formation (of soldiers)
8. **highwaymen.** People who rob travelers along roads
9. **singular fortune.** Surprisingly good luck

Words For Everyday Use

fa • ce • tious (fə sē´shəs) *adj.,* joking or jesting often inappropriately
throng (thrôŋ) *n.,* large number of assembled persons

ex • as • per • at • ed (eg zas´pər āt əd) *adj.,* enraged, irritated, annoyed
bawl (bôl) *vi.,* cry out at the top of one's voice

► What effect do the
fleeing soldiers have
on the youth's state
of mind?

► What does the
youth realize he
hasn't even seen yet?

of the critical veterans; but the retreating men apparently
were not even conscious of the presence of an audience.

The battle reflection that shone for an instant in the faces
on the mad current made the youth feel that forceful hands
from heaven would not have been able to have held him in
place if he could have got intelligent control of his legs.

There was an <u>appalling</u> imprint upon these faces. The
struggle in the smoke had pictured an exaggeration of itself
on the bleached cheeks and in the eyes wild with one desire.

The sight of this stampede exerted a floodlike force that
seemed able to drag sticks and stones and men from the
ground. They of the reserves had to hold on. They grew pale
and firm, and red and quaking.

The youth achieved one little thought in the midst of this
chaos. The composite[10] monster which had caused the other
troops to flee had not then appeared. He resolved to get a
view of it, and then, he thought he might very likely run better than the best of them.

---

10. **composite.** Made up of distinct parts

| Words
For
Everyday
Use | **ap • pall • ing** (ə pôl´iŋ) *adj.*, inspiring horror, dismay, or
disgust |

Chapter 5

There were moments of waiting. The youth thought of the village street at home before the arrival of the circus parade[1] on a day in the spring. He remembered how he had stood, a small, thrillful boy, prepared to follow the <u>dingy</u> lady upon the white horse, or the band in its faded chariot. He saw the yellow road, the lines of expectant people, and the <u>sober</u> houses. He particularly remembered an old fellow who used to sit upon a cracker box in front of the store and <u>feign</u> to despise such exhibition. A thousand details of color and form surged in his mind. The old fellow upon the cracker box appeared in middle <u>prominence</u>.

Some one cried, "Here they come!"

There was rustling and muttering among the men. They displayed a feverish desire to have every possible cartridge[2] ready to their hands. The boxes were pulled around into various positions, and adjusted with great care. It was as if seven hundred new bonnets were being tried on.

◀ *What do the soldiers do as soon as they know enemy soldiers are approaching?*

The tall soldier, having prepared his rifle, produced a red handkerchief of some kind. He was engaged in knotting it about his throat with exquisite attention to its position, when the cry was repeated up and down the line in a muffled roar of sound.

"Here they come! Here they come!" Gun locks clicked.

Across the smoke-infested fields came a brown swarm of running men who were giving shrill yells. They came on, stooping and swinging their rifles at all angles. A flag, tilted forward, sped near the front.

◀ *What does the youth see? What thought occurs to him?*

As he caught sight of them the youth was momentarily startled by a thought that perhaps his gun was not loaded. He stood trying to <u>rally</u> his faltering intellect so that he might recollect the moment when he had loaded, but he could not.

A hatless general pulled his dripping horse to a stand near the colonel of the 304th. He shook his fist in the other's face.

---

1. **circus parade.** In the nineteenth and early twentieth centuries, traveling circuses would advertise their arrival in town by parading through the main streets.
2. **cartridge.** Metal tube containing the charge for a firearm

Words For Everyday Use

din • gy (din´jē) *adj.*, dirty, shabby
so • ber (sō´bər) *adj.*, subdued in tone or color
feign (fān) *vi.*, pretend

prom • i • nence (prô´mə nən(t)s) *n.*, quality, state, or fact of being noticeable or conspicuous
ral • ly (ra´lē) *vt.*, arouse for action; rouse from depression or weakness

"You've got to hold 'em back!" he shouted, savagely; "you've got to hold 'em back!"

In his agitation the colonel began to stammer. "A-all r-right, General, all right, by Gawd! We-we'll do our—we-we'll d-d-do—do our best, General." The general made a passionate gesture and galloped away. The colonel, <u>perchance</u> to relieve his feelings, began to scold like a wet parrot. The youth, turning swiftly to make sure that the rear was unmolested, saw the commander regarding his men in a highly resentful manner, as if he regretted above everything his association with them.

The man at the youth's elbow was mumbling, as if to himself: "Oh, we're in for it now! oh, we're in for it now!"

The captain of the company had been pacing excitedly to and fro in the rear. He coaxed in schoolmistress fashion, as to a congregation of boys with primers. His talk was an endless repetition. "Reserve your fire, boys—don't shoot till I tell you—save your fire—wait till they get close up—don't be damned fools—"

Perspiration streamed down the youth's face, which was soiled like that of a weeping urchin. He frequently, with a nervous movement, wiped his eyes with his coat sleeve. His mouth was still a little ways open.

He got the one glance at the foe-swarming field in front of him, and instantly ceased to debate the question of his piece being loaded. Before he was ready to begin—before he had announced to himself that he was about to fight—he threw the obedient, well-balanced rifle into position and fired a first wild shot. Directly he was working at his weapon like an automatic affair.

He suddenly lost concern for himself, and forgot to look at a <u>menacing</u> fate. He became not a man but a member. He felt that something of which he was a part—a regiment, an army, a cause, or a country—was in a crisis. He was welded into a common personality which was dominated by a single desire. For some moments he could not flee no more than a little finger can commit a revolution from a hand.

If he had thought the regiment was about to be <u>annihilated</u> perhaps he could have amputated himself from it. But its noise gave him assurance. The regiment was like a firework that, once ignited, proceeds superior to circumstances

Words
For
Everyday
Use

per • chance (pər chan(t)s´) *adv.,* perhaps, possibly

men • ac • ing (me´nəs iŋ) *adj.,* threatening harm

an • ni • hi • late (ə nī´ə lāt) *vt.,* cause to cease to exist; kill

until its blazing vitality fades. It wheezed and banged with a mighty power. He pictured the ground before it as strewn with the <u>discomfited</u>.

There was a consciousness always of the presence of his comrades about him. He felt the subtle battle brotherhood more potent even than the cause for which they were fighting. It was a mysterious fraternity born of the smoke and danger of death.

He was at a task. He was like a carpenter who has made many boxes, making still another box, only there was furious haste in his movements. He, in his thoughts, was careering[3] off in other places, even as the carpenter who as he works whistles and thinks of his friend or his enemy, his home or a saloon. And these jolted dreams were never perfect to him afterward, but remained a mass of blurred shapes.

Presently he began to feel the effects of the war atmosphere—a blistering sweat, a sensation that his eyeballs were about to crack like hot stones. A burning roar filled his ears.

Following this came a red rage. He developed the acute exasperation of a pestered animal, a well-meaning cow worried by dogs. He had a mad feeling against his rifle, which could only be used against one life at a time. He wished to rush forward and strangle with his fingers. He craved a power that would enable him to make a world-sweeping gesture and brush all back. His impotency appeared to him, and made his rage into that of a driven beast.

Buried in the smoke of many rifles his anger was directed not so much against the men whom he knew were rushing toward him as against the swirling battle phantoms which were choking him, stuffing their smoke robes down his <u>parched</u> throat. He fought frantically for <u>respite</u> for his senses, for air, as a babe being smothered attacks the deadly blankets.

There was a blare of heated rage mingled with a certain expression of intentness on all faces. Many of the men were making low-toned noises with their mouths, and these subdued cheers, snarls, <u>imprecations</u>, prayers, made a wild, barbaric song that went as an undercurrent of sound, strange and chantlike with the resounding chords of the war march.

◄ *What does the youth find his mind doing as he keeps reloading his gun and shooting at the enemy?*

◄ *In what way does the youth's state of mind change after a while? What does he wish he could do?*

◄ *With whom or what is the youth angry?*

---

3. **careering.** Going at top speed, in a haphazard manner

The man at the youth's elbow was babbling. In it there was something soft and tender like the <u>monologue</u> of a babe. The tall soldier was swearing in a loud voice. From his lips came a black procession of curious oaths. Of a sudden another broke out in a <u>querulous</u> way like a man who has mislaid his hat. "Well, why don't they support us? Why don't they send supports? Do they think—"

The youth in his battle sleep heard this as one who dozes hears.

▶ What don't the men look like as they shoot?

There was a singular absence of heroic poses. The men bending and surging in their haste and rage were in every impossible attitude. The steel ramrods[4] clanked and clanged with incessant din as the men pounded them furiously into the hot rifle barrels. The flaps of the cartridge boxes were all unfastened, and bobbed idiotically with each movement. The rifles, once loaded, were jerked to the shoulder and fired without apparent aim into the smoke or at one of the blurred and shifting forms which upon the field before the regiment had been growing larger and larger like puppets under a magician's hand.

The officers, at their intervals, rearward, neglected to stand in <u>picturesque</u> attitudes. They were bobbing to and fro roaring directions and encouragements. The dimensions of their howls were extraordinary. They expended their lungs with <u>prodigal</u> wills. And often they nearly stood upon their heads in their anxiety to observe the enemy on the other side of the tumbling smoke.

▶ What has one soldier done already? Who confronts this soldier?

The lieutenant of the youth's company had encountered a soldier who had fled screaming at the first volley of his comrades. Behind the lines these two were acting a little isolated scene. The man was blubbering and staring with sheep-like eyes at the lieutenant, who had seized him by the collar and was pommeling[5] him. He drove him back into the ranks with many blows. The soldier went mechanically, dully, with his animal-like eyes upon the officer. Perhaps there was to him a divinity expressed in the voice of the other—stern, hard, with no reflection of fear in it. He tried to reload his

---

4. **Ramrods.** Rods used to push the charge into the muzzle of a gun. Most guns in this period had to be reloaded after each shot.
5. **pommeling.** Pummeling, or beating

Words For Everyday Use

mono • logue (mon´ə log) *n.*, long speech monopolizing conversation
quer • u • lous (kwer´yo͞o ləs) *adj.*, habitually complaining; whining

pic • tur • esque (pik chə resk´) *adj.*, resembling a picture; charming or quaint in appearance
prod • i • gal (prä´di gəl) *adj.*, recklessly extravagant

gun, but his shaking hands prevented. The lieutenant was obliged to assist him.

The men dropped here and there like bundles. The captain of the youth's company had been killed in an early part of the action. His body lay stretched out in the position of a tired man resting, but upon his face there was an astonished and sorrowful look, as if he thought some friend had done him an ill turn. The babbling man was grazed by a shot that made the blood stream widely down his face. He clapped both hands to his head. "Oh!" he said, and ran. Another grunted suddenly as if he had been struck by a club in the stomach. He sat down and gazed <u>ruefully</u>. In his eyes there was mute, indefinite <u>reproach</u>. Farther up the line a man, standing behind a tree, had had his knee joint splintered by a ball.[6] Immediately he had dropped his rifle and gripped the tree with both arms. And there he remained, clinging desperately and crying for assistance that he might withdraw his hold upon the tree.

◀ What is happening to some of the men in the youth's regiment? What different emotions does the youth see these people express?

At last an <u>exultant</u> yell went along the quivering line. The firing dwindled from an uproar to a last vindictive popping. As the smoke slowly <u>eddied</u> away, the youth saw that the charge had been repulsed. The enemy were scattered into reluctant groups. He saw a man climb to the top of the fence, straddle the rail, and fire a parting shot. The waves had receded, leaving bits of dark debris upon the ground.

◀ What has the youth's regiment managed to do?

Some in the regiment began to whoop frenziedly. Many were silent. Apparently they were trying to contemplate themselves.

After the fever had left his veins, the youth thought that at last he was going to suffocate. He became aware of the foul atmosphere in which he had been struggling. He was grimy and dripping like a laborer in a foundry.[7] He grasped his canteen and took a long swallow of the warmed water.

A sentence with variations went up and down the line. "Well, we 've helt 'em back. We 've helt 'em back; derned if we haven't." The men said it blissfully, <u>leering</u> at each other with dirty smiles.

---

6. **ball.** Musket ball, or round pellet from a heavy shoulder firearm used by foot soldiers

7. **foundry.** Place where hot metal is molded, known for being extremely hot

| Words For Everyday Use | **rue • ful • ly** (rōō´fə lē) *adv.*, mournfully, regretfully
re • proach (ri prōch´) *n.*, expression of blame or disapproval
ex • ul • tant (eg zul´tənt) *adj.*, filled with | or expressing great joy or triumph
ed • dy (e´dē) *vi.*, move in a circle, like a whirlpool
leer (lēr) *vi.*, glance at sidelong |

The youth turned to look behind him and off to the right and off to the left. He experienced the joy of a man who at last finds leisure in which to look about him.

▶ What is unusual about the way the dead lie?

Under foot there were a few ghastly forms motionless. They lay twisted in fantastic <u>contortions</u>. Arms were bent and heads were turned in incredible ways. It seemed that the dead men must have fallen from some great height to get into such positions. They looked to be dumped out upon the ground from the sky.

From a position in the rear of the grove a battery was throwing shells over it. The flash of the guns startled the youth at first. He thought they were aimed directly at him. Through the trees he watched the black figures of the gunners as they worked swiftly and intently. Their labor seemed a complicated thing. He wondered how they could remember its formula in the midst of confusion.

▶ What does the youth think the heavy guns are like? What does he think the men who work them are like?

The guns squatted in a row like savage chiefs. They argued with abrupt violence. It was a grim pow-wow.[8] Their busy servants ran hither and thither.

A small procession of wounded men were going drearily toward the rear. It was a flow of blood from the torn body of the brigade.

To the right and to the left were the dark lines of other troops. Far in front he thought he could see lighter masses protruding in points from the forest. They were suggestive of unnumbered thousands.

Once he saw a tiny battery go dashing along the line of the horizon. The tiny riders were beating the tiny horses.

From a sloping hill came the sound of cheerings and clashes. Smoke <u>welled</u> slowly through the leaves.

Batteries were speaking with thunderous <u>oratorical</u> effort. Here and there were flags, the red in the stripes dominating. They splashed bits of warm color upon the dark lines of troops.

▶ How does the youth feel about his regiment's flag? To what does he compare them?

The youth felt the old thrill at the sight of the emblems. They were like beautiful birds strangely <u>undaunted</u> in a storm.

As he listened to the din from the hillside, to a deep pul-

---

8. **pow-wow.** Meeting for discussion

Words For Everyday Use

con • tor • tion (kən tôr´shən) *n.*, twisted, strained shape
well (wel) *vi.*, rise like a flood of liquid
or • a • tor • i • cal (ôr ə tôr´i kəl) *adj.*, relating to, or characteristic of, a public

speaker or speeches
un • daunt • ed (ən dôn´təd) *adj.*, courageous and determined in the face of danger or difficulty

sating thunder that came from afar to the left, and to the lesser clamors which came from many directions, it occurred to him that they were fighting, too, over there, and over there, and over there. Heretofore he had supposed that all the battle was directly under his nose.

As he gazed around him the youth felt a flash of astonishment at the blue, pure sky and the sun gleamings on the trees and fields. It was surprising that Nature had gone tranquilly on with her golden process in the midst of so much devilment.

◄ What does the youth realize? What had he thought about the battle?

Chapter 6

The youth awakened slowly. He came gradually back to a position from which he could regard himself. For moments he had been <u>scrutinizing</u> his person in a dazed way as if he had never before seen himself. Then he picked up his cap from the ground. He wriggled in his jacket to make a more comfortable fit, and kneeling relaced his shoe. He thoughtfully mopped his reeking[1] features.

So it was all over at last! The supreme trial had been passed. The red, formidable difficulties of war had been vanquished.

He went into an ecstasy of self-satisfaction. He had the most delightful sensations of his life. Standing as if apart from himself, he viewed that last scene. He perceived that the man who had fought thus was magnificent.

He felt that he was a fine fellow. He saw himself even with those ideals which he had considered as far beyond him. He smiled in deep gratification.

Upon his fellows he beamed tenderness and good will. "Gee! ain't it, hot, hey?" he said <u>affably</u> to a man who was polishing his streaming face with his coat sleeves.

"You bet!" said the other, grinning sociably. "I never seen sech dumb hotness." He sprawled out luxuriously on the ground. "Gee, yes! An' I hope we don't have no more fightin' till a week from Monday."

There were some handshakings and deep speeches with men whose features were familiar, but with whom the youth now felt the bonds of tied hearts. He helped a cursing comrade to bind up a wound of the shin.

But, of a sudden, cries of amazement broke out along the ranks of the new regiment. "Here they come ag'in! Here they come ag'in!" The man who had sprawled upon the ground started up and said, "Gosh!"

The youth turned quick eyes upon the field. He <u>discerned</u> forms begin to swell in masses out of a distant wood. He again saw the tilted flag speeding forward.

The shells, which had ceased to trouble the regiment for a

> What does the youth think is over? What does he think he has vanquished?

> How does the youth feel about himself?

> What happens that amazes the new soldiers?

---

1. **reeking.** Steaming, sweating

Words For Everyday Use

scru • ti • nize (skrōō´t'n īz) *vt.*, examine closely and minutely
af • fa • bly (a´fə blē) *adv.*, pleasantly; in a friendly manner
dis • cern (di sərn´) *vt.*, detect with the eyes

time, came swirling again, and exploded in the grass or among the leaves of the trees. They looked to be strange war flowers bursting into fierce bloom.

◀ To what are the exploding shells compared?

The men groaned. The <u>luster</u> faded from their eyes. Their smudged countenances now expressed a profound dejection. They moved their stiffened bodies slowly, and watched in <u>sullen</u> mood the frantic approach of the enemy. The slaves toiling in the temple of this god began to feel rebellion at his harsh tasks.

◀ What attitude do the men have toward fighting again?

They fretted and complained each to each. "Oh, say, this is too much of a good thing! Why can't somebody send us supports?"

"We ain't never goin' to stand this second banging. I didn't come here to fight the hull damn' rebel army."

There was one who raised a <u>doleful</u> cry. "I wish Bill Smithers had trod on my hand, insteader me treddin' on his'n." The sore joints of the regiment creaked as it painfully floundered into position to repulse.

◀ What does one man wish? Why do you think the man who stepped on Bill Smithers's hand wishes this?

The youth stared. Surely, he thought, this impossible thing was not about to happen. He waited as if he expected the enemy to suddenly stop, apologize, and retire bowing. It was all a mistake.

But the firing began somewhere on the regimental line and ripped along in both directions. The level sheets of flame developed great clouds of smoke that tumbled and tossed in the mild wind near the ground for a moment, and then rolled through the ranks[2] as through a grate. The clouds were tinged an earthlike yellow in the sunrays and in the shadow were a sorry blue. The flag was sometimes eaten and lost in this mass of vapor, but more often it projected, sun-touched, <u>resplendent</u>.

Into the youth's eyes there came a look that one can see in the orbs of a <u>jaded</u> horse. His neck was quivering with nervous weakness and the muscles of his arms felt numb and bloodless. His hands, too, seemed large and awkward as if he was wearing invisible mittens. And there was a great uncertainty about his knee joints.

◀ How is the youth beginning to feel physically?

The words that comrades had uttered previous to the firing began to recur to him. "Oh, say, this is too much of a

---

2. **ranks.** Line of soldiers arranged side by side in close order

---

Words For Everyday Use	
lus • ter (lus´tər) *n.*, glow of reflected light	**re • splen • dent** (ri splen´dənt) *adj.*, shining brilliantly; characterized by a glowing splendor
sul • len (sə´lən) *adj.*, gloomily or resentfully silent or repressed	**jaded** (jād´əd) *adj.*, fatigued by overwork; exhausted
dole • ful (dōl´fəl) *adj.*, full of grief	

good thing! What do they take us for—why don't they send supports? I didn't come here to fight the hull damned rebel army."

He began to exaggerate the endurance, the skill, and the valor of those who were coming. Himself <u>reeling</u> from exhaustion, he was astonished beyond measure at such persistency. They must be machines of steel. It was very gloomy struggling against such affairs, wound up perhaps to fight until sundown.

He slowly lifted his rifle and catching a glimpse of the thickspread field he blazed at a cantering[3] cluster. He stopped then and began to peer as best he could through the smoke. He caught changing views of the ground covered with men who were all running like pursued imps, and yelling.

To the youth it was an <u>onslaught</u> of <u>redoubtable</u> dragons. He became like the man who lost his legs at the approach of the red and green monster. He waited in a sort of a horrified, listening attitude. He seemed to shut his eyes and wait to be gobbled.

A man near him who up to this time had been working feverishly at his rifle suddenly stopped and ran with howls. A lad whose face had borne an expression of exalted courage, the majesty of he who dares give his life, was, at an instant, smitten <u>abject</u>. He <u>blanched</u> like one who has come to the edge of a cliff at midnight and is suddenly made aware. There was a revelation. He, too, threw down his gun and fled. There was no shame in his face. He ran like a rabbit.

Others began to scamper away through the smoke. The youth turned his head, shaken from his trance by this movement as if the regiment was leaving him behind. He saw the few fleeting forms.

He yelled then with fright and swung about. For a moment, in the great clamor, he was like a proverbial[4] chicken. He lost the direction of safety. Destruction threatened him from all points.

Directly he began to speed toward the rear in great leaps. His rifle and cap were gone. His unbuttoned coat bulged in the wind. The flap of his cartridge box bobbed wildly, and

What does the youth think of the enemy?

What does the youth see? How does he feel about what he sees?

What do men who previously fought with an air of confidence begin to do?

What does the youth do?

---

3. **cantering**. Running
4. **proverbial**. Commonly spoken of

Words For Everyday Use

reel (rēl) *vt.*, walk or move unsteadily
on • slaught (on´slot) *n.*, especially fierce attack
re • doubt • able (ri dau´tə bəl) *adj.*, causing fear or alarm
ab • ject (ab´jekt) *adj.*, cast down in spirit
blanch (blanch) *vi.*, become white or pale

his canteen, by its slender cords, swung out behind. On his face was all the horror of those things which he imagined.

The lieutenant sprang forward bawling. The youth saw his features wrathfully red, and saw him make a dab[5] with his sword. His one thought of the incident was that the lieutenant was a peculiar creature to feel interested in such matters upon this occasion.

He ran like a blind man. Two or three times he fell down. Once he knocked his shoulder so heavily against a tree that he went <u>headlong</u>.

Since he had turned his back upon the fight his fears had been wondrously magnified. Death about to thrust him between the shoulder blades was far more dreadful than death about to smite him between the eyes. When he thought of it later, he conceived the impression that it is better to view the appalling than to be merely within hearing. The noises of the battle were like stones; he believed himself liable to be crushed.

◄ Does running from the battle make the youth more or less afraid? Why?

As he ran he mingled with others. He dimly saw men on his right and on his left, and he heard footsteps behind him. He thought that all the regiment was fleeing, pursued by these ominous crashes.

◄ Is the youth alone in running? What thought comforts him?

In his flight the sound of these following footsteps gave him his one meager relief. He felt vaguely that death must make a first choice of the men who were nearest; the initial <u>morsel</u> for the dragons would be then those who were following him. So he displayed the zeal of an insane sprinter in his purpose to keep them in the rear. There was a race.

As he, leading, went across a little field, he found himself in a region of shells. They hurtled over his head with long wild screams. As he listened he imagined them to have rows of cruel teeth that grinned at him. Once one lit before him and the livid lightning of the explosion effectually barred the way in his chosen direction. He groveled on the ground and then springing up went careering off through some bushes.

He experienced a thrill of amazement when he came within view of a battery in action. The men there seemed to be in conventional moods, altogether unaware of the

---

5. **dab.** Sudden blow or thrust

Words For Everyday Use

head • long (hed lôŋ´) *adv.*, headfirst
mor • sel (môr´səl) *n.*, small piece of food; bite

impending annihilation. The battery was disputing with a distant <u>antagonist</u> and the gunners were wrapped in admiration of their shooting. They were continually bending in coaxing postures over the guns. They seemed to be patting them on the back and encouraging them with words. The guns, <u>stolid</u> and undaunted, spoke with dogged valor.

The precise gunners were coolly enthusiastic. They lifted their eyes every chance to the smoke-wreathed hillock from whence the hostile battery addressed them. The youth pitied them as he ran. <u>Methodical</u> idiots! Machine-like fools! The refined joy of planting shells in the midst of the other battery's formation would appear a little thing when the infantry came swooping out of the woods.

The face of a youthful rider, who was jerking his frantic horse with an abandon of temper he might display in a placid barnyard, was impressed deeply upon his mind. He knew that he looked upon a man who would presently be dead.

Too, he felt a pity for the guns, standing, six good comrades, in a bold row.

He saw a brigade going to the relief of its pestered fellows. He scrambled upon a wee hill and watched it sweeping finely, keeping formation in difficult places. The blue of the line was crusted with steel color, and the brilliant flags projected. Officers were shouting.

This sight also filled him with wonder. The brigade was hurrying briskly to be gulped into the <u>infernal</u> mouths of the war god. What manner of men were they, anyhow? Ah, it was some wondrous breed! Or else they didn't comprehend—the fools.

A furious order caused commotion in the artillery. An officer on a bounding horse made <u>maniacal</u> motions with his arms. The teams went swinging up from the rear, the guns were whirled about, and the battery scampered away. The cannon with their noses poked slantingly at the ground grunted and grumbled like stout men, brave but with objections to hurry.

The youth went on, moderating his pace since he had left the place of noises.

Later he came upon a general of division seated upon a horse that pricked its ears in an interested way at the battle.

► What does the youth feel for the calm men who work the heavy artillery? What does he think will happen to these men?

► What does the youth think will happen to a young horseman he sees?

► What does the youth think of the brigade going to the relief of fellow soldiers?

► Whom does the youth come across?

Words For Everyday Use

an • tag • o • nist (an ta´gə nist) *n.*, one that contends with or opposes another

stol • id (stô´ləd) *adj.*, unemotional

me • thod • i • cal (mə thä´di kəl) *adj.*, habitually proceeding according to order

in • fer • nal (in fər´nəl) *adj.*, of or relating to a nether world of the dead

ma • ni • a • cal (mə nī´ə kəl) *adj.*, characterized by uncontrollable excitement or frenzy

There was a great gleaming of yellow and patent leather about the saddle and bridle. The quiet man astride looked mouse-colored upon such a splendid charger.[6]

A jingling staff was galloping hither and thither. Sometimes the general was surrounded by horsemen and at other times he was quite alone. He looked to be much harassed. He had the appearance of a business man whose market is swinging up and down.

◀ To what does the youth compare the general's appearance?

The youth went slinking around this spot. He went as near as he dared trying to overhear words. Perhaps the general, unable to comprehend chaos, might call upon him for information. And he could tell him. He knew all concerning it. Of a surety the force was in a fix, and any fool could see that if they did not retreat while they had opportunity— why—

◀ What does the youth hope he will have a chance to tell the general?

He felt that he would like to thrash the general, or at least approach and tell him in plain words exactly what he thought him to be. It was criminal to stay calmly in one spot and make no effort to stay[7] destruction. He loitered in a fever of eagerness for the division commander to apply to him.

As he warily moved about, he heard the general call out irritably: "Tompkins, go over an' see Taylor, an' tell him not t' be in such an all-fired hurry; tell him t' halt his brigade in th' edge of th' woods; tell him t' detach a reg'ment—say I think th' center 'll break if we don't help it out some; tell him t' hurry up."

A slim youth on a fine chestnut horse caught these swift words from the mouth of his superior. He made his horse bound into a gallop almost from a walk in his haste to go upon his mission. There was a cloud of dust.

A moment later the youth saw the general bounce excitedly in his saddle.

"Yes, by heavens, they have!" The officer leaned forward. His face was aflame with excitement. "Yes, by heavens, they've held 'em! They 've held 'em!"

◀ What good news does the general learn? How does he feel about the way the battle is progressing?

He began to blithely roar at his staff: "We 'll wallop 'em now. We 'll wallop 'em now. We 've got 'em sure." He turned suddenly upon an aide: "Here—you—Jones—quick—ride

---

6. **charger.** Battle horse
7. **stay.** Stop or delay the proceeding of

Words For Everyday Use

ha • rass (hə ras´) vt., annoy persistently

slink (sliŋk) vi., move stealthily or furtively (as in fear or shame)

loi • ter (lôi´tər) vi., remain in an area for no obvious reason

after Tompkins—see Taylor—tell him t' go in—everlastingly—like blazes—anything."

As another officer sped his horse after the first messenger, the general beamed upon the earth like a sun. In his eyes was a desire to chant a <u>paean</u>. He kept repeating, "They 've held 'em, by heavens!"

His excitement made his horse plunge, and he merrily kicked and swore at it. He held a little carnival of joy on horseback.

Words For Everyday Use

pae • an (pē´ən) *n.,* joyous song or hymn of praise, tribute, thanksgiving, or triumph

Chapter 7

The youth cringed as if discovered in a crime. By heavens, they had won after all! The imbecile line had remained and become victors. He could hear cheering.

◄ How does the youth feel about himself when he realizes his side has won?

He lifted himself upon his toes and looked in the direction of the fight. A yellow fog lay wallowing on the treetops. From beneath it came the clatter of musketry.[1] Hoarse cries told of an advance.

He turned away amazed and angry. He felt that he had been wronged.

He had fled, he told himself, because annihilation approached. He had done a good part in saving himself, who was a little piece of the army. He had considered the time, he said, to be one in which it was the duty of every little piece to rescue itself if possible. Later the officers could fit the little pieces together again, and make a battle front. If none of the little pieces were wise enough to save themselves from the flurry of death at such a time, why, then, where would be the army? It was all plain that he had proceeded according to very correct and commendable rules. His actions had been <u>sagacious</u> things. They had been full of strategy. They were the work of a master's legs.

◄ In what way does the youth justify his decision to run?

Thoughts of his comrades came to him. The brittle blue line had withstood the blows and won. He grew bitter over it. It seemed that the blind ignorance and stupidity of those little pieces had betrayed him. He had been overturned and crushed by their lack of sense in holding the position, when intelligent <u>deliberation</u> would have convinced them that it was impossible. He, the <u>enlightened</u> man who looks afar in the dark, had fled because of his superior perceptions and knowledge. He felt a great anger against his comrades. He knew it could be proved that they had been fools.

◄ According to the youth, what quality caused the other men to stay? What caused him to run?

He wondered what they would remark when later he appeared in camp. His mind heard howls of <u>derision</u>. Their density would not enable them to understand his sharper point of view.

---

1. **musketry.** Musket fire; noise from heavy, shoulder-borne guns carried by foot soldiers

| Words For Everyday Use | **sa • ga • cious** (sə gā′shəs) *adj.*, of keen and farsighted penetration and judgment | **en • light • ened** (en lī′tend) *adj.*, freed from ignorance and misinformation |
| | **de • lib • er • a • tion** (di li′bə rā′shən) *n.*, consideration, thought | **de • ri • sion** (di ri′zhən) *n.*, the use of ridicule or scorn to show contempt |

He began to pity himself acutely. He was ill used. He was trodden beneath the feet of an iron injustice. He had proceeded with wisdom and from the most righteous motives under heaven's blue only to be frustrated by hateful circumstances.

A dull, animal-like rebellion against his fellows, war in the abstract, and fate grew within him. He shambled along with bowed head, his brain in a tumult of agony and despair. When he looked <u>loweringly</u> up, quivering at each sound, his eyes had the expression of those of a criminal who thinks his guilt little and his punishment great, and knows that he can find no words.

▶ Where does the youth go?

He went from the fields into a thick woods, as if resolved to bury himself. He wished to get out of hearing of the crackling shots which were to him like voices.

The ground was cluttered with vines and bushes, and the trees grew close and spread out like bouquets. He was obliged to force his way with much noise. The creepers, catching against his legs, cried out harshly as their sprays² were torn from the barks of trees. The swishing saplings³ tried to make known his presence to the world. He could not <u>conciliate</u> the forest. As he made his way, it was always calling out protestations. When he separated embraces of trees and vines the disturbed <u>foliages</u> waved their arms and turned their face leaves toward him. He dreaded lest these noisy motions and cries should bring men to look at him. So he went far, seeking dark and intricate places.

▶ What type of place does the youth find?

After a time the sound of musketry grew faint and the cannon boomed in the distance. The sun, suddenly apparent, blazed among the trees. The insects were making rhythmical noises. They seemed to be grinding their teeth in unison. A woodpecker stuck his impudent head around the side of a tree. A bird flew on lighthearted wing.

Off was the rumble of death. It seemed now that Nature had no ears.

▶ What does the youth think would happen to this place if it witnessed the bloodshed of the battlefield?

This landscape gave him assurance. A fair field holding life. It was the religion of peace. It would die if its timid eyes

---

2. **sprays.** Flowering branches or shoots
3. **saplings.** Very young trees

Words For Everyday Use

low • er • ing • ly (lou´ər iŋ lē) *adv.*, in a dark and threatening manner

con • cil • i • ate (kən si´lē āt) *vt.*, gain (as goodwill) by pleasing acts

fo • liage (fō´lē ij) *n.*, cluster of leaves, flowers, and branches

were compelled to see blood. He conceived Nature to be a woman with a deep <u>aversion</u> to tragedy.

He threw a pine cone at a <u>jovial</u> squirrel, and he ran with chattering fear. High in a treetop he stopped, and, poking his head cautiously from behind a branch, looked down with an air of <u>trepidation</u>.

◄ What "experiment" does the youth perform? What does he see as the lesson of this experiment?

The youth felt triumphant at this exhibition. There was the law, he said. Nature had given him a sign. The squirrel, immediately upon recognizing danger, had taken to his legs without ado.[4] He did not stand stolidly baring his furry belly to the missile, and die with an upward glance at the sympathetic heavens. On the contrary, he had fled as fast as his legs could carry him; and he was but an ordinary squirrel, too— doubtless no philosopher of his race. The youth wended,[5] feeling that Nature was of his mind. She reenforced his argument with proofs that lived where the sun shone.

Once he found himself almost into a swamp. He was obliged to walk upon bog tufts[6] and watch his feet to keep from the oily <u>mire</u>. Pausing at one time to look about him he saw, out at some black water, a small animal pounce in and emerge directly with a gleaming fish.

The youth went again into the deep thickets. The brushed branches made a noise that drowned the sounds of cannon. He walked on, going from obscurity into promises of a greater obscurity.

At length he reached a place where the high, arching boughs made a chapel. He softly pushed the green doors aside and entered. Pine needles were a gentle brown carpet. There was a religious half light.

◄ To what does the youth compare this place in the woods?

Near the threshold he stopped, horror-stricken at the sight of a thing.

◄ What does the youth see that fills him with horror?

He was being looked at by a dead man who was seated with his back against a columnlike tree. The corpse was dressed in a uniform that once had been blue, but was now faded to a melancholy shade of green. The eyes, staring at the youth, had changed to the dull hue to be seen on the side of a dead fish. The mouth was open. Its red had changed

---

4. **ado.** Time-wasting bother over trivial details
5. **wended.** Traveled on his way
6. **bog tufts.** Marsh grass

Words For Everyday Use

a • ver • sion (ə vər´zhən) n., feeling of repulsion or distaste toward something with a desire to avoid or turn from it

jo • vial (jō´vē əl) adj., good-humored; merry

trep • i • da • tion (tre pə dā´shən) n., fearful uncertain agitation

mire (mīr) n., spongy earth (as of a bog or marsh)

► What detail attracts the youth's attention?

► What do the youth and the dead man do?

to an <u>appalling</u> yellow. Over the gray skin of the face ran little ants. One was trundling some sort of a bundle along the upper lip.

The youth gave a shriek as he confronted the thing. He was for moments turned to stone before it. He remained staring into the liquid-looking eyes. The dead man and the living man exchanged a long look. Then the youth cautiously put one hand behind him and brought it against a tree. Leaning upon this he retreated, step by step, with his face still toward the thing. He feared that if he turned his back the body might spring up and stealthily pursue him.

The branches, pushing against him, threatened to throw him over upon it. His unguided feet, too, caught aggravatingly in brambles; and with it all he received a subtle suggestion to touch the corpse. As he thought of his hand upon it he shuddered profoundly.

► What thought "pursues" the youth?

► What is the youth afraid he will hear? What does he actually hear?

At last he burst the bonds which had fastened him to the spot and fled, unheeding the underbrush. He was pursued by a sight of the black ants swarming greedily upon the gray face and venturing horribly near to the eyes.

After a time he paused, and, breathless and panting, listened. He imagined some strange voice would come from the dead throat and squawk after him in horrible menaces.

The trees about the portal of the chapel moved soughingly[7] in a soft wind. A sad silence was upon the little guarding <u>edifice</u>.

---

7. **soughingly.** With a moaning or sighing sound

| Words For Everyday Use | **ap • pall • ing** (ə pôl´iŋ) *adj.*, inspiring horror, dismay, or disgust |
| | **ed • i • fice** (e´dəfəs) *n.*, building |

Respond to the Selection

To what extent can you sympathize with Henry's (the youth's) decision to run? As a class, discuss decisions that people make based on fear. What are some examples? What do you think of the quality of decisions based on fear?

Investigate, Inquire, and Imagine

Recall: GATHERING FACTS

1a. In Chapter 4, what does the 304th regiment witness in the battle? What do they see another regiment do? What does seeing this make Henry think he will do? In Chapter 5, what does the 304th regiment do when the enemy charges? When the "red rage" comes over Henry, what does he wish he could do?

2a. As Chapter 6 begins, what does Henry think about war and himself? What does Henry begin to think about the enemy? What does Henry do once the battle begins again? Is he alone in doing this? What does he discover about the battle at the end of Chapter 6?

3a. In Chapter 7, what does Henry tell himself is the reason he fled? What does he think of the men who remained in position? Where does Henry go to escape from the sounds of battle? What "experiment" does Henry conduct there? To what is a small clearing in this place compared? What does the youth find in this clearing? What is Henry's reaction to finding this thing here?

Interpret: FINDING MEANING

→ 1b. Evaluate how Henry behaves in battle, in Chapter 5. How does he exceed his own expectations? What feelings motivate him to perform this way? At the end of Chapter 5, did you believe that Henry had conquered his fear of running from battle? Explain.

→ 2b. Are Henry's ideas about war and himself justified based on what he has experienced and done? Why, or why not? Explain why Henry reacts as he does to the battle. What does the news about the battle at the end of Chapter 6 reveal about Henry's fears? What does it reveal about what he has done?

→ 3b. Explain whether you agree with Henry's assessment of his decision. Why do you think he regards his decision in this way and seeks to support it in an "experiment"? Explain why the setting in which the thing is placed makes finding it there even more horrible. Why do you think Crane uses words like "it" and "thing" to describe what Henry finds?

Analyze: TAKING THINGS APART

4a. In what way is battle depicted in Chapters 4–7? In what way is death depicted? Identify some examples of vivid descriptions of battle scenes and of men being injured or dying.

Synthesize: BRINGING THINGS TOGETHER

→ 4b. Explain whether you believe that Crane is depicting war and its consequences realistically or whether his images of war are not convincing. What attitude toward war and its consequences do you think the author reveals in these chapters?

Evaluate: MAKING JUDGMENTS

5a. Explain whether Henry's actions make him a coward. What do you think about his decision to leave his regiment? Was it a smart decision? A moral or ethical decision? Explain whether you would have done the same thing in his position. Do you think you can truly know how you would react in such a situation without living through it? Why, or why not?

Extend: CONNECTING IDEAS

→ 5b. People in different time periods and cultures have held different attitudes about participating in a war. Desertion was viewed as a serious crime during the Civil War. People who ran from the battlefield were punished in many ways, and not always through proper military channels and trials. Some were publicly humiliated; others were branded or tortured; some were executed. Discuss how you think Henry's actions would be viewed by each of the following people: A) A commander of the Union army who wants to maintain strict order among his men; B) Henry's friend Wilson (the loud soldier) who has also admitted to feeling fear before battle; C) A protestor and conscientious objector to the Vietnam War in the year 1969; D) Someone you know whose mother or father has made a career in the military; E) Someone in your class who holds human life to be sacred

Understanding Literature

Foreshadowing. Foreshadowing is the act of hinting at events that will happen later in a poem, story, or play. In what way is Henry's decision to run from battle foreshadowed before he does so? Point to some examples of passages that might foreshadow Henry's action.

Metaphor. A **metaphor** is a figure of speech in which one thing is spoken or written about as if it were another. The figure of speech invites the reader to make a comparison between the two things. For example, in the line from Chapter 6, "The shells . . . looked to be strange war flowers bursting into fierce bloom," the exploding bombs launched by artillery are described as if they were blooming flowers. What two things are compared in each of the following lines? In what ways are they similar? In what ways are they different?

The men groaned. . . . watched in sullen mood the frantic approach of the enemy. The slaves toiling in the temple of this god began to feel rebellion at his harsh tasks.

To the youth it was an onslaught of redoubtable dragons. . . He seemed to shut his eyes and wait to be gobbled.

Chapter 8

The trees began softly to sing a hymn of twilight. The sun sank until slanted bronze rays struck the forest. There was a <u>lull</u> in the noises of insects as if they had bowed their beaks and were making a devotional pause. There was silence save for the chanted chorus of the trees.

Then, upon this stillness, there suddenly broke a tremendous clangor of sounds. A crimson roar came from the distance.

◄ What interrupts the stillness?

The youth stopped. He was transfixed by this terrific medley of all noises. It was as if worlds were being rended. There was the ripping sound of musketry and the breaking crash of the artillery.

His mind flew in all directions. He conceived the two armies to be at each other panther fashion.[1] He listened for a time. Then he began to run in the direction of the battle. He saw that it was an <u>ironical</u> thing for him to be running thus toward that which he had been at such pains to avoid. But he said, in substance, to himself that if the earth and the moon were about to clash, many persons would doubtless plan to get upon the roofs to witness the collision.

◄ Where does the youth run? What does he realize about his decision to run in this direction?

As he ran, he became aware that the forest had stopped its music, as if at last becoming capable of hearing the foreign sounds. The trees hushed and stood motionless. Everything seemed to be listening to the crackle and clatter and ear-shaking thunder. The chorus <u>pealed</u> over the still earth.

It suddenly occurred to the youth that the fight in which he had been was, after all, but <u>perfunctory</u> popping.[2] In the hearing of this present din he was doubtful if he had seen real battle scenes. This uproar explained a celestial battle; it was tumbling hordes a-struggle in the air.

◄ What does the youth realize about the battle he witnessed?

Reflecting, he saw a sort of a humor in the point of view of himself and his fellows during the late encounter. They had taken themselves and the enemy very seriously and had imagined that they were deciding the war. Individuals must have supposed that they were cutting the letters of their

◄ What thought amuses the youth?

---

1. **panther fashion.** Like panthers; exceptionally fierce
2. **popping.** Shooting

Words For Everyday Use

lull (ləl) *n.*, temporary pause or decline in activity
iron • i • cal (ī rä′ni kəl) *adj.*, incompatibility between the actual result of a sequence of events and the normal or expected result

peal (pēl) *vt.*, chime, ring out
per • func • to • ry (pər fəŋ(k) tə rē) *adj.*, characterized by routine or superficiality; mechanical

names deep into everlasting tablets of brass, or <u>enshrining</u> their reputations forever in the hearts of their countrymen, while, as to fact, the affair would appear in printed reports under a meek and <u>immaterial</u> title. But he saw that it was good, else, he said, in battle every one would surely run save forlorn hopes and their <u>ilk</u>.

He went rapidly on. He wished to come to the edge of the forest that he might peer out.

As he hastened, there passed through his mind pictures of stupendous conflicts. His accumulated thought upon such subjects was used to form scenes. The noise was as the voice of an <u>eloquent</u> being, describing.

Sometimes the brambles formed chains and tried to hold him back. Trees, confronting him, stretched out their arms and forbade him to pass. After its previous hostility this new resistance of the forest filled him with a fine bitterness. It seemed that Nature could not be quite ready to kill him.

But he obstinately took roundabout ways, and presently he was where he could see long gray walls of vapor where lay battle lines. The voices of cannon shook him. The musketry sounded in long irregular surges that played havoc with his ears. He stood regardant for a moment. His eyes had an awestruck expression. He gawked in the direction of the fight.

▶ To what does the youth compare war?

Presently he proceeded again on his forward way. The battle was like the grinding of an immense and terrible machine to him. Its complexities and powers, its grim processes, fascinated him. He must go close and see it produce corpses.

He came to a fence and clambered over it. On the far side, the ground was littered with clothes and guns. A newspaper, folded up, lay in the dirt. A dead soldier was stretched with his face hidden in his arm. Farther off there was a group of four or five corpses keeping mournful company. A hot sun had blazed upon the spot.

▶ How does the youth feel about entering the part of the battleground where only the dead remain?

In this place the youth felt that he was an invader. This forgotten part of the battle ground was owned by the dead men, and he hurried, in the vague apprehension that one of the swollen forms would rise and tell him to begone.

He came finally to a road from which he could see in the distance dark and agitated bodies of troops, smoke-fringed. In the lane was a blood-stained crowd streaming to the rear.

Words For Everyday Use

en • shrine (en shrīn´) vt., preserve or cherish as sacred

im • ma • te • ri • al (i mə tir´ē əl) adj., of no substantial consequence; unimportant

ilk (ilk) n., sort, kind

el • o • quent (e´lə kwənt) adj., marked by forceful and fluent expression

The wounded men were cursing, groaning, and wailing. In the air, always, was a mighty swell of sound that it seemed could sway the earth. With the courageous words of the artillery and the spiteful sentences of the musketry mingled red cheers. And from this region of noises came the steady current of the maimed.

◄ What type of men does the youth meet upon the road?

One of the wounded men had a shoeful of blood. He hopped like a schoolboy in a game. He was laughing hysterically.

◄ What is one wounded man doing? To what is he compared?

One was swearing that he had been shot in the arm through the commanding general's mismanagement of the army. One was marching with an air imitative of some <u>sublime</u> drum major. Upon his features was an unholy mixture of merriment and agony. As he marched he sang a bit of <u>doggerel</u> in a high and quavering voice:

"Sing a song 'a vic'try,
  A pocketful 'a bullets,
Five an' twenty dead men
  Baked in a—pie."[3]

◄ About what does one wounded man sing?

Parts of the procession limped and staggered to this tune.

Another had the gray seal of death already upon his face. His lips were curled in hard lines and his teeth were clinched. His hands were bloody from where he had pressed them upon his wound. He seemed to be awaiting the moment when he should pitch headlong. He stalked like the specter of a soldier, his eyes burning with the power of a stare into the unknown.

◄ What can the youth tell about what will happen to one of the injured men? How can he tell?

There were some who proceeded sullenly, full of anger at their wounds, and ready to turn upon anything as an obscure cause.

An officer was carried along by two privates. He was <u>peevish</u>. "Don't joggle so, Johnson, yeh fool," he cried. "Think m' leg is made of iron? If yeh can't carry me decent, put me down an' let some one else do it."

He bellowed at the <u>tottering</u> crowd who blocked the quick

---

3. "Sing . . . pie." The injured soldier is singing his own grim version of these lines from the nursery rhyme, "Sing a Song of Sixpence": "Sing a song of sixpence,/A pocket full of rye;/Four and twenty blackbirds/Baked in a pie."

| Words For Everyday Use | **sub • lime** (sə blīm´) *adj.,* lofty, grand, or exalted in thought, expression, or manner
dog • ger • el (dô´gə rəl) *n.,* verse styled for comic effect or to mock | **pee • vish** (pē´vish) *adj.,* marked by ill-temper
tot • ter • ing (tô´tər iŋ) *adj.,* being in an unstable condition |

march of his bearers. "Say, make way there, can't yeh? Make way, dickens take it all."

They sulkily parted and went to the roadsides. As he was carried past they made <u>pert</u> remarks to him. When he raged in reply and threatened them, they told him to be damned.

The shoulder of one of the tramping bearers knocked heavily against the spectral soldier who was staring into the unknown.

The youth joined this crowd and marched along with it. The torn bodies expressed the awful machinery in which the men had been entangled.

Orderlies and couriers occasionally broke through the throng in the roadway, scattering wounded men right and left, galloping on followed by howls. The melancholy march was continually disturbed by the messengers, and sometimes by bustling batteries that came swinging and thumping down upon them, the officers shouting orders to clear the way.

▶ Whom does the youth find at his side?

There was a tattered man, fouled with dust, blood and powder stain from hair to shoes, who trudged quietly at the youth's side. He was listening with eagerness and much humility to the lurid descriptions of a bearded sergeant. His lean features wore an expression of awe and admiration. He was like a listener in a country store to wondrous tales told among the sugar barrels. He eyed the story-teller with unspeakable wonder. His mouth was agape in yokel[4] fashion.

The sergeant, taking note of this, gave pause to his elaborate history while he administered a <u>sardonic</u> comment. "Be keerful, honey, you'll be a-ketchin' flies," he said.

The tattered man shrank back <u>abashed</u>.

▶ What does the tattered man seem to want of the youth?

▶ What does the youth notice about the tattered man?

After a time he began to <u>sidle</u> near to the youth, and in a diffident way try to make him a friend. His voice was gentle as a girl's voice and his eyes were pleading. The youth saw with surprise that the soldier had two wounds, one in the head, bound with a blood-soaked rag, and the other in the arm, making that member dangle like a broken bough.

After they had walked together for some time the tattered man mustered sufficient courage to speak. "Was pretty good

---

4. **yokel.** Demeaning term for a naïve or ignorant resident of a rural area or a small town

---

Words For Everyday Use

pert (pərt) *adj.,* rudely free and forward
sar • don • ic (sär də′nik) *adj.,* disdainfully or skeptically humorous
abash (ə bash′) *vt.,* destroy the self-possession or self-confidence of
si • dle (sī′d′l) *vi.,* go or move with one side foremost, especially in a furtive advance

fight, wa'n't it?" he timidly said. The youth, deep in thought, glanced up at the bloody and grim figure with its lamblike eyes. "What?"

"Was pretty good fight, wa'n't it?"

"Yes," said the youth shortly. He quickened his pace.

But the other hobbled industriously after him. There was an air of apology in his manner, but he evidently thought that he needed only to talk for a time, and the youth would perceive that he was a good fellow.

◀ What type of manner does the tattered man have?

"Was pretty good fight, wa'n't it?" he began in a small voice, and then he achieved the <u>fortitude</u> to continue. "Dern me if I ever see fellers fight so. Laws, how they did fight! I knowed th' boys 'd lick when they onct got square at it. Th' boys ain't had no fair chanct up t' now, but this time they showed what they was. I knowed it 'd turn out this way. Yeh can't lick them boys. No, sir! They're fighters, they be."

He breathed a deep breath of humble admiration. He had looked at the youth for encouragement several times. He received none, but gradually he seemed to get absorbed in his subject.

"I was talkin' 'cross pickets with a boy from Georgie, onct, an' that boy, he ses, 'Your fellers 'll all run like hell when they onct hearn a gun,' he ses. 'Mebbe they will,' I ses, 'but I don't b'lieve none of it,' I ses; 'an' b'jiminey,' I ses back t' 'um, 'mebbe your fellers 'll all run like hell when they onct hearn a gun,' I ses. He larfed. Well, they didn't run t' day, did they, hey? No, sir! They fit, an' fit, an' fit."

◀ What did a boy from Georgia tell the tattered man? About what is the tattered man proud?

His homely face was <u>suffused</u> with a light of love for the army which was to him all things beautiful and powerful.

After a time he turned to the youth. "Where yeh hit, ol' boy?" he asked in a brotherly tone.

The youth felt instant panic at this question, although at first its full import was not borne in upon him.

◀ What does the tattered man ask the youth? How does this question make the youth feel?

"What?" he asked.

"Where yeh hit?" repeated the tattered man.

"Why," began the youth, "I—I—that is—why—I—"

He turned away suddenly and slid through the crowd. His brow was heavily flushed, and his fingers were picking nervously at one of his buttons. He bent his head and fastened his eyes studiously upon the button as if it were a little problem.

The tattered man looked after him in astonishment.

Words For Everyday Use

for • ti • tude (fôr′tə tōod) *n.*, strength of mind that enables a person to encounter danger or bear pain or adversity with courage

suf • fuse (sə fyōoz′) *vt.*, spread over or through in the manner of fluid or light

Chapter 9

The youth fell back in the <u>procession</u> until the tattered soldier was not in sight. Then he started to walk on with the others.

But he was amid wounds. The mob of men was bleeding. Because of the tattered soldier's question he now felt that his shame could be viewed. He was continually casting sidelong glances to see if the men were contemplating the letters of guilt he felt burned into his brow.[1]

At times he regarded the wounded soldiers in an envious way. He conceived persons with torn bodies to be peculiarly happy. He wished that he, too, had a wound, a red badge of courage.

The spectral soldier was at his side like a stalking <u>reproach</u>. The man's eyes were still fixed in a stare into the unknown. His gray, appalling face had attracted attention in the crowd, and men, slowing to his <u>dreary</u> pace, were walking with him. They were discussing his plight, questioning him and giving him advice. In a dogged way he repelled them, signing to them to go on and leave him alone. The shadows of his face were deepening and his tight lips seemed holding in check the moan of great despair. There could be seen a certain stiffness in the movements of his body, as if he were taking infinite care not to arouse the passion of his wounds. As he went on, he seemed always looking for a place, like one who goes to choose a grave.

Something in the gesture of the man as he waved the bloody and pitying soldiers away made the youth start as if bitten. He yelled in horror. Tottering forward he laid a quivering hand upon the man's arm. As the latter slowly turned his waxlike features toward him, the youth screamed:

"Gawd! Jim Conklin!"

The tall soldier made a little <u>commonplace</u> smile. "Hello, Henry," he said.

The youth swayed on his legs and glared strangely. He

► What does the tattered man's question cause the youth to feel?

► For what does the youth wish?

► Whom does the youth run into again?

► What does the spectral soldier seem to be doing as he walks?

► Who is the spectral soldier?

---

1. **guilt . . . brow.** During the Civil War, deserters were sometimes punished in cruel ways; one method of punishment was branding, where the letter *D* for *deserter* would be branded with a hot iron onto the accused's face.

Words For Everyday Use

pro • ces • sion (prə se´shən) *n.*, group of individuals moving along in an orderly often ceremonial way
re • proach (ri prōch´) *n.*, expression of blame or disapproval

drea • ry (drir´ē) *adj.*, feeling, displaying, or reflecting listlessness or discouragement
com • mon • place (kä´mən plās) *n.*, something commonly found

stuttered and stammered. "Oh, Jim—oh, Jim—oh, Jim—oh Jim—"

The tall soldier held out his <u>gory</u> hand. There was a curious red and black combination of new blood and old blood upon it. "Where yeh been, Henry?" he asked. He continued in a monotonous voice, "I thought mebbe yeh got keeled over. There's been thunder t' pay t'-day. I was worryin' about it a good deal."

◀ About what does Jim, the tall soldier, say he has been worried?

The youth still lamented. "Oh, Jim—oh, Jim—oh, Jim—"

"Yeh know," said the tall soldier, "I was out there." He made a careful gesture. "An', Lord, what a circus! An', b'jiminey, I got shot—I got shot. Yes, b'jiminey, I got shot." He <u>reiterated</u> this fact in a bewildered way, as if he did not know how it came about.

◀ What does Jim say has happened to him? What does his mental state seem to be?

The youth put forth anxious arms to assist him, but the tall soldier went firmly on as if propelled. Since the youth's arrival as a guardian for his friend, the other wounded men had ceased to display much interest. They occupied themselves again in dragging their own tragedies toward the rear.

Suddenly, as the two friends marched on, the tall soldier seemed to be overcome by a terror. His face turned to a <u>semblance</u> of gray paste. He clutched the youth's arm and looked all about him, as if dreading to be overheard. Then he began to speak in a shaking whisper: "I tell yeh what I'm 'fraid of, Henry—I'll tell yeh what I'm 'fraid of. I'm 'fraid I'll fall down—an' then yeh know—them damned artillery wagons[2]—they like as not 'll run over me. That's what I'm 'fraid of—"

◀ Of what is Jim afraid?

The youth cried out to him hysterically: "I'll take care of yeh, Jim! I'll take care of yeh! I swear t' Gawd I will!"

"Sure—will yeh, Henry?" the tall soldier <u>beseeched</u>.

"Yes—yes—I tell yeh—I'll take care of yeh, Jim!" protested the youth. He could not speak accurately because of the gulpings in his throat.

But the tall soldier continued to beg in a lowly way. He now hung babelike to the youth's arm. His eyes rolled in the wildness of his terror. "I was allus a good friend t' yeh, wa'n't I, Henry? I've allus been a pretty good feller, ain't I? An' it

---

2. **artillery wagons.** Horse-drawn wagons in which the large guns were carried

---

Words For Everyday Use

gory (gōr´e) *adj.*, bloodstained
re • it • er • ate (rē i´tər āt) *vt.*, state or do over again or repeatedly sometimes with wearying effect

sem • blance (sem´blən(t)s) *n.*, outward appearance or show
be • seech (bi sēch´) *vt.*, beg for urgently or anxiously

ain't much t' ask, is it? Jest t' pull me along outer th' road? I'd do it fer you, wouldn't I, Henry?"

He paused in piteous anxiety to await his friend's reply.

The youth had reached an anguish where the sobs scorched him. He strove to express his loyalty, but he could only make fantastic gestures.

However, the tall soldier seemed suddenly to forget all those fears. He became again the grim, stalking specter of a soldier. He went stonily forward. The youth wished his friend to lean upon him, but the other always shook his head and strangely protested. "No—no—no—leave me be—leave me be—"

His look was fixed again upon the unknown. He moved with mysterious purpose, and all of the youth's offers he brushed aside. "No—no—leave me be—leave me be—"

The youth had to follow.

Presently the latter heard a voice talking softly near his shoulder. Turning he saw that it belonged to the tattered soldier. "Ye'd better take 'im outa th' road, pardner. There's a batt'ry comin' helitywhoop[3] down th' road an' he'll git runned over. He's a goner anyhow in about five minutes— yeh kin see that. Ye'd better take 'im outa th' road. Where th' blazes does he git his stren'th from?"

"Lord knows!" cried the youth. He was shaking his hands helplessly.

He ran forward presently and grasped the tall soldier by the arm. "Jim! Jim!" he coaxed, "come with me."

The tall soldier weakly tried to wrench himself free. "Huh," he said vacantly. He stared at the youth for a moment. At last he spoke as if dimly comprehending. "Oh! Inteh th' fields? Oh!"

He started blindly through the grass.

The youth turned once to look at the lashing riders and jouncing guns of the battery. He was startled from this view by a shrill outcry from the tattered man.

"Gawd! He's runnin'!"

Turning his head swiftly, the youth saw his friend running in a staggering and stumbling way toward a little clump of bushes. His heart seemed to wrench itself almost free from his body at this sight. He made a noise of pain. He and the tattered man began a pursuit. There was a singular race.

When he overtook the tall soldier he began to plead with all the words he could find. "Jim—Jim—what are you doing—what makes you do this way—you'll hurt yerself."

---

3. **helitywhoop.** Colorful term meaning "very quickly"

▶ Who reappears at the youth's side? What advice does this person give the youth? What does this person admire in Jim?

▶ What seems to be happening to Jim?

▶ What does the youth see Jim doing? How does it make him feel?

▶ What does the youth tell Jim about his actions? What is Jim's response?

The same purpose was in the tall soldier's face. He protested in a dulled way, keeping his eyes fastened on the mystic place of his intentions. "No—no—don't tech me—leave me be—leave me be—"

The youth, <u>aghast</u> and filled with wonder at the tall soldier, began quaveringly to question him. "Where yeh goin', Jim? What you thinking about? Where you going? Tell me, won't you, Jim?"

The tall soldier faced about as upon relentless pursuers. In his eyes there was a great appeal. "Leave me be, can't yeh? Leave me be fer a minnit."

The youth recoiled. "Why, Jim," he said, in a dazed way, "what's the matter with you?"

The tall soldier turned and, lurching dangerously, went on. The youth and the tattered soldier followed, sneaking as if whipped, feeling unable to face the stricken man if he should again confront them. They began to have thoughts of a solemn ceremony. There was something ritelike in these movements of the doomed soldier. And there was a resemblance in him to a <u>devotee</u> of a mad religion, blood-sucking, muscle-wrenching, bone-crushing. They were awed and afraid. They hung back lest he have at command a dreadful weapon.

◀ How do the youth and the tattered man feel about Jim and his actions?

At last, they saw him stop and stand motionless. Hastening up, they perceived that his face wore an expression telling that he had at last found the place for which he had struggled. His spare figure was erect; his bloody hands were quietly at his side. He was waiting with patience for something that he had come to meet. He was at the <u>rendezvous</u>. They paused and stood, expectant.

◀ What can they tell when they see Jim's face?

◀ Whom or what do you think Jim has come to meet at this place?

There was a silence.

Finally, the chest of the doomed soldier began to heave with a strained motion. It increased in violence until it was as if an animal was within and was kicking and tumbling furiously to be free.

This spectacle of gradual strangulation made the youth writhe, and once as his friend rolled his eyes, he saw something in them that made him sink wailing to the ground. He raised his voice in a last supreme call.

"Jim—Jim—Jim—"

Words
For
Everyday
Use

aghast (ə gast´) *adj.*, struck with terror, amazement, or horror

dev • o • tee (de vô tē´) *n.*, ardent follower, supporter, or enthusiast (as of a

religion, art form, or sport)

ren • dez • vous (rän´di vōō) *n.*, place appointed for assembling or meeting

The tall soldier opened his lips and spoke. He made a gesture. "Leave me be—don't tech me—leave me be—"

There was another silence while he waited.

Suddenly, his form stiffened and straightened. Then it was shaken by a prolonged <u>ague</u>. He stared into space. To the two watchers there was a curious and profound dignity in the firm lines of his awful face.

He was invaded by a creeping strangeness that slowly enveloped him. For a moment the tremor of his legs caused him to dance a sort of hideous hornpipe. His arms beat wildly about his head in expression of implike enthusiasm.

His tall figure stretched itself to its full height. There was a slight rending sound. Then it began to swing forward, slow and straight, in the manner of a falling tree. A swift muscular <u>contortion</u> made the left shoulder strike the ground first.

The body seemed to bounce a little way from the earth. "God!" said the tattered soldier.

The youth had watched, spellbound, this ceremony at the place of meeting. His face had been twisted into an expression of every agony he had imagined for his friend.

He now sprang to his feet and, going closer, gazed upon the pastelike face. The mouth was open and the teeth showed in a laugh.

As the flap of the blue jacket fell away from the body, he could see that the side looked as if it had been chewed by wolves.

The youth turned, with sudden, <u>livid</u> rage, toward the battlefield. He shook his fist. He seemed about to deliver a <u>philippic</u>.

"Hell—"

The red sun was pasted in the sky like a wafer.

▶ What is revealed about Jim's injury when he dies?

▶ How does the youth feel about what has happened to his friend?

Words
For
Everyday
Use

ague (āˊgyo͞o) *n.*, fit of shivering

con • tor • tion (kən tôrˊshən) *n.*, violent twist

liv • id (liˊvəd) *adj.*, very angry; enraged

phi • lip • pic (fə liˊpik) *n.*, discourse or declamation full of bitter condemnation; tirade

64 THE RED BADGE OF COURAGE

Chapter 10

The tattered man stood musing.

"Well, he was reg'lar jim-dandy[1] fer nerve, wa'n't he," said he finally in a little awestruck voice. "A reg'lar jim-dandy." He thoughtfully poked one of the <u>docile</u> hands with his foot. "I wonner where he got 'is stren'th from? I never seen a man do like that before. It was a funny thing. Well, he was a reg'lar jim-dandy."

The youth desired to screech out his grief. He was stabbed, but his tongue lay dead in the tomb of his mouth. He threw himself again upon the ground and began to <u>brood</u>.

The tattered man stood musing.

"Look-a-here, pardner," he said, after a time. He regarded the corpse as he spoke. "He's up an' gone, ain't 'e, an' we might as well begin t' look out fer ol' number one.[2] This here thing is all over. He's up an' gone, ain't 'e? An' he's all right here. Nobody won't bother 'im. An' I must say I ain't enjoying any great health m'self these days."

The youth, awakened by the tattered soldier's tone, looked quickly up. He saw that he was swinging uncertainly on his legs and that his face had turned to a shade of blue.

"Good Lord!" he cried, "you ain't goin' t'—not you, too."

The tattered man waved his hand. "Nary die,"[3] he said. "All I want is some pea soup an' a good bed. Some pea soup," he repeated dreamfully.

The youth arose from the ground. "I wonder where he came from. I left him over there." He pointed. "And now I find 'im here. And he was coming from over there, too." He indicated a new direction. They both turned toward the body as if to ask of it a question.

"Well," at length spoke the tattered man, "there ain't no use in our stayin' here an' tryin' t' ask him anything."

The youth nodded an <u>assent</u> wearily. They both turned to gaze for a moment at the corpse.

The youth murmured something.

---

1. **jim-dandy.** Something or someone excellent for its kind
2. **number one.** One's own interests or welfare
3. **Nary die.** Not going to die

Words For Everyday Use

doc • ile (dä´səl) *adj.,* easily led or managed; obedient
brood (brood) *vi.,* dwell gloomily on a subject
as • sent (ə sent´) *n.,* agreement

◄ What is the tattered man's reaction to the event he and the youth have witnessed?

◄ How does the youth feel about what has occurred? What is he unable to do? What does he do instead?

◄ What does the tattered man tell the youth they should do now? What does he say about his own health?

◄ What does the youth notice about the tattered soldier?

"Well, he was a jim-dandy, wa'n't 'e?" said the tattered man as if in response.

They turned their backs upon it and started away. For a time they stole softly, treading with their toes. It remained laughing there in the grass.

▶ What does the tattered man say about how he is feeling? What concerns the youth?

"I'm commencin' t' feel pretty bad," said the tattered man, suddenly breaking one of his little silences. "I'm commencin' t' feel pretty damn' bad."

The youth groaned. "O Lord!" He wondered if he was to be the tortured witness of another grim encounter.

▶ According to the tattered soldier, why can't he die yet?

But his companion waved his hand reassuringly. "Oh, I'm not goin' t' die yit! There too much dependin' on me fer me t' die yit. No, sir! Nary die! I *can't!* Ye'd oughta see th' swad[4] a' chil'ren I've got, an' all like that."

The youth glancing at his companion could see by the shadow of a smile that he was making some kind of fun.

As they plodded on the tattered soldier continued to talk. "Besides, if I died, I wouldn't die th' way that feller did. That was th' funniest thing. I'd jest flop down, I would. I never seen a feller die th' way that feller did.

▶ Who let the tattered man know he was injured? Where is the tattered man injured? What does the tattered man say he would be doing if not for this person?

"Yeh know Tom Jamison, he lives next door t' me up home. He's a nice feller, he is, an' we was allus good friends. Smart, too. Smart as a steel trap. Well, when we was a-fightin' this afternoon, all-of-a-sudden he begin t' rip up an' cuss an' beller at me. 'Yer shot, yeh blamed infernal!'—he swear horrible—he ses t' me. I put up m' hand t' m' head an' when I looked at m' fingers, I seen, sure 'nough, I was shot. I give a holler an' begin t' run, but b'fore I could git away another one hit me in th' arm an' whirl' me clean 'round. I got skeared[5] when they was all a-shootin' b'hind me an' I run t' beat all, but I cotch it pretty bad. I've an idee I'd a' been fightin' yit, if t'was n't fer Tom Jamison."

Then he made a calm announcement: "There's two of 'em[6]—little ones—but they 're beginnin' t' have fun with me now. I don't b'lieve I kin walk much furder."

▶ Whom does the tattered man think of? What does he say he is unable to do any longer?

▶ About what does the tattered man express concern?

They went slowly on in silence. "Yeh look pretty peaked yerself," said the tattered man at last. "I bet yeh've got a worser one than yeh think. Ye'd better take keer of yer hurt. It don't do t' let sech things go. It might be inside mostly, an' them plays thunder. Where is it located?" But he continued his harangue without waiting for a reply. "I see a feller git hit plum in th' head when my reg'ment was a-standin' at ease onct. An' everybody yelled out to 'im: Hurt, John? Are yeh

▶ According to the tattered man, what happened to another soldier who thought his injury wasn't serious?

---

4. **swad.** Bunch
5. **skeared.** Scared
6. **two of 'em.** The tattered man is referring to his children.

hurt much? 'No,' ses he. He looked kinder surprised, an' he went on tellin' 'em how he felt. He sed he didn't feel nothin'. But, by dad, th' first thing that feller knowed he was dead. Yes, he was dead—stone dead. So, yeh wanta watch out. Yeh might have some queer kind 'a hurt yerself. Yeh can't never tell. Where is your'n located?"

◀ What does the tattered man ask of the youth? How does the youth respond?

The youth had been wriggling since the introduction of this topic. He now gave a cry of exasperation and made a furious motion with his hand. "Oh, don't bother me!" he said. He was enraged against the tattered man, and could have strangled him. His companions seemed ever to play intolerable parts. They were ever upraising the ghost of shame on the stick of their curiosity. He turned toward the tattered man as one at bay. "Now, don't bother me," he repeated with desperate <u>menace</u>.

◀ How does the youth suddenly feel toward the tattered man? What does he tell him?

"Well, Lord knows I don't wanta bother anybody," said the other. There was a little accent of despair in his voice as he replied, "Lord knows I've gota 'nough m' own t' tend to."

The youth, who had been holding a bitter debate with himself and casting glances of hatred and contempt at the tattered man, here spoke in a hard voice. "Good-by," he said.

The tattered man looked at him in gaping amazement. "Why—why, pardner, where yeh goin'?" he asked unsteadily. The youth looking at him, could see that he, too, like that other one, was beginning to act dumb and animal-like. His thoughts seemed to be floundering about in his head. "Now—now—look—a—here, you Tom Jamison—now—I won't have this—this here won't do. Where—where yeh goin'?"

◀ What does the youth notice about the tattered man? For whom does the tattered man mistake the youth?

The youth pointed vaguely. "Over there," he replied.

"Well, now look—a—here—now," said the tattered man, rambling on in idiot fashion. His head was hanging forward and his words were slurred. "This thing won't do, now, Tom Jamison. It won't do. I know yeh, yeh pig-headed devil. Yeh wanta go trompin' off with a bad hurt. It ain't right—now—Tom Jamison—it ain't. Yeh wanta leave me take keer of yeh, Tom Jamison. It ain't—right—it ain't—fer yeh t' go—trompin' off—with a bad hurt—it ain't—ain't—ain't right—it ain't."

◀ About what is the tattered man still concerned? What does the tattered man wish to do for the youth?

In reply the youth climbed a fence and started away. He could hear the tattered man <u>bleating</u> <u>plaintively</u>.

◀ What does the youth do? What does the tattered man do?

Words For Everyday Use

men • ace (me´nəs) *n.*, show of intention to inflict harm; threat
bleat (blēt) *vi.*, whimper; talk complainingly or with a whine
plain • tive • ly (plān´tiv lē) *adv.*, in a manner expressing woe or suffering

Once he faced about angrily. "What?"

"Look—a—here, now, Tom Jamison—now—it ain't—"

The youth went on. Turning at a distance he saw the tattered man wandering about helplessly in the field.

He now thought that he wished he was dead. He believed that he envied those men whose bodies lay strewn over the grass of the fields and on the fallen leaves of the forest.

The simple questions of the tattered man had been knife thrusts to him. They asserted a society that <u>probes</u> pitilessly at secrets until all is apparent. His late companion's chance persistency made him feel that he could not keep his crime concealed in his bosom. It was sure to be brought plain by one of those arrows which cloud the air and are constantly pricking, discovering, proclaiming those things which are willed to be forever hidden. He admitted that he could not defend himself against this agency. It was not within the power of <u>vigilance</u>.

► *What does the youth wish? What did the tattered man's questions feel like to him?*

Words For Everyday Use

probe (prōb) *vt.,* search into and explore with great thoroughness

vig • i • lance (vi´jə lən(t)s) *n.,* quality or state of being alertly watchful, especially to avoid danger

Respond to the Selection

Think about a time when you did something and you later felt guilt or shame about your actions. Were you aware as you were acting that you would later feel guilt or shame? If you had a chance to act differently, would you do so?

Investigate, Inquire, and Imagine

Recall: GATHERING FACTS

1a. In Chapter 8, what sort of people does Henry (the youth) encounter in the road? Describe some of the actions of these men. What does the tattered man talk to Henry about? What questions does the tattered man ask that surprise Henry? What does Henry do after the tattered man asks these questions?

2a. In Chapter 9, what does Henry realize about the "spectral soldier"? What does the spectral soldier ask him to do? Who rejoins Henry, what does this person suggest, and what do they see the spectral soldier do? What happens to the spectral soldier at the end of Chapter 9?

3a. According to the tattered man, what attitude should they take toward the spectral soldier? What does Henry notice about the tattered man? What does Henry learn about the tattered man's home life? What does the tattered man ask about again? What does Henry say to the tattered man? What does Henry do to him? In what condition is the tattered man when Henry does this?

Interpret: FINDING MEANING

1b. Compare and contrast Henry's troubles to those of some of the wounded men. Based on the way the tattered man is described, his actions, and his words, what do you think of the tattered man as a character? How would you describe him? Why might all of the tattered man's words fill Henry with panic?

2b. How does Henry feel about what is happening to the spectral soldier? Why are the spectral soldier's actions surprising? How does Henry feel about what has happened at the end of Chapter 9? Why do you think Henry seems more affected emotionally by this event than by other similar events he has experienced this day?

3b. Do you believe that Henry had an obligation to help the tattered man? Why, or why not? Could Henry have done anything to help him? Why do you think Henry acts this way toward the tattered man? In what way have Henry's actions in Chapter 10 affected your view of him as a character?

Analyze: TAKING THINGS APART

4a. At the beginning of Chapter 8, Henry lingers about the battle lines because he thinks of the battle as "an immense and terrible machine" that he must see "produce corpses." In what way does his attitude about the results of battle—death and corpses—change throughout Chapter 8–10?

Synthesize: BRINGING THINGS TOGETHER

4b. Think back to the way Henry was at the beginning of Chapter 1—relatively innocent and naïve about war. In what way has the knowledge or experience that Henry has gathered since that time, and particularly in Chapters 8–10, affected him in the short-term? How do you think this knowledge and experience will affect him in the long-term?

Evaluate: MAKING JUDGMENTS

5a. Evaluate and explain the significance of the title of this novel, *The Red Badge of Courage*. Based on what you have read so far (look to Chapter 9 for clues), what is a red badge of courage and why is it significant to Henry? Why does he long for one?

Extend: CONNECTING IDEAS

5b. What potentially self-destructive actions can you think of that people do today? What do you think they are trying to prove through these actions? Can you think of better, less self-destructive ways the same people might prove the same things to themselves or to others? What might Henry do, other than get a red badge, to prove his courage?

Understanding Literature

Realism and Description. Realism is the attempt to portray in art or literature an accurate picture of reality. In the late nineteenth and early twentieth century, some writers reacted against earlier forms of literature by emphasizing the ordinary details of life. A **description** gives a picture in words of a character, object, or scene. Descriptions use sensory details—words and phrases that describe how things, look, sound, smell, taste, or feel. Explain whether you would consider the following examples of realism: the description of the wounded soldiers in Chapter 8, the description of the death of Jim Conklin in Chapter 9, and Henry's interactions with the tattered man in Chapter 10. Crane's writing style includes vivid descriptions full of sensory detail. Choose a sensory detail from each of the three scenes mentioned above that seems to be particularly vivid to you.

Symbol. A symbol is a thing that stands for or represents both itself and something else. Of what might the tattered man be a symbol? Think back on the questions he asks Henry in both Chapter 8 and Chapter 10.

Antihero. An antihero is a central character who lacks many of the qualities associated with heroes. An antihero may lack beauty, courage, grace, intelligence, or moral scruples. Many modern writers focus on antiheroes. Based on what you have read so far, would you classify Henry as a hero or an antihero?

Chapter 11

He became aware that the furnace roar of the battle was growing louder. Great brown clouds had floated to the still heights of air before him. The noise, too, was approaching. The woods filtered men and the fields became dotted.

As he rounded a hillock, he perceived that the roadway was now a crying mass of wagons, teams, and men. From the heaving tangle issued <u>exhortations</u>, commands, <u>imprecations</u>. Fear was sweeping it along. The cracking whips bit and horses plunged and tugged. The white-topped wagons strained and stumbled in their exertions like fat sheep.

◀ Who is in the road now? What is "sweeping" everyone along?

The youth felt comforted in a measure by this sight. They were all retreating. Perhaps, then, he was not so bad after all. He seated himself and watched the terror-stricken wagons. They fled like soft, ungainly animals. All the roarers and lashers served to help him to magnify the dangers and horrors of the engagement that he might try to prove to himself that the thing with which men could charge him was in truth a symmetrical act. There was an amount of pleasure to him in watching the wild march of this <u>vindication</u>.

◀ What are the men from his side doing? How does this make the youth feel about his own position?

Presently the calm head of a forward-going column of infantry appeared in the road. It came swiftly on. Avoiding the obstructions gave it the <u>sinuous</u> movement of a serpent. The men at the head butted[1] mules with their musket stocks. They prodded teamsters indifferent to all howls. The men forced their way through parts of the dense mass by strength. The blunt head of the column pushed. The raving teamsters swore many strange oaths.

◀ Who appears calm in the midst of the retreat?

The commands to make way had the ring of a great importance in them. The men were going forward to the heart of the din. They were to confront the eager rush of the enemy. They felt the pride of their onward movement when the remainder of the army seemed trying to dribble down this road. They tumbled teams about with a fine feeling that it was no matter so long as their column got to the front in time. This importance made their faces grave and stern. And the backs of the officers were very rigid.

◀ Why is this group of infantry moving forward rather than retreating?

---

1. **butted.** Struck or shoved

Words For Everyday Use	**ex • hor • ta • tion** (ek sôr tā´shən) *n.*, language intended to incite and encourage **im • pre • ca • tion** (im pri ka´shən) *n.*, curse	**vin • di • ca • tion** (vin də kā´shən) *n.*, justification against denial or censure **sin • u • ous** (sin´yə wəs) *adj.*, of a snakelike or wavy form

► How does the youth feel about himself in comparison to the men marching toward battle?

As the youth looked at them the black weight of his woe returned to him. He felt that he was regarding a procession of chosen beings. The separation was as great to him as if they had marched with weapons of flame and banners of sunlight. He could never be like them. He could have wept in his longings.

He searched about in his mind for an adequate <u>malediction</u> for the indefinite cause, the thing upon which men turn the words of final blame. It—whatever it was—was responsible for him, he said. There lay the fault.

The haste of the column to reach the battle seemed to the forlorn young man to be something much finer than stout fighting. Heroes, he thought, could find excuses in that long <u>seething</u> lane. They could retire with perfect self-respect and make excuses to the stars.

He wondered what those men had eaten that they could be in such haste to force their way to grim chances of death. As he watched his envy grew until he thought that he wished to change lives with one of them. He would have liked to have used a tremendous force, he said, throw off himself and become a better. Swift pictures of himself, apart, yet in himself, came to him—a blue desperate figure leading lurid charges with one knee forward and a broken blade high—a blue, determined figure standing before a crimson and steel assault, getting calmly killed on a high place before the eyes of all. He thought of the magnificent <u>pathos</u> of his dead body.

► How does the youth like to picture himself? What type of soldier would he like to be?

These thoughts uplifted him. He felt the quiver of war desire. In his ears, he heard the ring of victory. He knew the frenzy of a rapid successful charge. The music of the trampling feet, the sharp voices, the clanking arms of the column near him made him soar on the red wings of war. For a few moments he was sublime.

He thought that he was about to start for the front. Indeed, he saw a picture of himself, dust-stained, <u>haggard</u>, panting, flying to the front at the proper moment to seize and throttle the dark, leering witch of calamity.

Then the difficulties of the thing began to drag at him. He hesitated, balancing awkwardly on one foot.

He had no rifle; he could not fight with his hands, said he

Words For Everyday Use

mal • e • dic • tion (ma lə dik´shən) n., curse

seeth • ing (sēth´iŋ) adj., be in a state of rapid agitated movement

pa • thos (pā´thôs) n., element in experience or in artistic representation evoking pity or compassion

hag • gard (ha´gərd) adj., having a worn or emaciated appearance

resentfully to his plan. Well, rifles could be had for the picking. They were extraordinarily <u>profuse</u>.

Also, he continued, it would be a miracle if he found his regiment. Well, he could fight with any regiment.

He started forward slowly. He stepped as if he expected to tread upon some explosive thing. Doubts and he were struggling.

He would truly be a worm if any of his comrades should see him returning thus, the marks of his flight upon him. There was a reply that the intent fighters did not care for what happened rearward saving that no hostile bayonets[2] appeared there. In the battle-blur his face would, in a way, be hidden, like the face of a cowled[3] man.

But then he said that his tireless fate would bring forth, when the strife lulled for a moment, a man to ask of him an explanation. In imagination he felt the <u>scrutiny</u> of his companions as he painfully labored through some lies.

Eventually, his courage expended itself upon these objections. The debates drained him of his fire.

He was not cast down by this defeat of his plan, for, upon studying the affair carefully, he could not but admit that the objections were very formidable.

Furthermore, various ailments had begun to cry out. In their presence he could not persist in flying high with the wings of war; they rendered it almost impossible for him to see himself in a heroic light. He tumbled headlong.

He discovered that he had a scorching thirst. His face was so dry and grimy that he thought he could feel his skin crackle. Each bone of his body had an ache in it, and seemingly threatened to break with each movement. His feet were like two sores. Also, his body was calling for food. It was more powerful than a direct hunger. There was a dull, weight-like feeling in his stomach, and, when he tried to walk, his head swayed and he tottered. He could not see with distinctness. Small patches of green mist floated before his vision.

While he had been tossed by many emotions, he had not

----

2. **bayonets.** Steel blade attached to the end of a gun and used for hand-to-hand combat
3. **cowled.** Hooded

Words For Everyday Use

pro • fuse (prə fyo͞os′) *adj.,* exhibiting great abundance
scru • ti • ny (skro͞o′tə nē) *n.,* searching study, inquiry, or inspection

◄ What problems might prevent the youth from rejoining battle? What solutions does he find to these problems?

◄ According to the youth, why might his regiment not notice that he ran from battle?

◄ What "objection" to taking part in battle again makes the youth feel less eager to do so?

◄ Why does the youth feel that he is not physically able to rejoin the battle?

been aware of ailments. Now they <u>beset</u> him and made clamor. As he was at last compelled to pay attention to them, his capacity for self-hate was multiplied. In despair, he declared that he was not like those others. He now conceded it to be impossible that he should ever become a hero. He was a <u>craven</u> <u>loon</u>. Those pictures of glory were piteous things. He groaned from his heart and went staggering off.

A certain mothlike quality within him kept him in the vicinity of the battle. He had a great desire to see, and to get news. He wished to know who was winning.

He told himself that, despite his unprecedented suffering, he had never lost his greed for a victory, yet, he said, in a half-apologetic manner to his conscience, he could not but know that a defeat for the army this time might mean many favorable things for him. The blows of the enemy would splinter regiments into fragments. Thus, many men of courage, he considered, would be obliged to desert the colors and scurry like chickens. He would appear as one of them. They would be sullen brothers in distress, and he could then easily believe he had not run any farther or faster than they. And if he himself could believe in his virtuous perfection, he conceived that there would be small trouble in convincing all others.

He said, as if in excuse for this hope, that previously the army had encountered great defeats and in a few months had shaken off all blood and tradition of them, emerging as bright and valiant as a new one; thrusting out of sight the memory of disaster, and appearing with the valor and confidence of unconquered legions.[4] The shrilling voices of the people at home would pipe dismally for a time, but various generals were usually compelled to listen to these ditties.[5] He of course felt no <u>compunctions</u> for proposing a general as a sacrifice. He could not tell who the chosen for the <u>barbs</u> might be, so he could center no direct sympathy upon him. The people were afar and he did not conceive public opinion to be accurate at long range. It was quite probable they would hit the wrong man who, after he had recovered from his amazement would perhaps spend the rest of his days in

► *Why does the youth stay near the battle?*

► *Why does the youth begin to think it might be a good thing if his side loses the battle?*

---

4. **legions.** Large military forces; armies
5. **ditties.** Songs

Words For Everyday Use

be • set (bi set´) *vi.,* set upon; attack
cra • ven (krā´vən) *adj.,* lacking the least bit of courage
loon (lo͞on) *n.,* lout, idler, simpleton

com • punc • tion (kəm pəŋ(k)´shən) *n.,* anxiety arising from awareness of guilt
barb (bärb) *n.,* biting or pointedly critical remark or comment

writing replies to the songs of his alleged failure. It would be very unfortunate, no doubt, but in this case a general was of no consequence to the youth.

In a defeat there would be a roundabout vindication of himself. He thought it would prove, in a manner, that he had fled early because of his superior powers of perception. A serious prophet upon predicting a flood should be the first man to climb a tree. This would demonstrate that he was indeed a seer.

◄ What does the youth believe a defeat will prove about him?

A moral vindication was regarded by the youth as a very important thing. Without salve, he could not, he thought, wear the sore badge of his dishonor through life. With his heart continually assuring him that he was despicable, he could not exist without making it, through his actions, apparent to all men.

◄ Why does the youth believe he needs to be "vindicated"?

If the army had gone gloriously on he would be lost. If the din meant that now his army's flags were tilted forward he was a condemned wretch. He would be compelled to doom himself to isolation. If the men were advancing, their indifferent feet were trampling upon his chances for a successful life.

As these thoughts went rapidly through his mind, he turned upon them and tried to thrust them away. He denounced himself as a villain. He said that he was the most unutterably selfish man in existence. His mind pictured the soldiers who would place their defiant bodies before the spear of the yelling battle fiend, and as he saw their dripping corpses on an imagined field, he said that he was their murderer.

◄ What does the youth realize about his desire to see the army lose? What does he realize will happen to many of his fellow soldiers should this come to pass?

Again he thought that he wished he was dead. He believed that he envied a corpse. Thinking of the slain, he achieved a great contempt for some of them, as if they were guilty for thus becoming lifeless. They might have been killed by lucky chances, he said, before they had had opportunities to flee or before they had been really tested. Yet they would receive laurels from tradition. He cried out bitterly that their crowns were stolen and their robes of glorious memories were shams. However, he still said that it was a great pity he was not as they.

A defeat of the army had suggested itself to him as a means of escape from the consequences of his fall. He con-

| Words For Everyday Use | **salve** (sav) *n.,* healing or soothing influence or instrument
 de • spi • ca • ble (di spi´kə bəl) *adj.,* so worthless or obnoxious as to rouse moral indignation | **de • nounce** (di naun(t)s´) *vt.,* declare publicly to be blameworthy or evil
 lau • rel (lôr´əl) *n.,* crown of laurel, or the leaves of a plant; honor
 sham (sham) *n.,* cheap falseness |

▶ What has the
youth been taught
about his side in the
war?

▶ What plan of
action does the youth
form next?

▶ What does the
youth imagine his
regiment will do
when he returns?

sidered, now, however, that it was useless to think of such a possibility. His education had been that success for that mighty blue machine was certain; that it would make victories as a contrivance turns out buttons.[6] He presently discarded all his speculations in the other direction. He returned to the <u>creed</u> of soldiers.

When he perceived again that it was not possible for the army to be defeated, he tried to bethink him of a fine tale which he could take back to his regiment, and with it turn the expected shafts of derision.

But, as he mortally feared these shafts, it became impossible for him to invent a tale he felt he could trust. He experimented with many schemes, but threw them aside one by one as flimsy. He was quick to see vulnerable places in them all.

Furthermore, he was much afraid that some arrow of scorn might lay him mentally low before he could raise his protecting tale.

He imagined the whole regiment saying: "Where's Henry Fleming? He run, didn't 'e? Oh, my!" He recalled various persons who would be quite sure to leave him no peace about it. They would doubtless question him with sneers, and laugh at his stammering hesitation. In the next engagement they would try to keep watch of him to discover when he would run.

Wherever he went in camp, he would encounter insolent and lingeringly cruel stares. As he imagined himself passing near a crowd of comrades, he could hear some one say, "There he goes!"

Then, as if the heads were moved by one muscle, all the faces were turned toward him with wide, <u>derisive</u> grins. He seemed to hear some one make a humorous remark in a low tone. At it the others all crowed and cackled. He was a slang phrase.

---

6. **contrivance . . . buttons.** Machine makes buttons

Words
For
Everyday
Use

creed (krēd) *n.*, set of fundamental beliefs; guiding principle
de • ri • sive (di rī´siv) *adj.*, expressing or causing scorn or mockery

Chapter 12

The column that had butted stoutly at the obstacles in the roadway was barely out of the youth's sight before he saw dark waves of men come sweeping out of the woods and down through the fields. He knew at once that the steel fibers had been washed from their hearts. They were bursting from their coats and their equipments as from entanglements. They charged down upon him like terrified buffaloes.[1]

◄ What happens to the group of men who had been sent forward to fight the enemy?

Behind them blue smoke curled and clouded above the treetops, and through the thickets he could sometimes see a distant pink glare. The voices of the cannon were clamoring in interminable chorus.

The youth was horror-stricken. He stared in agony and amazement. He forgot that he was engaged in combating the universe. He threw aside his mental pamphlets on the philosophy of the retreated and rules for the guidance of the damned.

The fight was lost. The dragons were coming with <u>invincible</u> strides. The army, helpless in the matted thickets and blinded by the overhanging night, was going to be swallowed. War, the red animal, war, the blood-swollen god, would have bloated fill.

◄ What does the youth think about the way the battle is going for his side now?

Within him something bade to cry out. He had the impulse to make a <u>rallying</u> speech, to sing a battle hymn, but he could only get his tongue to call into the air: "Why—why—what—what 's th' matter?"

◄ What does the youth feel like doing? What does he ask the retreating soldiers?

Soon he was in the midst of them. They were leaping and scampering all about him. Their blanched faces shone in the dusk. They seemed, for the most part, to be very burly men. The youth turned from one to another of them as they galloped along. His incoherent questions were lost. They were <u>heedless</u> of his appeals. They did not seem to see him.

They sometimes <u>gabbled</u> insanely. One huge man was asking of the sky: "Say, where de plank road? Where de plank road!" It was as if he had lost a child. He wept in his pain and dismay.

---

1. **buffaloes.** Large horned animals that once roamed western states in large herds; when frightened they would stampede in a group

---

Words For Everyday Use

in • vin • ci • ble (in vin(t)´sə bəl) *adj.*, incapable of being conquered, overcome, or subdued
ral • ly • ing (ra´lē iŋ) *adj.*, arousing for action

heed • less (hēd´ləs) *adj.*, inconsiderate, thoughtless
gab • ble (ga´bəl) *vt.*, say with incoherent rapidity; babble

► Why does the youth stop one soldier? What do you think the youth wishes to ask? What is the soldier's reaction?

Presently, men were running hither and thither in all ways. The artillery booming, forward, rearward, and on the flanks made jumble of ideas of direction. Landmarks had vanished into the gathered gloom. The youth began to imagine that he had got into the center of the tremendous quarrel, and he could perceive no way out of it. From the mouths of the fleeing men came a thousand wild questions, but no one made answers.

The youth, after rushing about and throwing interrogations at the heedless bands of retreating infantry, finally clutched a man by the arm. They swung around face to face.

"Why—why—" stammered the youth struggling with his balking tongue.

The man screamed: "Let go me! Let go me!" His face was <u>livid</u> and his eyes were rolling uncontrolled. He was heaving and panting. He still grasped his rifle, perhaps having forgotten to release his hold upon it. He tugged frantically, and the youth being compelled to lean forward was dragged several paces.

"Let go me! Let go me!"

"Why—why—" stuttered the youth.

► What does the soldier do when the youth won't let go of him?

► What happens to the youth after having been struck? What is he unable to do?

"Well, then!" bawled the man in a <u>lurid</u> rage. He <u>adroitly</u> and fiercely swung his rifle. It crushed upon the youth's head. The man ran on.

The youth's fingers had turned to paste upon the other's arm. The energy was smitten from his muscles. He saw the flaming wings of lightning flash before his vision. There was a deafening rumble of thunder within his head.

Suddenly his legs seemed to die. He sank writhing to the ground. He tried to arise. In his efforts against the numbing pain he was like a man wrestling with a creature of the air.

There was a <u>sinister</u> struggle.

Sometimes he would achieve a position half erect, battle with the air for a moment, and then fall again, grabbing at the grass. His face was of a clammy <u>pallor</u>. Deep groans were wrenched from him.

At last, with a twisting movement, he got upon his hands and knees, and from thence, like a babe trying to walk, to his feet. Pressing his hands to his temples he went lurching over the grass.

He fought an intense battle with his body. His dulled

Words For Everyday Use

liv • id (liˊvəd) *adj.*, ashen, pale
lu • rid (lurˊəd) *adj.*, wan and ghastly pale in appearance
adroit • ly (ə drôitˊlē) *adv.*, skillfully, dexterously

sin • is • ter (siˊnəs tər) *adj.*, accompanied by or leading to disaster
pal • lor (paˊlər) *n.*, deficiency of color especially of the face

senses wished him to swoon and he opposed them stubbornly, his mind portraying unknown dangers and mutilations if he should fall upon the field. He went tall soldier fashion. He imagined secluded spots where he could fall and be unmolested. To search for one he strove against the tide of his pain.

Once he put his hand to the top of his head and timidly touched the wound. The scratching pain of the contact made him draw a long breath through his clinched teeth. His fingers were dabbled with blood. He regarded them with a fixed stare.

Around him he could hear the grumble of jolted cannon as the scurrying horses were lashed toward the front. Once, a young officer on a besplashed charger nearly ran him down. He turned and watched the mass of guns, men, and horses sweeping in a wide curve toward a gap in a fence. The officer was making excited motions with a gauntleted[2] hand. The guns followed the teams with an air of unwillingness, of being dragged by the heels.

Some officers of the scattered infantry were cursing and railing like fishwives.[3] Their scolding voices could be heard above the din. Into the unspeakable jumble in the roadway rode a squadron[4] of cavalry. The faded yellow of their facings shone bravely. There was a mighty altercation.

The artillery were assembling as if for a conference.

The blue haze of evening was upon the field. The lines of forest were long purple shadows. One cloud lay along the western sky partly smothering the red.

As the youth left the scene behind him, he heard the guns suddenly roar out. He imagined them shaking in black rage. They belched and howled like brass devils guarding a gate. The soft air was filled with the tremendous remonstrance. With it came the shattering peal of opposing infantry. Turning to look behind him, he could see sheets of orange light illumine the shadowy distance. There were subtle and sudden lightnings in the far air. At times he thought he could see heaving masses of men.

He hurried on in the dark. The day had faded until he

◄ Whom is the youth imitating? What does he wish to find?

◄ What happens when the youth tries to determine how serious his wound is?

---

2. **gauntleted.** Wearing a gauntlet, or a protective glove
3. **fishwives.** Women who sell fish, sometimes negatively characterized as vulgar and abusive
4. **squadron.** Unit of cavalry or horsemen

Words For Everyday Use

rail (rāl) *vi.*, scold in harsh, insolent, or abusive language

al • ter • ca • tion (äl tər kā´shən) *n.*, noisy heated angry quarrel

re • mon • strance (ri mən(t)´strən(t)s) *n.*, earnest presentation of reasons for opposition or protest

could barely distinguish place for his feet. The purple darkness was filled with men who lectured and <u>jabbered</u>. Sometimes he could see them <u>gesticulating</u> against the blue and somber sky. There seemed to be a great ruck[5] of men and munitions spread about in the forest and in the fields.

The little narrow roadway now lay lifeless. There were overturned wagons like sun-dried bowlders.[6] The bed of the former torrent was choked with the bodies of horses and splintered parts of war machines.

► After some time, how does the youth's wound feel? What is he careful to do?

It had come to pass that his wound pained him but little. He was afraid to move rapidly, however, for a dread of disturbing it. He held his head very still and took many precautions against stumbling. He was filled with anxiety, and his face was pinched and <u>drawn</u> in anticipation of the pain of any sudden mistake of his feet in the gloom.

His thoughts, as he walked, fixed intently upon his hurt. There was a cool, liquid feeling about it and he imagined blood moving slowly down under his hair. His head seemed swollen to a size that made him think his neck to be inadequate.

► How does this change in the wound make the youth feel about his injury?

The new silence of his wound made much worriment. The little blistering voices of pain that had called out from his scalp were, he thought, definite in their expression of danger. By them he believed that he could measure his plight. But when they remained <u>ominously</u> silent he became frightened and imagined terrible fingers that clutched into his brain.

► What times in his life does the youth think back on?

Amid it he began to reflect upon various incidents and conditions of the past. He bethought him of certain meals his mother had cooked at home, in which those dishes of which he was particularly fond had occupied prominent positions. He saw the spread table. The pine walls of the kitchen were glowing in the warm light from the stove. Too, he remembered how he and his companions used to go from the schoolhouse to the bank of a shaded pool. He saw his clothes in disorderly array upon the grass of the bank. He felt the swash of the fragrant water upon his body. The leaves of the overhanging maple rustled with melody in the wind of youthful summer.

---

5. **ruck.** Jumble or gathering
6. **bowlders.** Boulders or mass of rock

Words For Everyday Use

jab • ber (jaʹbər) *vi.,* talk rapidly, indistinctly, or unintelligibly

ges • tic • u • late (je stiʹkyo͞o lāt) *vi.,* make gestures especially when speaking

drawn (drôn) *adj.,* showing the effects of tension, pain, or illness

om • i • nous • ly (äʹmə nəs lē) *adv.,* in a manner that threatens evil

He was overcome presently by a dragging weariness. His head hung forward and his shoulders were stooped as if he were bearing a great bundle. His feet shuffled along the ground.

He held continuous arguments as to whether he should lie down and sleep at some near spot, or force himself on until he reached a certain <u>haven</u>. He often tried to dismiss the question, but his body persisted in rebellion and his senses nagged at him like pampered babies.

◀ What is the youth debating?

At last he heard a cheery voice near his shoulder: "Yeh seem t' be in a pretty bad way, boy?"

The youth did not look up, but he assented with thick tongue. "Uh!"

◀ What does one soldier with a "cheery voice" do for the youth?

The owner of the cheery voice took him firmly by the arm. "Well," he said, with a round laugh, "I'm goin' your way. Th' hull gang is goin' your way. An' I guess I kin give yeh a lift." They began to walk like a drunken man and his friend.

As they went along, the man questioned the youth and assisted him with the replies like one <u>manipulating</u> the mind of a child. Sometimes he interjected <u>anecdotes</u>. "What reg'-ment do yeh b'long teh? Eh? What's that? Th' 304th N' York? Why, what corps is that in? Oh, it is? Why, I thought they wasn't engaged t'-day—they're 'way over in th' center. Oh, they was, eh? Well, pretty nearly everybody got their share 'a fightin' t'-day. By dad, I give myself up fer dead any number 'a times. There was shootin' here an' shootin' there, an' hol-lerin' here an' hollerin' there, in th' damn' darkness, until I couldn't tell t' save m' soul which side I was on. Sometimes I thought I was sure 'nough from Ohier,[7] an' other times I could 'a swore I was from th' bitter end of Florida. It was th' most mixed up dern thing I ever see. An' these here hull woods is a reg'lar mess. It'll be a miracle if we find our reg'-ments t'-night. Pretty soon, though, we'll meet a-plenty of guards an' provost-guards,[8] an' one thing an' another. Ho! there they go with an off'cer, I guess. Look at his hand a-draggin'. He's got all th' war he wants, I bet. He won't be talkin' so big about his reputation an' all when they go t' sawin' off his leg. Poor feller! My brother's got whiskers jest

---

7. **Ohier.** Ohio
8. **provost-guards.** Police detail of soldiers

Words For Everyday Use

ha • ven (hā´vən) n., place of safety
ma • nip • u • late (mə ni´pyōō lāt) vt., control or play upon by artful or unfair means especially to one's own advantage

an • ec • dote (a´nik dōt) n., short account of an interesting, amusing, or biographical incident

like that. How did yeh git 'way over here, anyhow? Your reg'-
ment is a long way from here, ain't it? Well, I guess we can
find it. Yeh know there was a boy killed in my comp'ny t'-
day that I thought th' world an' all of. Jack was a nice feller.
By ginger, it hurt like thunder t' see ol' Jack jest git knocked
flat. We was a-standin' purty[9] peaceable fer a spell, 'though
there was men runnin' ev'ry way all 'round us, an' while we
was a-standin' like that, 'long come a big fat feller. He began
t' peck at Jack's elbow, an' he ses: 'Say, where's th' road t' th'
river?' An' Jack, he never paid no attention, an' th' feller kept
on a-peckin' at his elbow an' sayin': 'Say, where's th' road t'
th' river?' Jack was a-lookin' ahead all th' time tryin' t' see th'
Johnnies comin' through th' woods, an' he never paid no
attention t' this big fat feller fer a long time, but at last he
turned 'round an' he ses: 'Ah, go t' hell an' find th' road t' th'
river!' An' jest then a shot slapped him bang on th' side th'
head. He was a sergeant, too. Them was his last words.
Thunder, I wish we was sure 'a findin' our reg'ments t'-night.
It's goin' t' be long huntin'. But I guess we kin do it."

In the search which followed, the man of the cheery voice
seemed to the youth to possess a wand of a magic kind. He
threaded the mazes of the tangled forest with a strange fortune. In encounters with guards and patrols he displayed the
keenness of a detective and the valor of a gamin.[10] Obstacles
fell before him and became of assistance. The youth, with his
chin still on his breast, stood <u>woodenly</u> by while his companion beat ways and means out of sullen things.

The forest seemed a vast hive of men buzzing about in
frantic circles, but the cheery man conducted the youth
without mistakes, until at last he began to chuckle with glee
and self-satisfaction. "Ah, there yeh are! See that fire?"

The youth nodded stupidly.

"Well, there's where your reg'ment is. An' now, good-by,
ol' boy, good luck t' yeh."

A warm and strong hand clasped the youth's <u>languid</u> fingers for an instant, and then he heard a cheerful and auda-
cious whistling as the man strode away. As he who had so
befriended him was thus passing out of his life, it suddenly
occurred to the youth that he had not once seen his face.

► *What seems
magical to the youth
about the soldier
with the cheery
voice?*

► *Where does the
soldier successfully
lead the youth?*

► *What does the
youth realize about
the man who has
helped him?*

---

9. **purty.** Pretty
10. **gamin.** Boy who hangs around on the streets

Words For Everyday Use	**wood • en • ly** (wu´d'n lē) *adv.*, in an awkwardly stiff manner
	lan • guid (laŋ´gwəd) *adj.*, drooping or flagging from or as if from exhaustion; weak

Chapter 13

The youth went slowly toward the fire indicated by his departed friend. As he <u>reeled</u>, he bethought him of the welcome his comrades would give him. He had a conviction that he would soon feel in his sore heart the barbed missiles of ridicule. He had no strength to invent a tale; he would be a soft target.

He made vague plans to go off into the deeper darkness and hide, but they were all destroyed by the voices of exhaustion and pain from his body. His <u>ailments</u>, clamoring, forced him to seek the place of food and rest, at whatever cost.

◄ What does the youth plan to do? Why doesn't he go do this?

He swung unsteadily toward the fire. He could see the forms of men throwing black shadows in the red light, and as he went nearer it became known to him in some way that the ground was strewn with sleeping men.

Of a sudden he confronted a black and monstrous figure. A rifle barrel[1] caught some <u>glinting</u> beams. "Halt! halt!" He was <u>dismayed</u> for a moment, but he presently thought that he recognized the nervous voice. As he stood tottering before the rifle barrel, he called out: "Why, hello, Wilson, you—you here?"

◄ Whom does the youth encounter outside his regiment's camp?

The rifle was lowered to a position of caution and the loud soldier came slowly forward. He peered into the youth's face. "That you, Henry?"

"Yes, it's—it's me."

"Well, well, ol' boy," said the other, "by ginger, I'm glad t' see yeh! I give yeh up fer a goner. I thought yeh was dead sure enough." There was husky emotion in his voice.

◄ What did Wilson think had happened to Henry, the youth?

The youth found that now he could barely stand upon his feet. There was a sudden sinking of his forces. He thought he must hasten to produce his tale to protect him from the missiles already at the lips of his <u>redoubtable</u> comrades.

So, staggering before the loud soldier, he began: "Yes, yes. I've—I've had an awful time. I've been all over. Way over on th' right. Ter'ble fightin' over there. I had an awful time. I got separated from th' reg'ment. Over on th' right, I got shot. In

◄ What does Henry say has happened to him? How does he say he was injured?

---

1. **rifle barrel.** The tube of a gun that discharges

Words For Everyday Use

reel (rēl) *vi.*, waver; walk or move unsteadily
ail • ment (āl´mənt) *n.*, bodily disorder or chronic disease
glint • ing (glint´iŋ) *adj.*, reflecting in brilliant flashes; gleaming

dis • may (dis mā´) *vt.*, deprive of courage or resolution through fear or anxiety
re • doubt • able (ri dau´tə bəl) *adj.*, illustrious; worthy of respect

th' head. I never see sech fightin'. Awful time. I don't see how I could a' got separated from th' reg'ment. I got shot, too."

His friend had stepped forward quickly. "What? Got shot? Why didn't yeh say so first? Poor ol' boy, we must—hol' on a minnit; what am I doin'. I'll call Simpson."

Another figure at that moment loomed in the gloom. They could see that it was the corporal. "Who yeh talkin' to, Wilson?" he demanded. His voice was anger-toned. "Who yeh talkin' to? Yeh th' derndest sentinel²—why—hello, Henry, you here? Why, I thought you was dead four hours ago! Great Jerusalem, they keep turnin' up every ten minutes or so! We thought we'd lost forty-two men by straight count, but if they keep on a-comin' this way, we'll git th' comp'ny all back by mornin' yit. Where was yeh?"

"Over on th' right. I got separated"—began the youth with considerable <u>glibness</u>.

But his friend had interrupted hastily. "Yes, an' he got shot in th' head an' he's in a fix, an' we must see t' him right away." He rested his rifle in the hollow of his left arm and his right around the youth's shoulder.

"Gee, it must hurt like thunder!" he said.

The youth leaned heavily upon his friend. "Yes, it hurts—hurts a good deal," he replied. There was a <u>faltering</u> in his voice.

"Oh," said the corporal. He linked his arm in the youth's and drew him forward. "Come on, Henry. I'll take keer 'a yeh."

As they went on together the loud private called out after them: "Put 'im t' sleep in my blanket, Simpson. An'—hol' on a minnit—here's my canteen. It's full 'a coffee. Look at his head by th' fire an' see how it looks. Maybe it's a pretty bad un. When I git relieved in a couple 'a minnits, I'll be over an' see t' him."

The youth's senses were so deadened that his friend's voice sounded from afar and he could scarcely feel the pressure of the corporal's arm. He submitted <u>passively</u> to the latter's directing strength. His head was in the old manner hanging forward upon his breast. His knees wobbled.

---

2. **sentinel.** Soldier standing guard

Words For Everyday Use

glib • ness (glib´nəs) *n.*, ease and fluency in speaking or writing often to the point of being insincere or deceitful

fal • ter • ing (fôl´tər iŋ) *n.*, weak or broken stammer or hesitation

pas • sive • ly (pa´siv lē) *adv.*, in a manner that lacks energy or will

The corporal led him into the glare of the fire. "Now, Henry," he said, "let's have look at yer ol' head."

The youth sat down obediently and the corporal, laying aside his rifle, began to fumble in the bushy hair of his comrade. He was obliged to turn the other's head so that the full flush of the fire light would beam upon it. He puckered his mouth with a critical air. He drew back his lips and whistled through his teeth when his fingers came in contact with the splashed blood and the rare[3] wound.

"Ah, here we are!" he said. He awkwardly made further investigations. "Jest as I thought," he added, presently. "Yeh've been grazed by a ball. It's raised a queer lump jest as if some feller had lammed[4] yeh on th' head with a club. It stopped a-bleedin' long time ago. Th' most about it is that in th' mornin' yeh'll feel that a number ten hat wouldn't fit yeh. An' your head'll be all het up an' feel as dry as burnt pork. An' yeh may git a lot 'a other sicknesses, too, by mornin'. Yeh can't never tell. Still, I don't much think so. It's jest a damn' good belt on th' head, an' nothin' more. Now, you jest sit here an' don't move, while I go rout out th' relief. Then I'll send Wilson t' take keer 'a yeh."

The corporal went away. The youth remained on the ground like a parcel. He stared with a vacant look into the fire.

After a time he aroused, for some part, and the things about him began to take form. He saw that the ground in the deep shadows was cluttered with men, sprawling in every conceivable posture. Glancing narrowly into the more distant darkness, he caught occasional glimpses of visages that loomed pallid and ghostly, lit with a phosphorescent glow. These faces expressed in their lines the deep stupor of the tired soldiers. They made them appear like men drunk with wine. This bit of forest might have appeared to an ethereal wanderer as a scene of the result of some frightful debauch.

On the other side of the fire the youth observed an officer asleep, seated bolt upright, with his back against a tree. There was something perilous in his position. Badgered by dreams, perhaps, he swayed with little bounces and starts, like an old

◀ According to the corporal, what must have happened to Henry's head? What does the corporal say the injury looks like?

◀ According to the corporal, how serious is Henry's wound?

◀ What does the youth see all around the camp?

◀ In what position has one officer fallen asleep?

---

3. **rare.** Red, like rare cooked meat
4. **lammed.** Beat soundly

Words For Everyday Use	**vis • age** (viˊzij) *n.,* face, countenance, or appearance of a person	**ethe • re • al** (e thirˊē əl) *adj.,* of or relating to the regions beyond the earth
	stu • por (sto͞oˊpər) *n.,* state of extreme dullness or inactivity resulting often from stress or shock	**de • bauch** (di bôchˊ) *n.,* corrupt activity
		per • il • ous (perˊə ləs) *adj.,* dangerous

toddy-stricken[5] grandfather in a chimney corner. Dust and stains were upon his face. His lower jaw hung down as if lacking strength to assume its normal position. He was the picture of an exhausted soldier after a feast of war.

He had evidently gone to sleep with his sword in his arms. These two had slumbered in an embrace, but the weapon had been allowed in time to fall unheeded to the ground. The brass-mounted hilt lay in contact with some parts of the fire.

Within the gleam of rose and orange light from the burning sticks were other soldiers, snoring and <u>heaving</u>, or lying deathlike in slumber. A few pairs of legs were stuck forth, rigid and straight. The shoes displayed the mud or dust of marches and bits of rounded trousers, protruding from the blankets, showed rents and tears from hurried pitchings through the dense brambles.

The fire crackled musically. From it swelled light smoke. Overhead the foliage moved softly. The leaves, with their faces turned toward the blaze, were colored shifting hues of silver, often edged with red. Far off to the right, through a window in the forest could be seen a handful of stars lying, like glittering pebbles, on the black level of the night.

Occasionally, in this low-arched hall, a soldier would arouse and turn his body to a new position, the experience of his sleep having taught him of uneven and objectionable places upon the ground under him. Or, perhaps, he would lift himself to a sitting posture, blink at the fire for an unintelligent moment, throw a swift glance at his <u>prostrate</u> companion, and then cuddle down again with a grunt of sleepy content.

The youth sat in a forlorn heap until his friend the loud young soldier came, swinging two canteens by their light strings. "Well, now, Henry, ol' boy," said the latter, "we'll have yeh fixed up in jest about a minnit."

He had the bustling ways of an amateur nurse. He fussed around the fire and stirred the sticks to brilliant <u>exertions</u>. He made his patient drink largely from the canteen that contained the coffee. It was to the youth a delicious draught.[6] He

► What does Wilson, the loud soldier, do for Henry?

---

5. **toddy-stricken.** Drunken
6. **draught.** Draft, or drink

Words For Everyday Use

heave (hēv) *vi.*, rise and fall rhythmically
pros • trate (prô´strāt) *adj.*, completely overcome and lacking vitality, will, or power to rise

ex • er • tion (eg zər´shən) *n.*, laborious or perceptible effort

tilted his head afar back and held the canteen long to his lips. The cool mixture went caressingly down his blistered throat. Having finished, he sighed with comfortable delight.

The loud young soldier watched his comrade with an air of satisfaction. He later produced an extensive handkerchief from his pocket. He folded it into a manner of bandage and <u>soused</u> water from the other canteen upon the middle of it. This crude arrangement he bound over the youth's head, tying the ends in a queer knot at the back of the neck.

"There," he said, moving off and surveying his deed, "yeh look like th' devil, but I bet yeh feel better."

The youth contemplated his friend with grateful eyes. Upon his aching and swelling head the cold cloth was like a tender woman's hand.

"Yeh don't holler ner say nothin'," remarked his friend approvingly. "I know I'm a blacksmith at takin' keer 'a sick folks[7], an' yeh never squeaked. Yer a good un, Henry. Most 'a men would a' been in th' hospital long ago. A shot in th' head ain't foolin' business."

◄ What does Wilson say he admires about Henry?

The youth made no reply, but began to fumble with the buttons of his jacket.

"Well, come, now," continued his friend, "come on. I must put yeh t' bed an' see that yeh git a good night's rest."

The other got carefully erect, and the loud young soldier led him among the sleeping forms lying in groups and rows. Presently he stooped and picked up his blankets. He spread the rubber one upon the ground and placed the woolen one about the youth's shoulders.

"There now," he said, "lie down an' git some sleep."

The youth, with his manner of doglike obedience, got carefully down like a <u>crone</u> stooping. He stretched out with a murmur of relief and comfort. The ground felt like the softest couch.

But of a sudden he ejaculated: "Hol' on a minnit! Where you goin' t' sleep?"

◄ What does the youth realize as soon as he lies down in Wilson's blankets?

His friend waved his hand impatiently. "Right down there by yeh."

"Well, but hol' on a minnit," continued the youth. "What yeh goin' t' sleep in? I've got your—"

---

7. **blacksmith . . . sick folks.** Not gentle and skilled at taking care of sick people

| Words For Everyday Use | **souse** (sous) *vt.*, plunge in liquid; immerse |
| | **crone** (krōn) *n.*, withered old woman |

The loud young soldier snarled: "Shet up an' go on t' sleep. Don't be makin' a damn' fool 'a yerself," he said severely.

After the <u>reproof</u> the youth said no more. An exquisite drowsiness had spread through him. The warm comfort of the blanket enveloped him and made a gentle <u>languor</u>. His head fell forward on his crooked arm and his weighted lids went softly down over his eyes. Hearing a splatter of musketry from the distance, he wondered indifferently if those men sometimes slept. He gave a long sigh, snuggled down into his blanket, and in a moment was like his comrades.

Words For Everyday Use	**re • proof** (ri prōof) *n.*, criticism for a fault **lan • guor** (laŋ´gər) *n.*, weakness or weariness of body or mind

Chapter 14

When the youth awoke it seemed to him that he had been asleep for a thousand years, and he felt sure that he opened his eyes upon an unexpected world. Gray mists were slowly shifting before the first efforts of the sun rays. An <u>impending</u> splendor could be seen in the eastern sky. An icy dew had chilled his face, and immediately upon arousing he curled farther down into his blanket. He stared for a while at the leaves overhead, moving in a <u>heraldic</u> wind of the day.

The distance was splintering and blaring with the noise of fighting. There was in the sound an expression of a deadly persistency, as if it had not begun and was not to cease.

◀ What sounds does the youth hear upon awaking?

About him were the rows and groups of men that he had dimly seen the previous night. They were getting a last draught of sleep before the awakening. The <u>gaunt</u>, careworn features and dusty figures were made plain by this quaint light at the dawning, but it dressed the skin of the men in corpselike hues and made the tangled limbs appear pulseless and dead. The youth started up with a little cry when his eyes first swept over this motionless mass of men, thick-spread upon the ground, pallid, and in strange postures. His disordered mind interpreted the hall of the forest as a char-nel place.[1] He believed for an instant that he was in the house of the dead, and he did not dare to move lest these corpses start up, squalling and squawking. In a second, how-ever, he achieved his proper mind. He swore a complicated oath at himself. He saw that this somber picture was not a fact of the present, but a <u>mere</u> prophecy.

◀ In what way do the sleeping men appear to the youth?

He heard then the noise of a fire crackling briskly in the cold air, and, turning his head, he saw his friend pottering busily about a small blaze. A few other figures moved in the fog, and he heard the hard cracking of axe blows.

Suddenly there was a hollow rumble of drums. A distant bugle sang faintly. Similar sounds, varying in strength, came from near and far over the forest. The bugles called to each

---

1. **charnel place.** Building or chamber in which bodies or bones are placed

Words For Everyday Use		
im • pend • ing (im pend´iŋ) *adj.*, about to occur	**gaunt** (gônt) *adj.*, excessively thin and angular
he • ral • dic (he ral´dik) *adj.*, of or relating to a bearer of news	**mere** (mēr) *adj.*, being nothing more than

other like <u>brazen</u> gamecocks.[2] The near thunder of the regimental drums rolled.

The body of men in the woods rustled. There was a general uplifting of heads. A murmuring of voices broke upon the air. In it there was much bass[3] of grumbling oaths. Strange gods were addressed in condemnation of the early hours necessary to correct war. An officer's peremptory tenor[4] rang out and quickened the stiffened movement of the men. The tangled limbs unraveled. The corpse-hued faces were hidden behind fists that twisted slowly in the eye sockets.

The youth sat up and gave vent to an enormous yawn. "Thunder!" he remarked <u>petulantly</u>. He rubbed his eyes, and then putting up his hand felt carefully of the bandage over his wound. His friend, perceiving him to be awake, came from the fire. "Well, Henry, ol' man, how do yeh feel this mornin'?" he demanded.

► How does the youth's injury make him feel?

The youth yawned again. Then he puckered his mouth to a little pucker. His head, in truth, felt precisely like a melon, and there was an unpleasant sensation at his stomach.

"Oh, Lord, I feel pretty bad," he said.

"Thunder!" exclaimed the other. "I hoped ye'd feel all right this mornin'. Let's see th' bandage—I guess it's slipped." He began to tinker at the wound in rather a clumsy way until the youth exploded.

► What is the youth's response when Wilson tries to help him? What is Wilson's reaction to the youth's harsh words?

"Gosh-dern it!" he said in sharp irritation; "you're the hangdest man I ever saw! You wear muffs[5] on your hands. Why in good thunderation can't you be more easy? I'd rather you'd stand off an' throw guns at it. Now, go slow, an' don't act as if you was nailing down carpet."

He glared with insolent command at his friend, but the latter answered soothingly. "Well, well, come now, an' git some grub," he said. "Then, maybe, yeh'll feel better."

► How does the loud soldier, Wilson, treat his injured friend at breakfast?

At the fireside the loud young soldier watched over his comrade's wants with tenderness and care. He was very busy <u>marshaling</u> the little black vagabonds[6] of tin cups and pour-

---

2. **gamecocks.** Rooster trained for fighting
3. **bass.** Deep or low tones
4. **tenor.** High-pitched male voice
5. **muffs.** Warm tubular coverings for the hands
6. **vagabonds.** Things or people that wander; refers to the way the cups are passed about

---

Words For Everyday Use	
	bra • zen (brā´z'n) *adj.,* marked by contemptuous boldness
	pet • u • lant • ly (pe´chə lənt lē) *adv.,* characterized by temporary ill humor
	marshal (märsh´əl) *vt.,* place in proper rank or position

ing into them the streaming, iron-colored mixture from a small and sooty tin pail. He had some fresh meat, which he roasted hurriedly upon a stick. He sat down then and contemplated the youth's appetite with glee.

The youth took note of a remarkable change in his comrade since those days of camp life upon the river bank. He seemed no more to be continually regarding the proportions of his personal prowess. He was not furious at small words that pricked his <u>conceits</u>. He was no more a loud young soldier. There was about him now a fine <u>reliance</u>. He showed a quiet belief in his purposes and his abilities. And this inward confidence evidently enabled him to be indifferent to little words of other men aimed at him.

◀ What does the youth notice about his friend, the loud soldier?

The youth reflected. He had been used to regarding his comrade as a <u>blatant</u> child with an audacity grown from his inexperience, thoughtless, headstrong, jealous, and filled with a tinsel[7] courage. A swaggering babe accustomed to strut in his own dooryard. The youth wondered where had been born these new eyes; when his comrade had made the great discovery that there were many men who would refuse to be <u>subjected</u> by him. Apparently, the other had now climbed a peak of wisdom from which he could perceive himself as a very wee thing. And the youth saw that ever after it would be easier to live in his friend's neighborhood.

◀ What did the youth used to think of the loud soldier's character?

◀ What has the loud soldier apparently done? In what way has he changed for the better?

His comrade balanced his ebony coffee-cup on his knee. "Well, Henry," he said, "what d'yeh think th' chances are? D'yeh think we'll wallop 'em?"

The youth considered for a moment. "Day-b'fore-yesterday," he finally replied, with boldness, "you would 'a' bet you'd lick the hull kit-an'-boodle all by yourself."

His friend looked a trifle amazed. "Would I?" he asked. He pondered. "Well, perhaps I would," he decided at last. He stared humbly at the fire.

◀ What does Henry say Wilson would have said two days earlier? What does Wilson say about the way he was two days earlier?

The youth was quite disconcerted at this surprising reception of his remarks. "Oh, no, you wouldn't either," he said, hastily trying to retrace.

But the other made a <u>deprecating</u> gesture. "Oh, yeh needn't mind, Henry," he said. "I believe I was a pretty big fool in those days." He spoke as after a lapse of years.

---

7. **tinsel.** Superficial; false

Words For Everyday Use

con • ceit (kən sēt´) n., fanciful idea
re • li • ance (ri lī´an(t)s) n., confidence
bla • tant (blā´t'nt) adj., completely obvious, conspicuous, or obtrusive especially in a crass or offensive manner

sub • ject (səb jekt´) vt., bring under control or dominion
dep • re • cat • ing (de´pri kāt iŋ) adj., playing down; making little of

There was a little pause.

"All th' officers say we've got th' rebs[8] in a pretty tight box," said the friend, clearing his throat in a commonplace way. "They all seem t' think we've got 'em jest where we want 'em."

"I don't know about that," the youth replied. "What I seen over on th' right makes me think it was th' other way about. From where I was, it looked as if we was gettin' a good poundin' yestirday."

"D'yeh think so?" inquired the friend. "I thought we handled 'em pretty rough yestirday."

► What does the youth suddenly remember to tell his friend?

"Not a bit," said the youth. "Why, lord, man, you didn't see nothing of the fight. Why!" Then a sudden thought came to him. "Oh! Jim Conklin's dead."

His friend started. "What? Is he? Jim Conklin?"

The youth spoke slowly. "Yes. He's dead. Shot in th' side."

"Yeh don't say so. Jim Conklin. . . . poor cuss!"

All about them were other small fires surrounded by men with their little black utensils. From one of these near came sudden sharp voices in a row. It appeared that two light-footed soldiers had been teasing a huge, bearded man, causing him to spill coffee upon his blue knees. The man had gone into a rage and had sworn <u>comprehensively</u>. Stung by his language, his tormentors had immediately <u>bristled</u> at him with a great show of resenting unjust oaths. Possibly there was going to be a fight.

► What does Wilson tell the soldiers to break up their quarrel?

The friend arose and went over to them, making <u>pacific</u> motions with his arms. "Oh, here, now, boys, what's th' use?" he said. "We'll be at th' rebs in less'n an hour. What's th' good fightin' 'mong ourselves?"

One of the light-footed soldiers turned upon him red-faced and violent. "Yeh needn't come around here with yer preachin'. I s'pose yeh don't approve 'a fightin' since Charley Morgan licked yeh; but I don't see what business this here is 'a yours or anybody else."

"Well, it ain't," said the friend mildly. "Still I hate t' see—"

There was a tangled argument.

"Well, he—," said the two, indicating their opponent with accusative forefingers.

---

8. **rebs.** Rebels, members of the Confederate forces

Words For Everyday Use

com • pre • hen • sive • ly (kôm pri hen(t)´siv lē) *adv.*, completely or broadly

bris • tle (bri´səl) *vi.*, take on an aggressive attitude or appearance

pa • cif • ic (pə si´fik) *adj.*, tending to lessen conflict; peaceable

The huge soldier was quite purple with rage. He pointed at the two soldiers with his great hand, extended clawlike. "Well, they—"

But during this argumentative time the desire to deal blows seemed to pass, although they said much to each other. Finally the friend returned to his old seat. In a short while the three antagonists could be seen together in an amiable bunch.

"Jimmie Rogers ses I'll have t' fight him after th' battle t'-day," announced the friend as he again seated himself. "He ses he don't allow no interferin' in his business. I hate t' see th' boys fightin' 'mong themselves."

The youth laughed. "Yer changed a good bit. Yeh ain't at all like yeh was. I remember when you an' that Irish feller—" He stopped and laughed again.

"No, I didn't use t' be that way," said his friend thoughtfully. "That's true 'nough."

"Well, I didn't mean—" began the youth.

The friend made another deprecatory gesture. "Oh, yeh needn't mind, Henry."

There was another little pause.

"Th' reg'ment lost over half th' men yestirday," remarked the friend eventually. "I thought a course they was all dead, but, laws,[9] they kep' a-comin' back last night until it seems, after all, we didn't lose but a few. They'd been scattered all over, wanderin' around in th' woods, fightin' with other reg'-ments, an' everything. Jest like you done."

"So?" said the youth.

◄ What does Wilson say happened to many men in the regiment yesterday? Why do you think he says this?

9. **Laws.** Lord

Chapter 15

▶ What does the youth suddenly remember about Wilson?

The regiment was standing at order arms[1] at the side of a lane, waiting for the command to march, when suddenly the youth remembered the little packet enwrapped in a faded yellow envelope which the loud young soldier with <u>lugubrious</u> words had intrusted to him. It made him start. He uttered an exclamation and turned toward his comrade.

"Wilson!"

"What?"

His friend, at his side in the ranks, was thoughtfully staring down the road. From some cause his expression was at that moment very meek. The youth, regarding him with sidelong glances, felt <u>impelled</u> to change his purpose. "Oh, nothing," he said.

His friend turned his head in some surprise, "Why, what was yeh goin' t' say?"

"Oh, nothing," repeated the youth.

▶ What does the youth decide not to do?

▶ About what had the youth been concerned? Why isn't he as worried about this now?

He resolved not to deal the little blow. It was sufficient that the fact made him glad. It was not necessary to knock his friend on the head with the misguided packet.

He had been possessed of much fear of his friend, for he saw how easily questionings could make holes in his feelings. Lately, he had assured himself that the altered comrade would not <u>tantalize</u> him with a persistent curiosity, but he felt certain that during the first period of leisure his friend would ask him to relate his adventures of the previous day.

He now rejoiced in the possession of a small weapon with which he could <u>prostrate</u> his comrade at the first signs of a cross-examination. He was master. It would now be he who could laugh and shoot the shafts of derision.

The friend had, in a weak hour, spoken with sobs of his own death. He had delivered a melancholy <u>oration</u> previous to his funeral, and had doubtless in the packet of letters, presented various keepsakes to relatives. But he had not died, and thus he had delivered himself into the hands of the youth.

The latter felt immensely superior to his friend, but he

---

1. **order arms.** Position in which the rifle is held vertically beside the right leg with the butt resting on the ground

---

Words For Everyday Use

lu • gu • bri • ous (lu gōō´brē əs) *adj.,* exaggeratedly or affectedly mournful or sad
im • pel (im pel´) *vt.,* force
tan • ta • lize (tan´t'l īz) *vt.,* tease or torment

pros • trate (prô´strāt) *vt.,* put in a humble and submissive posture or state
o • ra • tion (ô ra´shən) *n.,* elaborate, formal, and dignified speech

inclined to <u>condescension</u>. He adopted toward him an air of <u>patronizing</u> good humor.

His self-pride was now entirely restored. In the shade of its flourishing growth he stood with braced and self-confident legs, and since nothing could now be discovered he did not shrink from an encounter with the eyes of judges, and allowed no thoughts of his own to keep him from an attitude of manfulness. He had performed his mistakes in the dark, so he was still a man.

◀ In the youth's mind, why is he still "a man"?

Indeed, when he remembered his fortunes of yesterday, and looked at them from a distance he began to see something fine there. He had license to be <u>pompous</u> and veteran-like.

◀ How is the youth beginning to feel about what happened yesterday?

His panting agonies of the past he put out of his sight.

In the present, he declared to himself that it was only the doomed and the damned who roared with sincerity at circumstance. Few but they ever did it. A man with a full stomach and the respect of his fellows had no business to scold about anything that he might think to be wrong in the ways of the universe, or even with the ways of society. Let the unfortunates rail; the others may play marbles.

He did not give a great deal of thought to these battles that lay directly before him. It was not essential that he should plan his ways in regard to them. He had been taught that many obligations of a life were easily avoided. The lessons of yesterday had been that <u>retribution</u> was a laggard and blind. With these facts before him he did not deem it necessary that he should become feverish over the possibilities of the ensuing twenty-four hours. He could leave much to chance. Besides, a faith in himself had secretly blossomed. There was a little flower of confidence growing within him. He was now a man of experience. He had been out among the dragons, he said, and he assured himself that they were not so hideous as he had imagined them. Also, they were inaccurate; they did not sting with precision. A stout heart often defied, and defying, escaped.

◀ What lessons did the youth learn the previous day?

And, furthermore, how could they kill him who was the chosen of gods and doomed to greatness?

He remembered how some of the men had run from the battle. As he recalled their terror-struck faces he felt a scorn for them. They had surely been more fleet and more wild

◀ For whom does the youth feel scorn? In what way does he differentiate his actions from theirs?

Words For Everyday Use	con • de • scen • sion (kən di sen(t)´shən) n., voluntary descent from one's rank or dignity in relations with an inferior pa • tron • iz • ing (pā´trə nīz iŋ) adj., treating haughtily or coolly	pomp • ous (pəm´pəs) adj., having or exhibiting self-importance; arrogant ret • ri • bu • tion (re trə byoo´shən) n., dispensing or receiving of reward or punishment

than was absolutely necessary. They were weak mortals. As for himself, he had fled with <u>discretion</u> and dignity.

He was aroused from this <u>reverie</u> by his friend, who, having hitched[2] about nervously and blinked at the trees for a time, suddenly coughed in an introductory way, and spoke.

"Fleming!"

"What?"

▶ What does Wilson ask of the youth? How does he feel about asking this?

The friend put his hand up to his mouth and coughed again. He fidgeted in his jacket.

"Well," he gulped, at last, "I guess yeh might as well give me back them letters." Dark, prickling blood had flushed into his cheeks and brow.

"All right, Wilson," said the youth. He loosened two buttons of his coat, thrust in his hand, and brought forth the packet. As he extended it to his friend the latter's face was turned from him.

He had been slow in the act of producing the packet because during it he had been trying to invent a remarkable comment upon the affair. He could conjure nothing of sufficient point. He was compelled to allow his friend to escape unmolested with his packet. And for this he took unto himself considerable credit. It was a generous thing.

▶ How does Wilson's shame make the youth feel?

His friend at his side seemed suffering great shame. As he contemplated him, the youth felt his heart grow more strong and stout. He had never been compelled to blush in such manner for his acts; he was an individual of extraordinary virtues.

He reflected, with condescending pity: "Too bad! Too bad! The poor devil, it makes him feel tough!"

After this incident, and as he reviewed the battle pictures he had seen, he felt quite competent to return home and make the hearts of the people glow with stories of war. He could see himself in a room of warm tints telling tales to listeners. He could exhibit laurels. They were insignificant; still, in a district where laurels were infrequent, they might shine.

▶ What does the youth look forward to doing one day?

He saw his gaping audience picturing him as the central figure in blazing scenes. And he imagined the <u>consternation</u> and the ejaculations of his mother and the young lady at the seminary as they drank his recitals. Their vague feminine <u>formula</u> for beloved ones doing brave deeds on the field of battle without risk of life would be destroyed.

---

2. **hitched.** Jerked

Words For Everyday Use

dis • cre • tion (dis kreˊshən) *n.,* ability to make responsible decisions
rev • er • ie (reˊvə rē) *n.,* daydream
con • ster • na • tion (kôn stər nāˊshən) *n.,* amazement or dismay that hinders or throws into confusion
for • mu • la (fôrˊmyo͞o lə) *n.,* conventionalized statement intended to express some fundamental truth or principle

Respond to the Selection

What is worse—being embarrassed in front of another person or suffering shame privately?

Investigate, Inquire, and Imagine

Recall: GATHERING FACTS

1a. In Chapter 11, what does Henry (the youth) see one calm and proud regiment doing? What does Henry wish would happen to his side in the battle? In Chapter 12, what happens to the calm and proud regiment described in Chapter 11? Describe the way in which Henry is injured in Chapter 12.

2a. What are the effects of Henry's injuries on him physically? Who volunteers to help Henry after he has been injured? What powers does this person seem to have to Henry? Where does this person lead him?

3a. What actions does Wilson (the loud soldier) perform for Henry once he returns to the regiment? What does Henry notice about Wilson? What does Wilson say about the way he acted this morning? What does the author call Wilson now instead of the "loud soldier"?

Interpret: FINDING MEANING

1b. What emotions does the loss of this particular battle create in Henry? In the regiment that retreats? Explain your reaction to how Henry was injured. Were you surprised that he was injured in this way? What does the way Henry was injured reveal about the effect that war and panic can have on people?

2b. In what way is Henry's position now similar to the tattered man's in previous chapters? In what way is it different? In what way do the actions of the person who helps Henry now compare with Henry's previous actions toward the tattered man?

3b. In what ways has Wilson changed? When Wilson speaks of his behavior that morning, he speaks of "those days," as if years have gone by instead of hours. Why might this day have had the effect of years passing? What does this new name reveal about the way Wilson has changed?

Analyze: TAKING THINGS APART

4a. Identify Henry's attitude toward his own position and what he perceives to be his own dishonor. In what way is Henry's injury a stroke of luck? What does it enable him to do that he might find to be more difficult if it were not for his injury?

Synthesize: BRINGING THINGS TOGETHER

4b. Explain whether Henry has in fact received a "red badge of courage." Think back to your responses about what a red badge of courage is in Chapters 8–10. In what way does Henry's injury help to teach him "that many obligations of a life were easily avoided"?

Evaluate: MAKING JUDGMENTS

5a. Who is the better friend: Henry to Wilson or Wilson to Henry? Consider that Henry feels that he is in a better position than his friend Wilson because he knows something shameful about him—Wilson told him that he feared he wouldn't make it through the battle and entrusted him with a packet of papers to give to his family. Wilson, on the other hand, seems to suspect what really happened to Henry. Why do you think the two don't poke fun at each other for their weaknesses?

Extend: CONNECTING IDEAS

→ 5b. Imagine that Henry's desertion has been discovered and his commanding officer wishes to try him in a military court to see if he can be punished for his actions. You have been hired as Henry's defense attorney. What would you say to defend him?

Understanding Literature

Crisis. The **crisis**, or turning point, is the point in a plot where something happens to determine the future course of events and the eventual fate of the main character. Based on what you have read so far, what do you think the crisis, or turning point, of this story may be?

Irony. Irony is a difference between appearance and reality. Explain why each of the following may be considered an example of irony:

- Henry's wishing for the Union troops to lose and then being filled with horror when he witnesses the regiment fleeing in panic
- Henry's being injured by a fellow soldier
- The corporal's assessment of Henry's wound, "Yeh've been grazed by a ball. It's raised a queer lump jest as if some feller had lammed yeh on th' head with a club."
- The youth's attitude the next day that "[i]ndeed, when he remembered his fortunes of yesterday, and looked at them from a distance he began to see something fine there. He had license to be pompous and veteranlike."
- Henry's remembering "how some of the men had run from the battle. As he recalled their terror-struck faces he felt a scorn for them. They had surely been more fleet and more wild than was absolutely necessary. They were weak mortals. As for himself, he had fled with discretion and dignity."

Chapter 16

A sputtering of musketry was always to be heard. Later, the cannon had entered the dispute. In the fog-filled air their voices made a thudding sound. The <u>reverberations</u> were continual. This part of the world led a strange, battleful existence.

◄ *Where is the youth's regiment sent?*

The youth's regiment was marched to relieve a command that had lain long in some damp trenches. The men took positions behind a curving line of rifle pits[1] that had been turned up, like a large <u>furrow</u>, along the line of woods. Before them was a level stretch, peopled with short, deformed stumps. From the woods beyond came the dull popping of the skirmishers and pickets,[2] firing in the fog. From the right came the noise of a terrific <u>fracas</u>.

◄ *What does the youth's friend do as soon as the regiment takes their position in the trenches?*

The men cuddled[3] behind the small embankment and sat in easy attitudes awaiting their turn. Many had their backs to the firing. The youth's friend lay down, buried his face in his arms, and almost instantly, it seemed, he was in a deep sleep.

The youth leaned his breast against the brown dirt and peered over at the woods and up and down the line. Curtains of trees interfered with his ways of vision. He could see the low line of trenches but for a short distance. A few idle flags were perched on the dirt hills. Behind them were rows of dark bodies with a few heads sticking curiously over the top.

Always the noise of skirmishers came from the woods on the front and left, and the din on the right had grown to frightful proportions. The guns were roaring without an instant's pause for breath. It seemed that the cannon had come from all parts and were engaged in a <u>stupendous</u> wrangle. It became impossible to make a sentence heard.

The youth wished to launch a joke—a quotation from newspapers. He desired to say, "All quiet on the Rappahannock,"[4] but the guns refused to permit even a com-

---

1. **rifle pits.** Pits or slashes in the earth from which one can fire a weapon and take cover from enemy attack
2. **pickets.** Body of soldiers that defends an army from surprise attack
3. **cuddled.** Lay close to the ground
4. **"All . . . Rappahannock."** During the Civil War Northern newspapers mocked the inactivity of Northern forces by writing, "All quiet on the Potomac." The Potomac is a river in Virginia; the Rappahannock, another river in Virginia.

Words For Everyday Use

re • ver • ber • a • tion (ri vər bə rā´shən) n., act of echoing or resounding

fur • row (fər´ō) n., trench in the earth, usually made by a plow

fra • cas (frā´kəs) n., noisy quarrel; brawl

stu • pen • dous (stu pen´dəs) adj., causing astonishment or wonder

ment upon their uproar. He never successfully concluded the sentence. But at last the guns stopped, and among the men in the rifle pits rumors again flew, like birds, but they were now for the most part black creatures who flapped their wings drearily near to the ground and refused to rise on any wings of hope. The men's faces grew <u>doleful</u> from the interpreting of omens. Tales of hesitation and uncertainty on the part of those high in place and responsibility came to their ears. Stories of disaster were borne into their minds with many proofs. This din of musketry on the right, growing like a released genie[5] of sound, expressed and emphasized the army's plight.

The men were disheartened and began to mutter. They made gestures expressive of the sentence: "Ah, what more can we do?" And it could always be seen that they were <u>bewildered</u> by the <u>alleged</u> news and could not fully comprehend a defeat.

Before the gray mists had been totally <u>obliterated</u> by the sun rays, the regiment was marching in a spread column that was retiring carefully through the woods. The disordered, hurrying lines of the enemy could sometimes be seen down through the groves and little fields. They were yelling, shrill and exultant.

At this sight the youth forgot many personal matters and became greatly enraged. He exploded in loud sentences. "B'jiminey, we're generaled by a lot 'a lunkheads."[6]

"More than one feller has said that t'-day," observed a man.

His friend, recently aroused, was still very drowsy. He looked behind him until his mind took in the meaning of the movement. Then he sighed. "Oh, well, I s'pose we got licked," he remarked sadly.

The youth had a thought that it would not be handsome for him to freely condemn other men. He made an attempt to restrain himself, but the words upon his tongue were too bitter. He presently began a long and intricate <u>denunciation</u> of the commander of the forces.

▶ What does the regiment learn about the way the battle is going?

▶ Whom does the youth condemn?

---

5. **released genie.** Legendary magic spirit, often described as living in an enclosed container, that when released serves the person who calls or releases it
6. **lunkheads.** Stupid persons

Words For Everyday Use

dole • ful (dōl´fəl) adj., full of grief
be • wil • der (bi wil´dər) vt., perplex or confuse
al • leged (ə lejd´) adj., asserted without proof or before proving

o • blit • er • ate (ô bli´tə rāt) vt., remove from existence
de • nun • ci • a • tion (di nən(t) sē ā´shən) n., public condemnation

"Mebbe, it wa'n't all his fault—not all together. He did th' best he knowed. It's our luck t' git licked often," said his friend in a weary tone. He was trudging along with stooped shoulders and shifting eyes like a man who has been caned[7] and kicked.

"Well, don't we fight like the devil? Don't we do all that men can?" demanded the youth loudly.

◀ What does the youth's friend say about the commander?

He was secretly <u>dumfounded</u> at this sentiment when it came from his lips. For a moment his face lost its valor and he looked guiltily about him. But no one questioned his right to deal in such words, and presently he recovered his air of courage. He went on to repeat a statement he had heard going from group to group at the camp that morning. "The brigadier[8] said he never saw a new reg'ment fight the way we fought yesterday, didn't he? And we didn't do better than many another reg'ment, did we? Well, then, you can't say it's th' army's fault, can you?"

In his reply, the friend's voice was stern. "'A course not," he said. "No man dare say we don't fight like th' devil. No man will ever dare say it. Th' boys fight like hell-roosters. But still—still, we don't have no luck."

"Well, then, if we fight like the devil an' don't ever whip, it must be the general's fault," said the youth grandly and decisively. "And I don't see any sense in fighting and fighting and fighting, yet always losing through some derned old lunkhead of a general."

◀ According to the youth, why is the way the battle is going the general's fault?

A sarcastic man who was tramping at the youth's side, then spoke lazily. "Mebbe yeh think yeh fit th' hull battle yestirday, Fleming," he remarked.

The speech pierced the youth. Inwardly he was reduced to an <u>abject</u> <u>pulp</u> by these chance words. His legs quaked privately. He cast a frightened glance at the sarcastic man.

◀ What sarcastic comment does one man make after hearing the youth blame the general? How does this remark make the youth feel?

"Why, no," he hastened to say in a <u>conciliating</u> voice, "I don't think I fought the whole battle yesterday."

But the other seemed innocent of any deeper meaning. Apparently, he had no information. It was merely his habit. "Oh!" he replied in the same tone of calm derision.

The youth, nevertheless, felt a threat. His mind shrank

---

7. **caned.** Beaten with a cane
8. **brigadier.** Certain rank of officer in the armed forces

| Words For Everyday Use | **dumb • found** or **dum • found** (dəm faund´) vt., perplex; puzzle | **pulp** (pulp) n., soft mass of vegetable matter |
| | **ab • ject** (ab´jekt) adj., sunk to or existing in a low state or condition | **con • cil • i • at • ing** (kən si´lē āt iŋ) adj., compatible; reconciling; appeasing |

from going near to the danger, and thereafter he was silent. The significance of the sarcastic man's words took from him all loud moods that would make him appear <u>prominent</u>. He became suddenly a modest person.

There was low-toned talk among the troops. The officers were impatient and snappy, their countenances clouded with the tales of misfortune. The troops, sifting through the forest, were sullen. In the youth's company once a man's laugh rang out. A dozen soldiers turned their faces quickly toward him and frowned with vague displeasure.

The noise of firing <u>dogged</u> their footsteps. Sometimes, it seemed to be driven a little way, but it always returned again with increased insolence. The men muttered and cursed, throwing black looks in its direction.

▶ Where is the regiment halted? What happens here as soon as the sun comes up?

In a clear space the troops were at last halted. Regiments and brigades, broken and detached through their encounters with thickets, grew together again and lines were faced toward the pursuing bark of the enemy's infantry.

This noise, following like the yellings of eager, metallic hounds, increased to a loud and joyous burst, and then, as the sun went serenely up the sky, throwing illuminating rays into the gloomy thickets, it broke forth into prolonged pealings. The woods began to crackle as if afire.

"Whoop-a-dadee," said a man, "here we are! Everybody fightin'. Blood an' destruction."

"I was willin' t' bet they'd attack as soon as th' sun got fairly up," savagely asserted the lieutenant who commanded the youth's company. He jerked without mercy at his little mustache. He strode to and fro with dark dignity in the rear of his men, who were lying down behind whatever protection they had collected.

A battery had <u>trundled</u> into position in the rear and was thoughtfully shelling the distance. The regiment, unmolested as yet, awaited the moment when the gray shadows of the woods before them should be slashed by the lines of flame. There was much growling and swearing.

▶ How does the youth feel about being marched to this new position?

"Good Gawd," the youth grumbled, "we're always being chased around like rats! It makes me sick. Nobody seems to know where we go or why we go. We just get fired around from pillar to post and get licked here and get licked there, and nobody knows what it's done for. It makes a man feel

Words For Everyday Use	**prom • i • nent** (prô´mə nənt) *adj.*, readily noticeable
	dog (dôg) *vt.*, hunt or track like a dog
	trun • dle (trən´d'l) *vt.*, roll; transport in or as if in a wheeled vehicle

like a damn' kitten in a bag. Now, I'd like to know what the eternal thunders we was marched into these woods for anyhow, unless it was to give the rebs a regular pot shot[9] at us. We came in here and got our legs all tangled up in these cussed briers, and then we begin to fight and the rebs had an easy time of it. Don't tell me it's just luck! I know better. It's this derned old—"

The friend seemed jaded, but he interrupted his comrade with a voice of calm confidence. "It'll turn out all right in th' end," he said.

◄ What does the youth's friend tell him?

"Oh, the devil it will! You always talk like a dog-hanged parson.[10] Don't tell me! I know—"

At this time there was an <u>interposition</u> by the savage-minded lieutenant, who was obliged to vent some of his inward dissatisfaction upon his men. "You boys shut right up! There no need 'a your wastin' your breath in long-winded arguments about this an' that an' th' other. You've been jawin' like a lot 'a old hens.[11] All you've got t' do is to fight, an' you'll get plenty 'a that t' do in about ten minutes. Less talkin' an' more fightin' is what's best for you boys. I never saw sech gabbling jackasses."

◄ What does the lieutenant find to criticize in the youth and the other soldiers?

He paused, ready to pounce upon any man who might have the <u>temerity</u> to reply. No words being said, he resumed his dignified pacing.

◄ What is the lieutenant's opinion about what is wrong with the war?

"There's too much chin music[12] an' too little fightin' in this war, anyhow," he said to them, turning his head for a final remark.

The day had grown more white, until the sun shed his full radiance upon the thronged forest. A sort of a gust of battle came sweeping toward that part of the line where lay the youth's regiment. The front shifted a trifle to meet it squarely. There was a wait. In this part of the field there passed slowly the intense moments that precede the <u>tempest</u>.

A single rifle flashed in a thicket before the regiment. In an instant it was joined by many others. There was a mighty song of clashes and crashes that went sweeping through the

---

9. **pot shot.** Shot taken from ambush at an easy target
10. **parson.** Clergyman
11. **jawin' . . . hens.** Contemptuous phrase meaning, "talking like old women"
12. **chin music.** Talking

Words For Everyday Use

in • ter • po • si • tion (in tər pə zi´shən) *n.,* interruption; interjection

te • mer • i • ty (tə mer´ə tē) *n.,* unreasonable or foolhardy contempt of danger

or opposition

tem • pest (tem´pəst) *n.,* violent storm

woods. The guns in the rear, aroused and enraged by shells that had been thrown burr-like[13] at them, suddenly involved themselves in a hideous <u>altercation</u> with another band of guns. The battle roar settled to a rolling thunder, which was a single, long explosion.

► *What is the regiment's reaction just before they must begin to fight?*

In the regiment there was a peculiar kind of hesitation <u>denoted</u> in the attitudes of the men. They were worn, exhausted, having slept but little and labored much. They rolled their eyes toward the advancing battle as they stood awaiting the shock. Some shrank and <u>flinched</u>. They stood as men tied to stakes.

---

13. **burr-like.** Like burrs, or prickly seeds or pods

Words For Everyday Use	**al • ter • ca • tion** (äl tər kā´shən) *n.*, noisy heated angry dispute
	de • note (di nōt´) *vt.*, make known
	flinch (flinch) *vt.*, withdraw or shrink from or as if from pain

Chapter 17

This advance of the enemy had seemed to the youth like a ruthless hunting. He began to <u>fume</u> with rage and exasperation. He beat his foot upon the ground, and scowled with hate at the swirling smoke that was approaching like a phantom flood. There was a maddening quality in this seeming resolution of the foe to give him no rest, to give him no time to sit down and think. Yesterday he had fought and had fled rapidly. There had been many adventures. For to-day he felt that he had earned opportunities for <u>contemplative</u> <u>repose</u>. He could have enjoyed portraying to uninitiated listeners various scenes at which he had been a witness or ably discussing the processes of war with other proved men. Too it was important that he should have time for physical recuperation. He was sore and stiff from his experiences. He had received his fill of all exertions, and he wished to rest.

But those other men seemed never to grow weary; they were fighting with their old speed. He had a wild hate for the relentless foe. Yesterday, when he had imagined the universe to be against him, he had hated it, little gods and big gods; to-day he hated the army of the foe with the same great hatred. He was not going to be badgered of his life, like a kitten chased by boys, he said. It was not well to drive men into final corners; at those moments they could all develop teeth and claws.

He leaned and spoke into his friend's ear. He menaced the words with a gesture. "If they keep on chasing us, by Gawd, they'd better watch out. Can't stand *too* much."

The friend twisted his head and made a calm reply. "If they keep on a-chasin' us they'll drive us all inteh th' river."

The youth cried out savagely at this statement. He crouched behind a little tree, with his eyes burning hatefully and his teeth set in a curlike[1] snarl. The awkward bandage was still about his head, and upon it, over his wound, there was a spot of dry blood. His hair was wondrously <u>tousled</u>, and some straggling, moving locks hung over the cloth of

◄ Why does the enemy make the youth angry? What does he think he deserves to do today?

◄ What words might you use to describe the youth's appearance?

---

1. **curlike.** Like a dog

| Words For Everyday Use | **fume** (fyo͞om) *vi.*, be in a state of excited irritation or anger | **re • pose** (ri pōz´) *n.*, state of resting after activity or strain |
| | **con • tem • pla • tive** (kən tem´plə tiv) *adj.*, marked by or given to thought or consideration | **tou • sled** (tau´zəld) *adj.*, disheveled; rumpled |

the bandage down toward his forehead. His jacket and shirt were open at the throat, and exposed his young bronzed neck. There could be seen spasmodic gulpings at his throat.

His fingers twined nervously about his rifle. He wished that it was an engine of annihilating power. He felt that he and his companions were being taunted and derided from sincere convictions that they were poor and puny. His knowledge of his inability to take vengeance for it made his rage into a dark and stormy specter, that possessed him and made him dream of abominable cruelties. The tormentors were flies sucking insolently at his blood, and he thought that he would have given his life for a revenge of seeing their faces in pitiful plights.

The winds of battle had swept all about the regiment, until the one rifle, instantly followed by brothers, flashed in its front. A moment later the regiment roared forth its sudden and valiant retort. A dense wall of smoke settled slowly down. It was furiously slit and slashed by the knifelike fire from the rifles.

► What do the fighting men look like to the youth?

To the youth the fighters resembled animals tossed for a death struggle into a dark pit. There was a sensation that he and his fellows, at bay, were pushing back, always pushing fierce onslaughts of creatures who were slippery. Their beams of crimson seemed to get no purchase upon the bodies of their foes; the latter seemed to evade them with ease, and come through, between, around, and about with unopposed skill.

► What emotion fills the youth in the battle?

When, in a dream, it occurred to the youth that his rifle was an impotent stick, he lost sense of everything but his hate, his desire to smash into pulp the glittering smile of victory which he could feel upon the faces of his enemies.

The blue smoke-swallowed line curled and writhed like a snake stepped upon. It swung its ends to and fro in an agony of fear and rage.

The youth was not conscious that he was erect upon his feet. He did not know the direction of the ground. Indeed, once he even lost the habit of balance and fell heavily. He was up again immediately. One thought went through the chaos of his brain at the time. He wondered if he had fallen because he had been shot. But the suspicion flew away at once. He did not think more of it.

Words For Everyday Use

spas • mod • ic (spaz mô´dik) *adj.*, affected or characterized by involuntary muscular contractions
spec • ter (spek´tər) *n.*, something that haunts or perturbs the mind

abom • i • na • ble (ə bəm´nə bəl) *adj.*, of or causing disgust or hatred
val • iant (val´yənt) *adj.*, courageous
bay (bā) *n.*, position of one unable to retreat and forced to face danger

He had taken up a first position behind the little tree, with a direct determination to hold it against the world. He had not deemed it possible that his army could that day succeed, and from this he felt the ability to fight harder. But the throng had surged in all ways, until he lost directions and locations, save that he knew where lay the enemy.

The flames bit him, and the hot smoke broiled his skin. His rifle barrel grew so hot that ordinarily he could not have borne it upon his palms; but he kept on stuffing cartridges into it, and pounding them with his clanking, bending ramrod. If he aimed at some changing form through the smoke, he pulled his trigger with a fierce grunt, as if he were dealing a blow of the fist with all his strength.

When the enemy seemed falling back before him and his fellows, he went instantly forward, like a dog who, seeing his foes lagging, turns and insists upon being pursued. And when he was compelled to retire again, he did it slowly, sullenly, taking steps of wrathful despair.

◄ What does the youth do when the enemy falls back? When the enemy advances?

Once he, in his intent hate, was almost alone, and was firing, when all those near him had ceased. He was so engrossed in his occupation that he was not aware of a lull.

He was recalled by a hoarse laugh and a sentence that came to his ears in a voice of contempt and amazement. "Yeh infernal fool, don't yeh know enough t' quit when there ain't anything t' shoot at? Good Gawd!"

He turned then and, pausing with his rifle thrown half into position, looked at the blue line of his comrades. During this moment of leisure they seemed all to be engaged in staring with astonishment at him. They had become spectators. Turning to the front again he saw, under the lifted smoke, a deserted ground.

◄ What action does the youth perform that surprises his fellow soldiers? What does the youth realize when the smoke clears?

He looked bewildered for a moment. Then there appeared upon the glazed vacancy of his eyes a diamond point of intelligence. "Oh," he said, comprehending.

He returned to his comrades and threw himself upon the ground. He sprawled like a man who had been thrashed. His flesh seemed strangely on fire, and the sounds of the battle continued in his ears. He groped blindly for his canteen.

The lieutenant was crowing. He seemed drunk with fighting. He called out to the youth: "By heavens, if I had ten thousand wild cats like you I could tear th' stomach outa this war in less'n a week!" He puffed out his chest with large dignity as he said it.

◄ How does the lieutenant feel about the fight? About the youth's actions in the fight?

Some of the men muttered and looked at the youth in awe-struck ways. It was plain that as he had gone on loading

► How do the men now regard the youth? Why do you think the youth's friend asks him if he is "all right"?

and firing and cursing without the proper intermission, they had found time to regard him. And they now looked upon him as a war devil.

The friend came staggering to him. There was some fright and dismay in his voice. "Are yeh all right, Fleming? Do yeh feel all right? There ain't nothin' th' matter with yeh, Henry, is there?"

"No," said the youth with difficulty. His throat seemed full of knobs and burrs.

► What does the youth suddenly realize about his actions?

These incidents made the youth ponder. It was revealed to him that he had been a barbarian, a beast. He had fought like a pagan who defends his religion. Regarding it, he saw that it was fine, wild, and, in some ways, easy. He had been a tremendous figure, no doubt. By this struggle he had overcome obstacles which he had admitted to be mountains. They had fallen like paper peaks, and he was now what he called a hero. And he had not been aware of the process. He had slept and, awakening, found himself a knight.

He lay and basked in the occasional stares of his comrades. Their faces were varied in degrees of blackness from the burned powder. Some were utterly smudged. They were reeking with perspiration, and their breaths came hard and wheezing. And from these soiled expanses they peered at him.

"Hot work![2] Hot work!" cried the lieutenant deliriously. He walked up and down, restless and eager. Sometimes his voice could be heard in a wild, incomprehensible laugh.

► With whom does the lieutenant now discuss his thoughts about the war?

When he had a particularly profound thought upon the science of war he always unconsciously addressed himself to the youth.

There was some grim rejoicing by the men. "By thunder, I bet this army'll never see another new reg'ment like us!"

"You bet!"

"A dog, a woman, an' a walnut tree,
Th' more yeh beat 'em, th' better they be!

That's like us."

---

2. **Hot work.** Good work

| Words For Everyday Use | **pa • gan** (pā´gən) *n.*, follower of a religion that worships more than one god **bask** (bask) *vi.*, take pleasure or obtain enjoyment | **de • lir • i • ous • ly** (di lir´ē əs lē) *adv.*, in an irrational manner **pro • found** (prə faund´) *adj.*, having intellectual depth and insight |

"Lost a piler[3] men, they did. If an' ol' woman swep' up th' woods she'd git a dustpanful."

"Yes, an' if she'll come around ag'in in 'bout an hour she'll git a pile more."

The forest still bore its burden of clamor. From off under the trees came the rolling clatter of the musketry. Each distant thicket seemed a strange porcupine[4] with quills of flame. A cloud of dark smoke, as from smoldering ruins, went up toward the sun now bright and gay in the blue, <u>enameled</u> sky.

---

3. **piler.** Pile of
4. **porcupine.** Large rodent with sharp erect bristles

Words For Everyday Use

e • nam • eled (e na´məld) *adj.,* covered with a glossy, hard surface

Chapter 18

The ragged line had <u>respite</u> for some minutes, but during its pause the struggle in the forest became magnified until the trees seemed to quiver from the firing and the ground to shake from the rushing of the men. The voices of the cannon were mingled in a long and <u>interminable</u> row. It seemed difficult to live in such an atmosphere. The chests of the men strained for a bit of freshness, and their throats craved water.

There was one shot through the body, who raised a cry of bitter <u>lamentation</u> when came this lull. Perhaps he had been calling out during the fighting also, but at that time no one had heard him. But now the men turned at the woeful complaints of him upon the ground.

"Who is it? Who is it?"

"It's Jimmie Rogers. Jimmie Rogers."

When their eyes first encountered him there was a sudden halt, as if they feared to go near. He was thrashing about in the grass, twisting his shuddering body into many strange <u>postures</u>. He was screaming loudly. This instant's hesitation seemed to fill him with a tremendous, fantastic contempt, and he damned them in shrieked sentences.

The youth's friend had a geographical illusion concerning a stream, and he obtained permission to go for some water. Immediately canteens were showered upon him. "Fill mine, will yeh?" "Bring me some, too." "And me, too." He departed, <u>ladened</u>. The youth went with his friend, feeling a desire to throw his heated body into the stream and, soaking there, drink quarts.[1]

They made a hurried search for the supposed stream, but did not find it. "No water here," said the youth. They turned without delay and began to retrace their steps.

From their position as they again faced toward the place of the fighting, they could of course comprehend a greater amount of the battle than when their visions had been blurred by the hurlyng smoke of the line. They could see dark stretches winding along the land, and on one cleared space there was a row of guns making gray clouds, which

---

1. **quarts.** Many cups full

▶ What do the soldiers notice once they stop fighting for a few moments?

▶ What do the youth and his friend leave the regiment to do? Are they successful?

Words For Everyday Use

re • spite (res´pət) *n.*, period of rest or relief

in • ter • mi • na • ble (in tərm´nə bəl) *adj.*, having or seeming to have no end

lam • en • ta • tion (la mən tā´shən) *n.*, act

or instance of mourning, grieving, sobbing

pos • ture (pôs´chər) *n.*, position or bearing of the body

lad • ened (lād´end) *vt.*, heavily loaded

were filled with large flashes of orange-colored flame. Over some foliage they could see the roof of a house. One window, glowing a deep murder red, shone squarely through the leaves. From the <u>edifice</u> a tall leaning tower of smoke went far into the sky.

◄ What do the youth and his friend see happening to a house?

Looking over their own troops, they saw mixed masses slowly getting into regular form. The sunlight made twinkling points of the bright steel. To the rear there was a glimpse of a distant roadway as it curved over a slope. It was crowded with retreating infantry. From all the interwoven forest arose the smoke and <u>bluster</u> of the battle. The air was always occupied by a <u>blaring</u>.

Near where they stood shells were flip-flapping and hooting.[2] Occasional bullets buzzed in the air and spanged[3] into tree trunks. Wounded men and other stragglers were slinking through the woods.

Looking down an aisle of the grove, the youth and his companion saw a jangling general and his staff almost ride upon a wounded man, who was crawling on his hands and knees. The general reined strongly at his charger's opened and foamy mouth and guided it with dexterous horsemanship past the man. The latter scrambled in wild and torturing haste. His strength evidently failed him as he reached a place of safety. One of his arms suddenly weakened, and he fell, sliding over upon his back. He lay stretched out, breathing gently.

◄ What do they see happen in a grove?

A moment later the small, creaking cavalcade[4] was directly in front of the two soldiers. Another officer, riding with the skillful abandon of a cowboy, galloped his horse to a position directly before the general. The two unnoticed foot soldiers made a little show of going on, but they lingered near in the desire to overhear the conversation. Perhaps, they thought, some great inner historical things would be said.

◄ Whom are the youth and his friend near? Why do they linger near these people?

The general, whom the boys knew as the commander of their division, looked at the other officer and spoke coolly, as if he were criticizing his clothes. "Th' enemy's formin' over

---

2. **flip-flapping and hooting.** Flipping in the air and making a loud clamorous mechanical sound
3. **spanged.** Hit squarely
4. **cavalcade.** Procession of riders

Words For Everyday Use

ed • i • fice (e´də fəs) *n.*, building
blus • ter (bləs´tər) *n.*, violent commotion
blar • ing (blar´iŋ) *n.*, loud sound

► What do the two soldiers learn about the enemy's plans and what the general plans to do?

there for another charge," he said. "It'll be directed against Whiterside, an' I fear they'll break through there unless we work like thunder t' stop them."

The other swore at his <u>restive</u> horse, and then cleared his throat. He made a gesture toward his cap. "It'll be hell t' pay stoppin' them," he said shortly.

"I <u>presume</u> so," remarked the general. Then he began to talk rapidly and in a lower tone. He frequently illustrated his words with a pointing finger. The two infantrymen could hear nothing until finally he asked: "What troops can you spare?"

► Which troop does the officer say he can spare? In what way does he describe this troop?

The officer who rode like a cowboy reflected for an instant. "Well," he said, "I had to order in th' 12th to help th' 76th, an' I haven't really got any. But there's th' 304th. They fight like a lot 'a mule drivers.[5] I can spare them best of any."

► How do the youth and his friend feel about what they have learned? Whose troop is the 304th?

The youth and his friend exchanged glances of astonishment.

The general spoke sharply. "Get 'em ready, then. I'll watch developments from here, an' send you word when t' start them. It'll happen in five minutes."

► What does the general say to the officer about the chosen group of soldiers?

As the other officer tossed his fingers toward his cap and <u>wheeling</u> his horse, started away, the general called out to him in a sober voice: "I don't believe many of your mule drivers will get back."

The other shouted something in reply. He smiled.

With scared faces, the youth and his companion hurried back to the line.

► What does the youth find startling?

These happenings had occupied an incredibly short time, yet the youth felt that in them he had been made aged. New eyes were given to him. And the most startling thing was to learn suddenly that he was very insignificant. The officer spoke of the regiment as if he referred to a broom. Some part of the woods needed sweeping, perhaps, and he merely indicated a broom in a tone properly <u>indifferent</u> to its fate. It was war, no doubt, but it appeared strange.

As the two boys approached the line, the lieutenant perceived them and swelled with wrath. "Fleming—Wilson—

---

5. **mule drivers.** The officer is implying that the 304th regiment does not contain the most valuable, skillful soldiers.

Words For Everyday Use

res • tive (res´tiv) *adj.*, stubbornly resisting control

pre • sume (pri zoom´) *vt.*, expect or assume especially with confidence

wheel (wēl) *vt.*, cause to change direction as in a circle

in • dif • fer • ent (in dif´rənt) *adj.*, marked by a lack of interest, enthusiasm, or concern for something

how long does it take yeh to git water, anyhow—where yeh been to."

But his oration ceased as he saw their eyes, which were large with great tales. "We're goin' t' charge—we're goin' t' charge!" cried the youth's friend, hastening with his news.

◀ What do the two soldiers tell the lieutenant when they return? How does the lieutenant feel about this news?

"Charge?" said the lieutenant. "Charge? Well, b'Gawd! Now, this is real fightin'." Over his soiled countenance there went a boastful smile. "Charge? Well, b'Gawd!"

A little group of soldiers surrounded the two youths. "Are we, sure 'nough? Well, I'll be derned! Charge? What fer? What at? Wilson, you're lyin'."

"I hope to die," said the youth, pitching his tones to the key of angry <u>remonstrance</u>. "Sure as shooting, I tell you."

And his friend spoke in re-enforcement. "Not by a blame sight, he ain't lyin'. We heard 'em talkin'."

They caught sight of two mounted figures a short distance from them. One was the colonel of the regiment and the other was the officer who had received orders from the commander of the division. They were gesticulating at each other. The soldier, pointing at them, interpreted the scene.

One man had a final objection: "How could yeh hear 'em talkin'?" But the men, for a large part, nodded, admitting that previously the two friends had spoken truth.

They settled back into reposeful attitudes with airs of having accepted the matter. And they mused upon it, with a hundred varieties of expression. It was an <u>engrossing</u> thing to think about. Many tightened their belts carefully and hitched at their trousers.

A moment later the officers began to bustle among the men, pushing them into a more compact mass and into a better alignment. They chased those that straggled and fumed at a few men who seemed to show by their attitudes that they had decided to remain at that spot. They were like critical shepherds struggling with sheep.

◀ What actions do the officers take to ready the soldiers for battle?

Presently, the regiment seemed to draw itself up and heave a deep breath. None of the men's faces were mirrors of large thoughts. The soldiers were bended and stooped like <u>sprinters</u> before a signal. Many pairs of glinting eyes peered from the grimy faces toward the curtains of the deeper woods. They seemed to be engaged in deep calculations of time and distance.

Words
For
Everyday
Use

re • mon • strance (ri mən(t)´strən(t)s) *n.*, presentation of reasons for opposition or complaint

en • gross • ing (en grō´siŋ) *adj.*, occupying the attention completely

sprint • er (sprint´ər) *n.*, person who runs a fast race for a short distance

▶ What secret do the youth and his friend share?

They were surrounded by the noises of the monstrous altercation between the two armies. The world was fully interested in other matters. Apparently, the regiment had its small affair to itself.The youth, turning, shot a quick, inquiring glance at his friend. The latter returned to him the same manner of look. They were the only ones who possessed an inner knowledge. "Mule drivers—hell t' pay—don't believe many will get back." It was an ironical secret. Still, they saw no hesitation in each other's faces, and they nodded a mute and unprotesting <u>assent</u> when a shaggy man near them said in a meek voice: "We'll git swallowed."

Words
For
Everyday
Use

as • sent (ə sent´) *n.,* agreement; consent

Chapter 19

The youth stared at the land in front of him. Its foliages now seemed to veil powers and horrors. He was unaware of the machinery of orders that started the charge, although from the corners of his eyes he saw an officer, who looked like a boy a-horseback, come galloping, waving his hat. Suddenly he felt a straining and heaving among the men. The line fell slowly forward like a toppling wall, and, with a <u>convulsive</u> gasp that was intended for a cheer, the regiment began its journey. The youth was pushed and jostled for a moment before he understood the movement at all, but directly he lunged ahead and began to run.

◀ What does the youth's regiment begin to do?

He fixed his eye upon a distant and prominent clump of trees where he had concluded the enemy were to be met, and he ran toward it as toward a goal. He had believed throughout that it was a mere question of getting over an unpleasant matter as quickly as possible, and he ran desperately, as if pursued for a murder. His face was drawn hard and tight with the stress of his endeavor. His eyes were fixed in a lurid glare. And with his soiled and disordered dress, his red and inflamed features <u>surmounted</u> by the dingy rag with its spot of blood, his wildly swinging rifle and banging <u>accouterments</u>, he looked to be an insane soldier.

◀ In what direction does the youth run? What is his attitude toward the charge?

◀ What makes the youth look like an "insane soldier"?

As the regiment swung from its position out into a cleared space the woods and thickets before it awakened. Yellow flames leaped toward it from many directions. The forest made a tremendous objection.

◀ What happens as the regiment runs into a "cleared space"?

The line lurched straight for a moment. Then the right wing[1] swung forward; it in turn was surpassed by the left. Afterward the center careered to the front until the regiment was a wedge-shaped mass, but an instant later the opposition of the bushes, trees, and uneven places on the ground split the command and scattered it into detached clusters.

The youth, light-footed, was unconsciously in advance. His eyes still kept note of the clump of trees. From all places near it the <u>clannish</u> yell of the enemy could be heard. The little flames of rifles leaped from it. The song of the bullets was

---

1. **wing.** Section of an army to the right or to the left

Words For Everyday Use	**con • vul • sive** (kən vəl′siv) *adj.*, violent, sudden, frantic, or spasmodic **sur • mount** (sər maunt′) *vt.*, stand or lie at the top of	**ac • cou • tre • ment** *or* **ac • cou • ter • ment** (ə ko͞o′trə mənt) *n.*, equipment, trappings **clan • nish** (kla′nish) *adj.*, of or relating to a close group

in the air and shells snarled among the treetops. One tumbled directly into the middle of a hurrying group and exploded in crimson fury. There was an instant's spectacle of a man, almost over it, throwing up his hands to shield his eyes.

Other men, punched by bullets, fell in grotesque agonies. The regiment left a <u>coherent</u> trail of bodies.

They had passed into a clearer atmosphere. There was an effect like a <u>revelation</u> in the new appearance of the landscape. Some men working madly at a battery were plain to them, and the opposing infantry's lines were defined by the gray walls and fringes of smoke.

It seemed to the youth that he saw everything. Each blade of the green grass was bold and clear. He thought that he was aware of every change in the thin, transparent vapor that floated idly in sheets. The brown or gray trunks of the trees showed each roughness of their surfaces. And the men of the regiment, with their starting eyes and sweating faces, running madly, or falling, as if thrown headlong, to queer, heaped-up corpses—all were comprehended. His mind took a mechanical but firm impression, so that afterward everything was pictured and explained to him, save why he himself was there.

But there was a frenzy made from this furious rush. The men, pitching forward insanely, had burst into cheerings, moblike and barbaric, but tuned in strange keys that can arouse the dullard[2] and the <u>stoic</u>. It made a mad enthusiasm that, it seemed, would be incapable of checking itself before granite and brass. There was the <u>delirium</u> that encounters despair and death, and is heedless and blind to the odds. It is a temporary but sublime absence of selfishness. And because it was of this order was the reason, perhaps, why the youth wondered, afterward, what reasons he could have had for being there.

Presently the straining pace ate up the energies of the men. As if by agreement, the leaders began to slacken their speed. The volleys directed against them had had a seeming windlike effect. The regiment snorted and blew. Among some stolid trees it began to falter and hesitate. The men, staring intently, began to wait for some of the distant walls of smoke to move and disclose to them the scene. Since

---

2. **dullard.** Stupid or unimaginative person

▶ What can be seen once they charge into a less smoke-filled area?

▶ What does the youth seem to think is happening to his senses?

▶ What are the men encountering? What are they "heedless" to? What human emotion do the men become free of, temporarily, in their charge?

▶ What happens as soon as the regiment slows their pace?

Words For Everyday Use

co • her • ent (cō hir´ənt) *adj.*, logically ordered; consistent

rev • e • la • tion (re və la´shən) *n.*, act of revealing or communicating divine truth

sto • ic (stō´ik) *n.*, one apparently or professedly indifferent to pleasure or pain

de • lir • i • um (di lir´ē əm) *n.*, frenzied excitement

much of their strength and their breath had vanished, they returned to caution. They were become men again.

The youth had a vague belief that he had run miles, and he thought, in a way, that he was now in some new and unknown land.

The moment the regiment ceased its advance the protesting splutter of musketry became a steadied roar. Long and accurate fringes of smoke spread out. From the top of a small hill came level belchings of yellow flame that caused an inhuman whistling in the air.

The men, halted, had opportunity to see some of their comrades dropping with moans and shrieks. A few lay under foot, still or wailing. And now for an instant the men stood, their rifles slack in their hands, and watched the regiment dwindle. They appeared dazed and stupid. This spectacle seemed to paralyze them, overcome them with a fatal fascination. They stared woodenly at the sights, and, lowering their eyes, looked from face to face. It was a strange pause, and a strange silence.

Then, above the sounds of the outside commotion, arose the roar of the lieutenant. He strode suddenly forth, his infantile features black with rage.

"Come on, yeh fools!" he bellowed. "Come on! Yeh can't stay here. Yeh must come on." He said more, but much of it could not be understood.

He started rapidly forward, with his head turned toward the men. "Come on," he was shouting. The men stared with blank and yokel-like eyes at him. He was obliged to halt and retrace his steps. He stood then with his back to the enemy and delivered gigantic curses into the faces of the men. His body vibrated from the weight and force of his imprecations. And he could string oaths with the facility of a maiden who strings beads.

The friend of the youth aroused. Lurching suddenly forward and dropping to his knees, he fired an angry shot at the persistent woods. This action awakened the men. They huddled no more like sheep. They seemed suddenly to bethink them of their weapons, and at once commenced firing. Belabored by their officers, they began to move forward. The regiment, involved like a cart involved in mud and muddle, started unevenly with many jolts and jerks. The men

What happens to the men halted in front of enemy fire? What do the men seem to be unable to do?

Who tries to urge the men to move? Is he successful at first?

What does the youth's friend do? What is the effect of this action on the rest of the regiment?

Words For Everyday Use

be • la • bor (bi lā´bər) *vt.*, attack verbally
mud • dle (mə´d'l) *n.*, confused mess

stopped now every few paces to fire and load, and in this manner moved slowly on from trees to trees.

▶ What happens to slow the regiment's forward progress?

The flaming opposition in their front grew with their advance until it seemed that all forward ways were barred by the thin leaping tongues, and off to the right an ominous demonstration could sometimes be dimly <u>discerned</u>. The smoke lately generated was in confusing clouds that made it difficult for the regiment to proceed with intelligence. As he passed through each curling mass the youth wondered what would confront him on the farther side.

The command went painfully forward until an open space interposed between them and the <u>lurid</u> lines. Here, crouching and cowering behind some trees, the men clung with desperation, as if threatened by a wave. They looked wild-eyed, and as if amazed at this furious disturbance they had stirred. In the storm there was an ironical expression of their importance. The faces of the men, too, showed a lack of certain feeling of responsibility for being there. It was as if they had been driven. It was the dominant animal failing to remember in the supreme moments the forceful causes of various superficial qualities. The whole affair seemed incomprehensible to many of them.

As they halted thus the lieutenant again began to bellow profanely. Regardless of the vindictive threats of the bullets, he went about coaxing, <u>berating</u>, and bedamning. His lips, that were habitually in a soft and childlike curve, were now writhed into unholy contortions. He swore by all possible deities.

▶ What does the lieutenant tell the youth?

Once he grabbed the youth by the arm. "Come on, yeh lunkhead!" he roared. "Come on! We'll all git killed if we stay here. We've on'y got t' go across that lot. An' then"—the remainder of his idea disappeared in a blue haze of curses.

The youth stretched forth his arm. "Cross there?" His mouth was puckered in doubt and awe.

"Certainly. Jest 'cross th' lot! We can't stay here," screamed the lieutenant. He poked his face close to the youth and waved his bandaged hand. "Come on!" Presently he grappled with him as if for a wrestling bout. It was as if he planned to drag the youth by the ear on to the assault.

The private felt a sudden unspeakable <u>indignation</u> against his officer. He wrenched fiercely and shook him off.

Words For Everyday Use

dis • cern (di sərn´) vt., detect with the eyes strongly and at length

lu • rid (lur´əd) adj., shining with the red glow of fire seen through smoke or cloud

be • rate (bi rāt´) vt., scold or condemn

in • dig • na • tion (in dig nā´shən) n., anger aroused by something unjust, unworthy, or mean

"Come on yerself, then," he yelled. There was a bitter challenge in his voice.

They galloped together down the regimental front. The friend scrambled after them. In front of the colors the three men began to bawl: "Come on! come on!" They danced and <u>gyrated</u> like tortured savages.

The flag, obedient to these appeals, bended its glittering form and swept toward them. The men wavered in indecision for a moment, and then with a long, wailful cry the dilapidated regiment surged forward and began its new journey.

Over the field went the scurrying mass. It was a handful of men splattered into the faces of the enemy. Toward it instantly sprang the yellow tongues. A vast quantity of blue smoke hung before them. A mighty banging made ears valueless.

The youth ran like a madman to reach the woods before a bullet could discover him. He ducked his head low, like a football player. In his haste his eyes almost closed, and the scene was a wild blur. Pulsating saliva stood at the corners of his mouth.

Within him, as he hurled himself forward, was born a love, a despairing fondness for this flag which was near him. It was a creation of beauty and <u>invulnerability</u>. It was a goddess, radiant, that bended its form with an <u>imperious</u> gesture to him. It was a woman, red and white, hating and loving, that called him with the voice of his hopes. Because no harm could come to it he <u>endowed</u> it with power. He kept near, as if it could be a saver of lives, and an imploring cry went from his mind.

In the mad scramble he was aware that the color sergeant flinched suddenly, as if struck by a bludgeon.[3] He faltered, and then became motionless, save for his quivering knees.

He made a spring and a clutch at the pole. At the same instant his friend grabbed it from the other side. They jerked at it, stout and furious, but the color sergeant was dead, and the corpse would not <u>relinquish</u> its trust. For a moment there was a grim encounter. The dead man, swinging with bended

◄ What challenge does the youth offer the lieutenant? What do the youth, the lieutenant, and the youth's friend do then?

◄ What do the three men inspire the rest of the regiment to do? How do the number of soldiers in the regiment compare to the numbers of the enemy?

◄ How does the youth feel about his regiment's flag? What does it seem to be to him?

◄ What happens to the color sergeant who carries the flag? What do the youth and his friend do? What does the dead man seem to be doing?

---

3. **bludgeon.** Short stick used as a weapon

Words For Everyday Use

gy • rate (jī´rāt) *vi.*, swing with a circular or spiral motion
in • vul • ner • a • bil • I • ty (in vəl nə rə bil´ə tē) *n.*, quality of being immune to attack

im • pe • ri • ous (im pir´ē əs) *adj.*, commanding; intensely compelling
en • dow (en dau´) *vt.*, provide with something freely or naturally
re • lin • quish (ri liŋ´kwish) *vt.*, give up

back, seemed to be obstinately tugging, in <u>ludicrous</u> and awful ways, for the possession of the flag.

It was past in an instant of time. They wrenched the flag furiously from the dead man, and, as they turned again, the corpse swayed forward with bowed head. One arm swung high, and the curved hand fell with heavy protest on the friend's unheeding shoulder.

**Words
For
Everyday
Use**

lu • di • crous (lōō´də krəs) *adj.,* amusing or laughable through obvious absurdity, incongruity, exaggeration, or eccentricity

Chapter 20

When the two youths turned with the flag they saw that much of the regiment had crumbled away, and the dejected remnant was coming slowly back. The men, having hurled themselves in projectile fashion,[1] had presently expended their forces. They slowly retreated, with their faces still toward the spluttering woods, and their hot rifles still replying to the din. Several officers were giving orders, their voices keyed to screams.

◀ What are the youth and his friend forced to do?

"Where in hell yeh goin'?" the lieutenant was asking in a sarcastic howl. And a red-bearded officer, whose voice of triple brass[2] could plainly be heard, was commanding: "Shoot into 'em! Shoot into 'em, Gawd damn their souls!" There was a <u>melee</u> of screeches, in which the men were ordered to do conflicting and impossible things.

The youth and his friend had a small scuffle over the flag. "Give it t' me!" "No, let me keep it!" Each felt satisfied with the other's possession of it, but each felt bound to declare, by an offer to carry the emblem, his willingness to further risk himself. The youth roughly pushed his friend away.

◀ Why do the youth and his friend fight over the flag? Why might it be risky to carry the flag? Who gets the flag?

The regiment fell back to the stolid trees. There it halted for a moment to blaze at some dark forms that had begun to steal upon its track. Presently it <u>resumed</u> its march again, curving among the tree trunks. By the time the depleted regiment had again reached the first open space they were receiving a fast and merciless fire. There seemed to be mobs all about them.

◀ Describe the situation for the remaining men of the youth's regiment.

The greater part of the men, discouraged, their spirits worn by the turmoil, acted as if stunned. They accepted the <u>pelting</u> of the bullets with bowed and weary heads. It was of no purpose to strive against walls. It was of no use to batter themselves against granite. And from this consciousness that they had attempted to conquer an unconquerable thing there seemed to arise a feeling that they had been betrayed. They glowered with bent brows, but dangerously, upon some

◀ What attitude do the soldiers now have toward the enemy fire? What do they think of their attempt to conquer the enemy?

---

1. **in projectile fashion.** Like missiles
2. **triple brass.** The officer's voice is as clear and easily heard as a brass instrument, such as a trumpet.

Words For Everyday Use

me • lee (māˊlā) *n.*, confused struggle; hand-to-hand fight among several people

re • sume (ri zo͞omˊ) *vt.*, return to or begin again after interruption

pelt • ing (peltˊiŋ) *n.*, succession of blows or missiles

of the officers, more particularly upon the red-bearded one with the voice of triple brass.

However, the rear of the regiment was fringed with men, who continued to shoot irritably at the advancing foes. They seemed resolved to make every trouble. The youthful lieutenant was perhaps the last man in the disordered mass. His forgotten back was toward the enemy. He had been shot in the arm. It hung straight and rigid. Occasionally he would cease to remember it, and be about to emphasize an oath with a sweeping gesture. The multiplied pain caused him to swear with incredible power.

▶ What has happened to the lieutenant of the regiment?

The youth went along with slipping, uncertain feet. He kept watchful eyes rearward. A scowl of <u>mortification</u> and rage was upon his face. He had thought of a fine revenge upon the officer who had referred to him and his fellows as mule drivers. But he saw that it could not come to pass. His dreams had collapsed when the mule drivers, dwindling rapidly, had wavered and hesitated on the little clearing, and then had recoiled. And now the retreat of the mule drivers was a march of shame to him.

▶ Why does the youth feel rage and shame? What "revenge" do you think the youth had in mind, or in other words, what do you think the youth hoped his regiment would accomplish?

A dagger-pointed gaze from without his blackened face was held toward the enemy, but his greater hatred was <u>riveted</u> upon the man, who, not knowing him, had called him a mule driver.

▶ Whom does the youth hate even more than the enemy?

When he knew that he and his comrades had failed to do anything in successful ways that might bring the little pangs of a kind of remorse upon the officer, the youth allowed the rage of the baffled to possess him. This cold officer upon a monument, who dropped epithets unconcernedly down, would be finer as a dead man, he thought. So <u>grievous</u> did he think it that he could never possess the secret right to taunt truly in answer.

▶ How had the youth hoped his regiment's actions would make the officer feel?

He had pictured red letters of curious revenge. "We *are* mule drivers, are we?" And now he was compelled to throw them away.

He presently wrapped his heart in the cloak of his pride and kept the flag erect. He harangued his fellows, pushing against their chests with his free hand. To those he knew well he made frantic appeals, <u>beseeching</u> them by name. Between him and the lieutenant, scolding and near to losing his mind with rage, there was felt a subtle fellowship and equality.

▶ What does the youth join the lieutenant in doing?

Words For Everyday Use

mor • ti • fi • ca • tion (môr tə fə kā´shən) *n.*, sense of humiliation and shame caused by something that wounds one's pride or self-respect
ri • vet (ri´vət) *vt.*, fasten firmly

griev • ous (grē´vəs) *adj.*, serious; burdensome
be • seech (bi sēch´) *vt.*, beg for urgently or anxiously

They supported each other in all manner of hoarse, howling protests.

But the regiment was a machine run down. The two men babbled at a forceless thing. The soldiers who had heart to go slowly were continually shaken in their resolves by a knowledge that comrades were slipping with speed back to the lines. It was difficult to think of reputation when others were thinking of skins. Wounded men were left crying on this black journey.

◄ What makes it difficult for the soldiers to hold their ground and retreat as slowly as possible? Whom do the soldiers have to leave behind?

The smoke fringes and flames blustered always. The youth, peering once through a sudden rift in a cloud, saw a brown mass of troops, interwoven and magnified until they appeared to be thousands. A fierce-hued flag flashed before his vision.

Immediately, as if the uplifting of the smoke had been prearranged, the discovered troops burst into a rasping yell, and a hundred flames jetted toward the retreating band. A rolling gray cloud again interposed as the regiment doggedly replied. The youth had to depend again upon his misused ears, which were trembling and buzzing from the melee of musketry and yells.

The way seemed eternal. In the clouded haze men became panic-stricken with the thought that the regiment had lost its path, and was proceeding in a <u>perilous</u> direction. Once the men who headed the wild procession turned and came pushing back against their comrades, screaming that they were being fired upon from points which they had considered to be toward their own lines. At this cry a hysterical fear and dismay beset the troops. A soldier, who <u>heretofore</u> had been ambitious to make the regiment into a wise little band that would proceed calmly amid the huge-appearing difficulties, suddenly sank down and buried his face in his arms with an air of bowing to a doom. From another a shrill lamentation rang out filled with profane allusions to a general. Men ran hither and thither, seeking with their eyes roads of escape. With serene regularity, as if controlled by a schedule, bullets buffed into men.[3]

◄ What difficulties does the smoke of battles cause for the regiment?

The youth walked stolidly into the midst of the mob, and with his flag in his hands took a stand as if he expected an

---

3. **buffed.** Abbreviation of *buffet,* meaning "strike"

Words
For
Everyday
Use

per • il • ous (per´ə ləs) *adj.,* dangerous
here • to • fore (hir´tə fōr) *adv.,* up to this time

attempt to push him to the ground. He unconsciously assumed the attitude of the color bearer in the fight of the preceding day. He passed over his brow a hand that trembled. His breath did not come freely. He was choking during this small wait for the crisis.

His friend came to him. "Well, Henry, I guess this is good-bye John."

"Oh, shut up, you damned fool!" replied the youth, and he would not look at the other.

The officers labored like politicians to beat the mass into a proper circle to face the <u>menaces</u>. The ground was uneven and torn. The men curled into depressions and fitted themselves snugly behind whatever would frustrate a bullet.

The youth noted with vague surprise that the lieutenant was standing mutely with his legs far apart and his sword held in the manner of a cane. The youth wondered what had happened to his vocal organs that he no more cursed.

There was something curious in this little intent pause of the lieutenant. He was like a babe which, having wept its fill, raises its eyes and fixes upon a distant toy. He was engrossed in this contemplation, and the soft under lip quivered from self-whispered words.

Some lazy and ignorant smoke curled slowly. The men, hiding from the bullets, waited anxiously for it to lift and disclose the plight of the regiment.

The silent ranks were suddenly thrilled by the eager voice of the youthful lieutenant bawling out: "Here they come! Right onto us, b'Gawd!" His further words were lost in a roar of wicked thunder from the men's rifles.

The youth's eyes had instantly turned in the direction indicated by the awakened and agitated lieutenant, and he had seen the haze of <u>treachery</u> disclosing a body of soldiers of the enemy. They were so near that he could see their features. There was a recognition as he looked at the types of faces. Also he perceived with dim amazement that their uniforms were rather gay in effect, being light gray, accented with a brilliant-hued facing. Too, the clothes seemed new.

These troops had apparently been going forward with caution, their rifles held in readiness, when the youthful lieutenant had discovered them and their movement had been interrupted by the volley from the blue regiment. From the

► What isn't the youth willing to do yet?

► What warning does the lieutenant give? What does the youth see when he turns?

Words For Everyday Use	men • ace (me´nəs) *n.*, threat, danger
	treach • ery (tre´chə rē) *n.*, violation of allegiance or of faith and confidence; treason

moment's glimpse, it was derived[4] that they had been unaware of the <u>proximity</u> of their darksuited foes or had mistaken the direction. Almost instantly they were shut utterly from the youth's sight by the smoke from the energetic rifles of his companions. He strained his vision to learn the accomplishment of the volley, but the smoke hung before him.

◀ Of what had the enemy troops also been unaware?

The two bodies of troops exchanged blows in the manner of a pair of boxers. The fast angry firings went back and forth. The men in blue were intent with the despair of their circumstances and they seized upon the revenge to be had at close range. Their thunder swelled loud and <u>valiant</u>. Their curving front bristled with flashes and the place resounded with the clangor of their ramrods. The youth ducked and dodged for a time and achieved a few unsatisfactory views of the enemy. There appeared to be many of them and they were replying swiftly. They seemed moving toward the blue regiment, step by step. He seated himself gloomily on the ground with his flag between his knees.

As he noted the vicious, wolflike temper of his comrades he had a sweet thought that if the enemy was about to swallow the regimental broom as a large prisoner, it could at least have the consolation of going down with bristles forward.

But the blows of the antagonist began to grow more weak. Fewer bullets ripped the air, and finally, when the men slackened to learn of the fight, they could see only dark, floating smoke. The regiment lay still and gazed. Presently some chance whim came to the pestering[5] blur, and it began to coil heavily away. The men saw a ground vacant of fighters. It would have been an empty stage if it were not for a few corpses that lay thrown and twisted into fantastic shapes upon the sward.[6]

◀ What begins to happen to the enemy? What do the men see when they stop shooting?

◀ What has happened to the enemy?

At sight of this <u>tableau</u>, many of the men in blue sprang from behind their covers and made an <u>ungainly</u> dance of joy. Their eyes burned and a hoarse cheer of <u>elation</u> broke from their dry lips.

It had begun to seem to them that events were trying to prove that they were impotent. These little battles had evi-

---

4. **derived.** Concluded
5 **pestering.** Bothersome
6. **sward.** Grassy land

Words For Everyday Use

prox • im • i • ty (prək si´mə tē) *n.,* closeness
val • iant (val´yənt) *adj.,* possessing or acting with bravery or boldness
tab • leau (ta´blō) *n.,* graphic description or representation; picture
un • gain • ly (ən gān´lē) *adj.,* clumsy, awkward
ela • tion (e lā´shən) *n.,* extreme joy

dently endeavored to demonstrate that the men could not fight well. When on the verge of submission to these opinions, the small duel had showed them that the proportions were not impossible, and by it they had revenged themselves upon their <u>misgivings</u> and upon the foe.

The <u>impetus</u> of enthusiasm was theirs again. They gazed about them with looks of uplifted pride, feeling new trust in the grim, always confident weapons in their hands. And they were men.

► How does this victory make the regiment feel?

Words
For
Everyday
Use

mis • giv • ing (mis gi´viŋ) *n.*, feeling of doubt or suspicion especially concerning a future event

im • pe • tus (im´pə təs) *n.*, driving force

Respond to the Selection

How does it feel to win despite many difficulties or obstacles that stand in your way? Describe a time in your life when you persevered to achieve a success.

Investigate, Inquire, and Imagine

Recall: GATHERING FACTS

1a. In Chapter 16, whom does Henry (the youth) publicly blame for his side's losses in battle? To what evidence does he point? What attitude does Wilson (his friend) have toward the upcoming battle? In Chapter 17, when Henry's regiment is fighting the enemy, which of Henry's actions surprise his fellow soldiers? What does the lieutenant say in praise of Henry's actions? What does the youth think of his own actions?

2a. In Chapter 18, why do Henry and Wilson leave their regiment? What do they overhear the general and an officer saying about Henry's regiment, the 304th? What do they plan to have the 304th do? What does the general think of the regiment's chances?

3a. What do Henry and the lieutenant do in Chapter 19, when the regiment begins to lose its energy in its charge against the enemy? What do Henry and Wilson struggle over at the end of Chapter 19 and the beginning of Chapter 20? In Chapter 20, what makes it look as if the regiment will be defeated? What happens to change this situation for the 304th regiment?

Interpret: FINDING MEANING

1b. What do Henry and Wilson's different reactions to the nerve-wracking moments before a battle reveal about their characters? Explain whether you agree with Henry's own assessment of his actions in Chapter 17. Why might Henry feel this way about himself, considering what he has overcome?

2b. Why do you think this description of their regiment surprises Henry and Wilson? What is the "ironical secret" Henry and Wilson keep from their regiment? Why do you think they keep this information secret?

3b. What words would you use to describe Henry's actions in this charge against the enemy? Why do you think Henry and Wilson struggle over possession of this thing? What does carrying it symbolize or represent to them? Why is Henry especially upset about the idea of being defeated by the enemy? Explain whether the regiment's feeling of pride at the end of Chapter 20 is justified.

Analyze: Taking Things Apart

4a. In what way has Henry changed as a soldier? Identify how he has grown or changed since the last battle in which he took part.

Synthesize: Bringing Things Together

4b. Explain whether you think Henry would behave the way he does in these chapters if he hadn't run in terror from battle earlier. How would he have fought if his fellow soldiers hadn't labeled him a hero?

Evaluate: Making Judgments

5a. Crane ends Chapter 20 with the line, "And they were men." Decide what you think Crane means by this line. Why might Crane say this about the soldiers of the 304th regiment at this point in the story?

Extend: Connecting Ideas

5b. During the Civil War, as in previous times and in other cultures, young men came of age or proved themselves by enlisting in war. In what ways do young people today come of age or prove themselves? What do you see as the most important milestones on the road from childhood to adulthood?

Understanding Literature

Description. A **description** gives a picture in words of a character, object, or scene. In Chapter 17, Henry is described as "crouched behind a little tree, with his eyes burning hatefully and his teeth set in a curlike snarl. The awkward bandage was still upon his head, and upon it, over his wound, there was a spot of dry blood. . . . There could be seen spasmodic gulpings at his throat." What does this physical description of Henry reveal about his state of mind? What details in this description help to make his state of mind clear to you?

Suspense. Suspense is a feeling of anxiousness or curiosity. Writers create suspense by raising questions in the reader's mind and by using details that create strong emotions. In what way does Crane build suspense in Chapters 16–20?

Chapter 21

Presently they knew that no firing threatened them. All ways seemed once more opened to them. The dusty blue lines of their friends were disclosed a short distance away. In the distance there were many colossal noises, but in all this part of the field there was a sudden stillness.

They perceived that they were free. The <u>depleted</u> band drew a long breath of relief and gathered itself into a bunch to complete its trip.

In this last length of journey the men began to show strange emotions. They hurried with nervous fear. Some who had been dark and <u>unfaltering</u> in the grimmest moments now could not conceal an anxiety that made them frantic. It was perhaps that they dreaded to be killed in insignificant ways after the times for proper military deaths had passed. Or, perhaps, they thought it would be too ironical to get killed at the portals[1] of safety. With backward looks of <u>perturbation</u>, they hastened.

As they approached their own lines there was some sarcasm exhibited on the part of a gaunt and bronzed regiment that lay resting in the shade of trees. Questions were wafted[2] to them.

"Where th' hell yeh been?"

"What yeh comin' back fer?"

"Why didn't yeh stay there?"

"Was it warm out there, sonny?"

"Goin' home now, boys?"

One shouted in taunting mimicry: "Oh, mother, come quick an' look at th' sojers!"

There was no reply from the bruised and battered regiment, save that one man made broadcast challenges to fist fights and the red-bearded officer walked rather near and glared in great <u>swashbuckler</u> style at a tall captain in the other regiment. But the lieutenant suppressed the man who wished to fist fight, and the tall captain, flushing at the little fanfare of the red-bearded one, was obliged to look intently at some trees.

◀ What does the regiment notice? What are they now able to do?

◀ Why are some men more nervous now than they were in battle?

◀ In what way is the regiment treated by a "gaunt and bronzed" regiment when they rejoin their forces?

---

1. **portals.** Doors, entrances
2. **wafted.** Tossed; asked in a light tone

Words For Everyday Use	de • plet • ed (di plēt´əd) *adj.*, reduced in number	per • tur • ba • tion (pər tər bā´shən) *n.*, disturbance, uneasiness
	un • fal • ter • ing (ən fôl´tə riŋ) *adj.*, firm; not weakening	swash • buck • ler (swəsh´bə klər) *n.*, daring soldier or adventurer

The youth's tender flesh was deeply stung by these remarks. From under his creased brows he glowered with hate at the mockers. He meditated upon a few revenges. Still, many in the regiment hung their heads in criminal fashion, so that it came to pass that the men trudged with sudden heaviness, as if they bore upon their bended shoulders the coffin of their honor. And the youthful lieutenant, recollecting himself, began to mutter softly in black curses.

They turned when they arrived at their old position to regard the ground over which they had charged.

► What does the youth realize when he looks back at the place where they charged and fought?

The youth in this contemplation was smitten[3] with a large astonishment. He discovered that the distances, as compared with the brilliant measurings of his mind, were trivial and ridiculous. The stolid trees, where much had taken place, seemed incredibly near. The time, too, now that he reflected, he saw to have been short. He wondered at the number of emotions and events that had been crowded into such little spaces. Elfin[4] thoughts must have exaggerated and enlarged everything, he said.

It seemed, then, that there was bitter justice in the speeches of the gaunt and bronzed veterans. He veiled a glance of disdain at his fellows who strewed the ground, choking with dust, red from perspiration, misty-eyed, disheveled.

► How does the youth feel about the comments of the veteran regiment now?

They were gulping at their canteens, fierce to wring every mite[5] of water from them, and they polished at their swollen and watery features with coat sleeves and bunches of grass.

However, to the youth there was a considerable joy in musing upon his performances during the charge. He had had very little time previously in which to appreciate himself, so that there was now much satisfaction in quietly thinking of his actions. He recalled bits of color that in the flurry had stamped themselves unawares upon his engaged senses.

► How does the youth feel about his own actions in the charge?

As the regiment lay heaving from its hot exertions the officer who had named them as mule drivers came galloping along the line. He had lost his cap. His tousled hair streamed wildly, and his face was dark with vexation and wrath. His

► Who rides up to the regiment? What does this person's state of mind seem to be?

---

3. **smitten.** Hit
4. **Elfin.** Otherworldly
5. **mite.** Tiny bit

Words For Everyday Use

trudge (trəj) *vi.,* walk or march steadily on
veil (vā(ə)l) *vt.,* cover, provide, obscure, or conceal with or as if with a veil

dis • dain (dis dān´) *n.,* contempt, scorn
vex • a • tion (vek sā´shən) *n.,* irritation

temper was displayed with more clearness by the way in which he managed his horse. He jerked and wrenched savagely at his bridle,[6] stopping the hard-breathing animal with a furious pull near the colonel of the regiment. He immediately exploded in reproaches which came unbidden to the ears of the men. They were suddenly alert, being always curious about black words between officers.

"Oh, thunder, MacChesnay, what an awful bull you made of this thing!" began the officer. He attempted low tones, but his indignation caused certain of the men to learn the sense of his words. "What an awful mess you made! Good Lord, man, you stopped about a hundred feet this side of a very pretty success! If your men had gone a hundred feet farther you would have made a great charge, but as it is—what a lot of mud diggers you've got anyway!"

◀ What does the officer say about the regiment's charge?

The men, listening with <u>bated</u> breath, now turned their curious eyes upon the colonel. They had a ragamuffin[7] interest in this affair.

The colonel was seen to straighten his form and put one hand forth in oratorical fashion. He wore an injured air; it was as if a deacon[8] had been accused of stealing. The men were wiggling in an ecstasy of excitement.

But of a sudden the colonel's manner changed from that of a deacon to that of a Frenchman.[9] He shrugged his shoulders. "Oh, well, general, we went as far as we could," he said calmly.

◀ What does the colonel say in defense of the regiment?

"'As far as you could? Did you, b'Gawd?" snorted the other. "Well, that wasn't very far, was it?" he added, with a glance of cold contempt into the other's eyes. "Not very far, I think. You were intended to make a <u>diversion</u> in favor of Whiterside. How well you succeeded your own ears can now tell you." He wheeled his horse and rode stiffly away.

The colonel, bidden to hear the jarring noises of an engagement in the woods to the left, broke out in vague damnations.

The lieutenant, who had listened with an air of impotent

◀ What does the officer say the regiment was supposed to do? What is the proof that they failed in this mission?

---

6. **bridle.** Headgear with which a rider governs a horse
7. **ragamuffin.** Like ragged and dirty, but curious, street children
8. **deacon.** Officer in a Christian church
9. **Frenchman.** The author is stereotyping Frenchmen as nonchalant, or aloof and detached.

Words For Everyday Use

bat • ed (bāt´əd) *adj.,* restrained; reduced in force or intensity

di • ver • sion (də vər´zhən) *n.,* attack that draws the attention and force of an enemy from the point of the main operation

► What does the lieutenant say in defense of the regiment?

rage to the interview, spoke suddenly in firm and <u>undaunted</u> tones. "I don't care what a man is—whether he is a general or what—if he says th' boys didn't put up a good fight out there he's a damned fool."

"Lieutenant," began the colonel, severely, "this is my own affair, and I'll trouble you—"

The lieutenant made an obedient gesture. "All right, colonel, all right," he said. He sat down with an air of being content with himself.

► How do the men of the regiment feel when they realize they have been reproached, not praised for their actions?

The news that the regiment had been reproached went along the line. For a time the men were bewildered by it. "Good thunder!" they ejaculated, staring at the vanishing form of the general. They conceived it to be a huge mistake.

Presently, however, they began to believe that in truth their efforts had been called <u>light</u>. The youth could see this conviction weigh upon the entire regiment until the men were like cuffed[10] and cursed animals, but <u>withal</u> rebellious.

The friend, with a grievance in his eye, went to the youth. "I wonder what he does want," he said. "He must think we went out there an' played marbles! I never see sech a man!"

The youth developed a <u>tranquil</u> philosophy for these moments of irritation. "Oh, well," he rejoined, "he probably didn't see nothing of it at all and got mad as blazes,[11] and concluded we were a lot of sheep, just because we didn't do what he wanted done. It's a pity old Grandpa Henderson got killed yestirday—he'd have known that we did our best and fought good. It's just our awful luck, that's what."

► What does the youth's friend find unjust? What does he say he feels like doing "next time"?

"I should say so," replied the friend. He seemed to be deeply wounded at an injustice. "I should say we did have awful luck! There's no fun in fightin' fer people when every-thing yeh do—no matter what—ain't done right. I have a notion t' stay behind next time an' let 'em take their ol' charge an' go t' th' devil with it."

The youth spoke soothingly to his comrade. "Well, we both did good. I'd like to see the fool what'd say we both did-n't do as good as we could!"

► What has the friend overheard other soldiers saying?

"Of course we did," declared the friend stoutly. "An' I'd break th' feller's neck if he was as big as a church. But we're

---

10. **cuffed.** Beaten
11. **as blazes.** Slang for "very"

| Words For Everyday Use | **un • daunt • ed** (ən dôn´təd) *adj.*, coura-geous in the face of danger or difficulty **light** (līt) *adj.*, of little importance | **with • al** (wi thôl´) *adv.*, together with this; besides **tran • quil** (tran´kwəl) *adj.*, free from agi-tation of mind or spirit |

all right, anyhow, for I heard one feller say that we two fit th' best in th' reg'ment, an' they had a great argument 'bout it. Another feller, 'a course, he had t' up an' say it was a lie—he seen all what was goin' on an' he never seen us from th' beginnin' t' th' end. An' a lot more struck in an' ses it wasn't a lie—we did fight like thunder, an' they give us quite a send-off.[12] But this is what I can't stand—these everlastin' ol' soldiers, titterin' an' laughin', an' then that general, he's crazy."

The youth exclaimed with sudden exasperation: "He's a lunkhead! He makes me mad. I wish he'd come along next time. We'd show 'im what—"

He ceased because several men had come hurrying up. Their faces expressed a bringing of great news.

"O Flem, yeh jest oughta heard!" cried one, eagerly.

"Heard what?" said the youth.

"Yeh jest oughta heard!" repeated the other, and he arranged himself to tell his <u>tidings</u>. The others made an excited circle. "Well, sir, th' colonel met your lieutenant right by us—it was damnedest thing I ever heard—an' he ses: 'Ahem! ahem!' he ses. 'Mr. Hasbrouck!' he ses, 'by th' way, who was that lad what carried th' flag?' he ses. There, Flemin', what d' yeh think 'a that? 'Who was th' lad what carried th' flag?' he ses, an' th' lieutenant, he speaks up right away: 'That's Flemin', an' he's a jimhickey,' he ses, right away. What? I say he did. 'A jimhickey,'[13] he ses—those 'r his words. He did, too. I say he did. If you kin tell this story better than I kin, go ahead an' tell it. Well, then, keep yer mouth shet. Th' lieutenant, he ses: 'He's a jimhickey,' an' th' colonel, he ses: 'Ahem! ahem! he is, indeed, a very good man t' have, ahem! He kep' th' flag 'way t' th' front. I saw 'im. He's a good un,' ses th' colonel. 'You bet,' ses th' lieutenant, 'he an' a feller named Wilson was at th' head 'a th' charge, an' howlin' like Indians all th' time,' he ses. 'Head a' th' charge all th' time,' he ses. 'A feller named Wilson,' he ses. There, Wilson, m'boy, put that in a letter an' send it hum t' yer mother, hay? 'A feller named Wilson,' he ses. An' th' colonel, he ses: 'Were they, indeed? Ahem! ahem! My sakes!' he ses. 'At th' head 'a th' reg'ment?' he ses. 'They were,' ses

◄ What has this soldier overheard the colonel and the lieutenant saying?

---

12. **send-off.** Showing of goodwill on the start of a journey
13. **jimhickey.** Similar to *jim-dandy,* meaning "an excellent fellow"

Words For Everyday Use

tid • ing (tī´diŋ) *n.,* piece of news

► What does the colonel say in praise of the youth and his friend?

► How does this compliment make the youth and his friend feel? What does this compliment make them forget?

th' lieutenant. 'My sakes!' ses th' colonel. He ses: 'Well, well, well,' he ses, 'those two babies?' 'They were,' ses th' lieutenant. 'Well, well,' ses th' colonel, 'they deserve t' be major-generals,'[14] he ses. 'They deserve t' be major-generals.'"

The youth and his friend had said: "Huh!" "Yer lyin', Thompson." "Oh, go t' blazes!" "He never sed it." "Oh, what a lie!" "Huh!" But despite these youthful scoffings and embarrassments, they knew that their faces were deeply <u>flushing</u> from thrills of pleasure. They exchanged a secret glance of joy and congratulation.

They speedily forgot many things. The past held no pictures of error and disappointment. They were very happy, and their hearts swelled with grateful affection for the colonel and the youthful lieutenant.

---

14. **major generals.** Generals with a fairly high rank; commanders

Words For Everyday Use   **flush** (fləsh) *vi.,* blush

Chapter 22

When the woods again began to pour forth the dark-hued masses of the enemy the youth felt serene self-confidence. He smiled briefly when he saw men dodge and duck at the long screechings of shells that were thrown in giant handfuls over them. He stood, erect and tranquil, watching the attack begin against a part of the line that made a blue curve along the side of an adjacent hill. His vision being unmolested by smoke from the rifles of his companions, he had opportunities to see parts of the hard fight. It was a relief to perceive at last from whence[1] came some of these noises which had been roared into his ears.

◀ How does the youth feel when the enemy again begins to attack?

Off a short way he saw two regiments fighting a little separate battle with two other regiments. It was in a cleared space, wearing a set-apart look. They were blazing as if upon a wager, giving and taking tremendous blows. The firings were incredibly fierce and rapid. These intent regiments apparently were <u>oblivious</u> of all larger purposes of war, and were slugging each other as if at a matched game.

In another direction he saw a magnificent brigade going with the evident intention of driving the enemy from a wood. They passed in out of sight and presently there was a most awe-inspiring racket in the wood. The noise was unspeakable. Having stirred this prodigious uproar, and, apparently, finding it too <u>prodigious</u>, the brigade, after a little time, came marching <u>airily</u> out again with its fine formation in nowise disturbed. There were no traces of speed in its movements. The brigade was <u>jaunty</u> and seemed to point a proud thumb[2] at the yelling wood.

◀ What does the youth see one proud regiment do? Are they successful in their goal?

On a slope to the left there was a long row of guns, gruff and maddened, denouncing the enemy, who, down through the woods, were forming for another attack in the pitiless monotony of conflicts. The round red discharges from the guns made a crimson flare and a high, thick smoke. Occasional glimpses could be caught of groups of the toiling artillerymen. In the rear of this row of guns stood a house,

---

1. **whence.** What place, source, or cause
2. **proud thumb.** Gesture of scorn or defiance

Words For Everyday Use	**o • bliv • i • ous** (ə bliv´vē əs) *adj.,* lacking active conscious knowledge or awareness **pro • di • gious** (prə di´jəs) *adj.,* exciting amazement or wonder	**air • i • ly** (ar´ə lē) *adv.,* in a light and graceful manner; proudly **jaun • ty** (jôn´tē) *adj.,* lively in manner or appearance

calm and white, amid bursting shells. A congregation of horses, tied to a long railing, were tugging <u>frenziedly</u> at their bridles. Men were running hither and thither.[3]

▶ Who wins the battle between the four regiments?

The detached battle between the four regiments lasted for some time. There chanced to be no interference, and they settled their dispute by themselves. They struck savagely and powerfully at each other for a period of minutes, and then the lighter-hued regiments faltered and drew back, leaving the dark-blue lines shouting.[4] The youth could see the two flags shaking with laughter amid the smoke remnants.

Presently there was a stillness, <u>pregnant</u> with meaning. The blue lines shifted and changed a trifle and stared expectantly at the silent woods and fields before them. The hush was solemn and churchlike, save for a distant battery[5] that, evidently unable to remain quiet, sent a faint rolling thunder over the ground. It irritated, like the noises of unimpressed boys. The men imagined that it would prevent their perched[6] ears from hearing the first words of the new battle.

Of a sudden the guns on the slope roared out a message of warning. A spluttering sound had begun in the woods. It swelled with amazing speed to a <u>profound</u> clamor that involved the earth in noises. The splitting crashes swept along the lines until an interminable roar was developed. To those in the midst of it became a din fitted to the universe. It was the whirring and thumping of gigantic machinery, complications among the smaller stars. The youth's ears were filled cups. They were incapable of hearing more.

▶ To what are the rushes of the soldiers compared?

On an incline over which a road wound he saw wild and desperate rushes of men perpetually backward and forward in <u>riotous</u> <u>surges</u>. These parts of the opposing armies were two long waves that pitched upon each other madly at dictated points. To and fro they swelled. Sometimes, one side by its yells and cheers would proclaim decisive blows, but a moment later the other side would be all yells and cheers. Once the youth saw a spray of light forms go in houndlike

---

3. **hither and thither.** To this place and to that place
4. **lighter-hued . . . shouting.** The Union troops, of which the youth Henry is a member, push back the Confederate troops.
5. **battery.** Artillery unit of an army, or the persons who operate the heavy guns
6. **perched.** Raised; eager to hear

Words For Everyday Use

fren • zied • ly (fren´zēd lē) *adv.*, in a furious and wild manner

preg • nant (preg´nənt) *adj.*, full, teeming

pro • found (prə faund´) *adj.*, coming from, reaching to, or situated at a depth

ri • ot • ous (rī´ə təs) *adj.*, violent, disorderly

surge (sərj) *n.*, swelling, rolling, or sweeping forward like that of a wave

leaps toward the waving blue lines. There was much howling, and presently it went away with a vast mouthful of prisoners. Again, he saw a blue wave dash with such thunderous force against a gray obstruction that it seemed to clear the earth of it and leave nothing but trampled sod. And always in their swift and deadly rushes to and fro the men screamed and yelled like maniacs.

Particular pieces of fence or secure positions behind collections of trees were wrangled over, as gold thrones or pearl bedsteads. There were desperate lunges at these chosen spots seemingly every instant, and most of them were <u>bandied</u> like light toys between the contending forces. The youth could not tell from the battle flags flying like crimson foam in many directions which color of cloth was winning.

◀ *What do men find positions behind fences or trees as valuable as?*

His emaciated regiment bustled forth with undiminished fierceness when its time came. When assaulted again by bullets, the men burst out in a barbaric cry of rage and pain. They bent their heads in aims of intent hatred behind the projected hammers of their guns. Their ramrods clanged loud with fury as their eager arms pounded the cartridges into the rifle barrels. The front of the regiment was a smoke-wall penetrated by the flashing points of yellow and red.

◀ *How does the youth's regiment act when needed to fight again?*

Wallowing in the fight, they were in an astonishingly short time resmudged.[7] They surpassed in stain and dirt all their previous appearances. Moving to and fro with strained <u>exertion</u>, jabbering the while, they were, with their swaying bodies, black faces, and glowing eyes, like strange and ugly fiends jigging[8] heavily in the smoke.

The lieutenant, returning from a tour after a bandage,[9] produced from a hidden receptacle of his mind new and <u>portentous</u> oaths suited to the emergency. Strings of <u>expletives</u> he swung lashlike over the backs of his men, and it was evident that his previous efforts had in nowise[10] impaired his resources.

The youth, still the bearer of the colors, did not feel his idleness. He was deeply absorbed as a spectator. The crash and swing of the great drama made him lean forward,

---

7. **resmudged.** Covered again with the grime of smoke, dirt, and sweat
8. **jigging.** Moving with rapid and jerky motions
9. **tour after a bandage.** Journey in search of a bandage (for his injured hand)
10. **nowise.** No way

Words For Everyday Use		
ban • dy (ban´dē) *vt.*, toss from side to side carelessly	**por • ten • tous** (pôr ten´təs) *adj.*, grave or serious
ex • er • tion (eg zər´shən) *n.*, fatiguing effort	**ex • ple • tive** (ek´splə tiv) *n.*, exclamatory word or phrase, especially a swear or a curse

intent-eyed, his face working in small contortions. Sometimes he prattled,[11] words coming unconsciously from him in grotesque exclamations. He did not know that he breathed; that the flag hung silently over him, so absorbed was he.

A <u>formidable</u> line of the enemy came within dangerous range. They could be seen plainly—tall, gaunt men with excited faces running with long strides toward a wandering fence.

► What do the men of the regiment no longer need before they attack?

At sight of this danger the men suddenly ceased their cursing monotone. There was an instant of strained silence before they threw up their rifles and fired a plumping volley at the foes. There had been no order given; the men, upon recognizing the <u>menace</u>, had immediately let drive their flock[12] of bullets without waiting for word of command.

But the enemy were quick to gain the protection of the wandering line of fence. They slid down behind it with remarkable <u>celerity</u>, and from this position they began briskly to slice up the blue men.

These latter braced their energies for a great struggle. Often, white clinched[13] teeth shone from the dusky faces. Many heads surged to and fro, floating upon a pale sea of smoke. Those behind the fence frequently shouted and yelped in taunts and gibelike[14] cries, but the regiment main-

► On what are the men of the regiment intent? What makes their situation "thrice bitter"?

tained a stressed silence. Perhaps, at this new assault the men recalled the fact that they had been named mud diggers, and it made their situation thrice[15] bitter. They were breathlessly intent upon keeping the ground and thrusting away the rejoicing body of the enemy. They fought swiftly and with a despairing savageness <u>denoted</u> in their expressions.

► What does the youth see as his revenge upon the officer who insulted his regiment?

The youth had resolved not to budge whatever should happen. Some arrows of scorn that had buried themselves in his heart had generated strange and unspeakable hatred. It was clear to him that his final and absolute revenge was to be achieved by his dead body lying, torn and gluttering,[16] upon the field. This was to be a <u>poignant</u> retaliation upon

---

11. **prattled.** Made meaningless sounds suggestive of children's chatter
12. **flock.** Large number
13. **clinched.** Clenched, or closed tightly
14. **gibelike.** Taunting, mocking
15. **thrice.** Three times as
16. **gluttering.** Guttering, or dripping fluid as a candle does wax

---

Words For Everyday Use

for • mi • da • ble (fôr′mə də bəl) adj., causing fear, dread, or apprehension
men • ace (me′nəs) n., threat, danger
ce • ler • i • ty (sə ler′ə tē) n., quickness of motion or action
de • note (di nōt′) vt., make known
poi • gnant (pôi′nyənt) adj., designed to make an impression

the officer who had said "mule drivers," and later "mud diggers," for in all the wild graspings of his mind for a unit responsible for his sufferings and commotions he always seized upon the man who had dubbed him wrongly. And it was his idea, vaguely formulated, that his corpse would be for those eyes a great and salt[17]reproach.

◄ What effect does the youth believe his corpse would have on the officer?

The regiment bled extravagantly. Grunting bundles of blue began to drop. The orderly sergeant[18] of the youth's company was shot through the cheeks. Its supports being injured, his jaw hung afar down, disclosing in the wide cavern of his mouth a pulsing mass of blood and teeth. And with it all he made attempts to cry out. In his <u>endeavor</u> there was a dreadful earnestness, as if he conceived that one great shriek would make him well.

◄ What happens to the orderly sergeant?

The youth saw him presently go rearward. His strength seemed in nowise impaired. He ran swiftly, casting wild glances for <u>succor</u>.

Others fell down about the feet of their companions. Some of the wounded crawled out and away, but many lay still, their bodies twisted into impossible shapes.

The youth looked once for his friend. He saw a vehement young man, powder-smeared and frowzled,[19] whom he knew to be him. The lieutenant, also, was <u>unscathed</u> in his position at the rear. He had continued to curse, but it was now with the air of a man who was using his last box of oaths.

For the fire of the regiment had begun to <u>wane</u> and drip. The <u>robust</u> voice, that had come strangely from the thin ranks, was growing rapidly weak.

◄ What is happening to the youth's regiment?

---

17. **salt.** Bitter
18. **orderly sergeant.** Sergeant in charge of carrying messages for superior officers
19. **frowzled.** Having a sloppy, uncared for appearance

Words For Everyday Use

en • deav • or (en de´vər) *n.*, serious determined effort
suc • cor (sə´kər) *n.*, relief, help, aid
un • scathed (ən skāthd´) *adj.*, wholly unharmed; not injured

wane (wān) *vi.*, decrease in size, extent, or degree
ro • bust (rō bəst´) *adj.*, having or showing power, strength, or firmness; healthy

Chapter 23

▶ What is the regiment ordered to do? According to the youth, why is this a good decision?

The colonel came running along back of the line. There were other officers following him. "We must charge 'm!" they shouted. "We must charge 'm!" they cried with resentful voices, as if anticipating a rebellion against this plan by the men.

The youth, upon hearing the shouts, began to study the distance between him and the enemy. He made vague calculations. He saw that to be firm soldiers they must go forward. It would be death to stay in the present place, and with all the circumstances to go backward would <u>exalt</u> too many others. Their hope was to push the <u>galling</u> foes away from the fence.

▶ What is the youth surprised to see in his regiment? To what is their eagerness to move forward compared?

He expected that his companions, weary and stiffened, would have to be driven to this assault, but as he turned toward them he perceived with a certain surprise that they were giving quick and unqualified expressions of assent. There was an ominous, clanging <u>overture</u> to the charge when the shafts of the bayonets rattled upon the rifle barrels.[1] At the yelled words of command the soldiers sprang forward in eager leaps. There was new and unexpected force in the movement of the regiment. A knowledge of its faded and jaded condition made the charge appear like a <u>paroxysm</u>, a display of the strength that comes before a final feebleness. The men scampered in insane fever of haste, racing as if to achieve a sudden success before an exhilarating fluid should leave them. It was a blind and despairing rush by the collection of men in dusty and tattered blue, over a green sward[2] and under a sapphire sky, toward a fence, dimly outlined in smoke, from behind which spluttered the fierce rifles of enemies.

▶ What does the youth do during the charge?

The youth kept the bright colors to the front. He was waving his free arm in furious circles, the while shrieking mad calls and appeals, urging on those that did not need to be urged, for it seemed that the mob of blue men hurling them-

---

1. **shafts . . . barrels.** Blades like knives rattle against the parts of the guns that discharge, to which they are attached.
2. **sward.** Grass-covered land

Words For Everyday Use

ex • alt (eg zôlt´) vt., raise in rank, power, or character

gall • ing (gô´liŋ) adj., especially irritating

o • ver • ture (ō və(r)´chur) n., orchestral introduction to a musical dramatic work

par • ox • ysm (par´ək si zəm) n., fit, attack, or sudden increase or recurrence of symptoms

selves on the dangerous group of rifles were again grown suddenly wild with an enthusiasm of unselfishness. From the many firings started toward them, it looked as if they would merely succeed in making a great sprinkling of corpses on the grass between their former position and the fence. But they were in a state of frenzy, perhaps because of forgotten <u>vanities</u>, and it made an exhibition of sublime recklessness. There was no obvious questioning, nor figurings, nor diagrams.[3] There was, apparently, no considered loopholes. It appeared that the swift wings of their desires would have shattered against the iron gates of the impossible.

◀ What does it appear will happen to the regiment?

◀ What have the men forgotten? In what way don't they look at their situation?

He himself felt the daring spirit of a savage, religion-mad. He was capable of profound sacrifices, a tremendous death. He had not time for <u>dissections</u>, but he knew that he thought of the bullets only as things that could prevent him from reaching the place of his endeavor. There were subtle flashings of joy within him that thus should be his mind.

◀ What is the youth's state of mind? What is he capable of doing?

He strained all his strength. His eyesight was shaken and dazzled by the tension of thought and muscle. He did not see anything excepting the mist of smoke gashed by the little knives of fire, but he knew that in it lay the aged fence of a vanished farmer protecting the snuggled bodies of the gray men.

As he ran a thought of the shock of contact gleamed in his mind. He expected a great concussion when the two bodies of troops crashed together. This became a part of his wild battle madness. He could feel the onward swing of the regiment about him and he conceived of a thunderous, crushing blow that would prostrate the resistance and spread <u>consternation</u> and amazement for miles. The flying regiment was going to have a catapultian[4] effect. This dream made him run faster among his comrades, who were giving vent[5] to hoarse and frantic cheers.

◀ What does the youth imagine will happen when his regiment meets the enemy forces?

But presently he could see that many of the men in gray did not intend to <u>abide</u> the blow. The smoke, rolling, disclosed men who ran, their faces still turned. These grew to a

◀ What do the enemy troops do to contradict what the youth had imagined?

---

3. **There . . . diagrams.** The soldiers did not question or analyze what they were doing.
4. **catapultian.** Like a catapult, or device that hurls missiles
5. **giving vent.** Letting forth

Words For Everyday Use

van • i • ty (va nə′tē) *n.*, something that is vain, empty, or valueless

dis • sec • tion (di sek′shən) *n.*, act or process of analyzing and interpreting something in detail

con • ster • na • tion (kən(t) stər na′shən) *n.*, amazement or dismay that hinders or throws into confusion

abide (ə bīd′) *vt.*, bear patiently; accept without objection

crowd, who retired stubbornly. Individuals wheeled frequently to send a bullet at the blue wave.

But at one part of the line there was a grim and <u>obdurate</u> group that made no movement. They were settled firmly down behind posts and rails. A flag, ruffled and fierce, waved over them and their rifles dinned fiercely.

The blue whirl of men got very near, until it seemed that in truth there would be a close and frightful scuffle. There was an expressed disdain in the opposition of the little group, that changed the meaning of the cheers of the men in blue. They became yells of wrath, directed, personal. The cries of the two parties were now in sound an interchange of scathing insults.

They in blue showed their teeth; their eyes shone all white. They launched themselves as at the throats of those who stood resisting. The space between dwindled to an insignificant distance.

▶ What does the youth wish to do?

The youth had centered the gaze of his soul upon that other flag. Its possession would be high pride. It would express bloody minglings, near blows. He had a gigantic hatred for those who made great difficulties and complications. They caused it to be as a craved treasure of mythology, hung amid tasks and <u>contrivances</u> of danger.

▶ What does the youth do to achieve his goal?

He plunged like a mad horse at it. He was resolved it should not escape if wild blows and darings of blows could seize it. His own emblem, quivering and aflare, was winging toward the other. It seemed there would shortly be an encounter of strange beaks and claws, as of eagles.[6]

The swirling body of blue men came to a sudden halt at close and disastrous range and roared a swift volley. The group in gray was split and broken by this fire, but its <u>riddled</u> body still fought. The men in blue yelled again and rushed in upon it.

The youth, in his leapings, saw, as through a mist, a picture of four or five men stretched upon the ground or writhing upon their knees with bowed heads as if they had been stricken by bolts from the sky. Tottering among them was the rival color bearer, whom the youth saw had been bitten <u>vitally</u> by the bullets of the last formidable volley. He per-

▶ What has happened to the color bearer who carries the enemy's flag?

---

6. **strange beaks . . . eagles.** Refers to the animals depicted on the flags

---

Words For Everyday Use

ob • du • rate (əbˊdə rət) *adj.,* stubbornly persistent in wrongdoing

con • triv • ance (kən trīˊvən(t)s) *n.,* artificial arrangement or development

rid • dled (ridˊləd) *adj.,* pierced with many holes

vi • tal • ly (vīˊtˊl ē) *adv.,* in a manner that is destructive to life; mortally; fatally

ceived this man fighting a last struggle, the struggle of one whose legs are grasped by demons. It was a ghastly battle. Over his face was the bleach of death, but set upon it was the dark and hard lines of desperate purpose. With this terrible grin of resolution he hugged his precious flag to him and was stumbling and staggering in his design to go the way that led to safety for it.

But his wounds always made it seem that his feet were retarded, held, and he fought a grim fight, as with invisible ghouls[7] fastened greedily upon his limbs. Those in advance of the scampering blue men, howling cheers, leaped at the fence. The despair of the lost was in his eyes as he glanced back at them.

The youth's friend went over the obstruction in a tumbling heap and sprang at the flag as a panther at prey. He pulled at it and, wrenching it free, swung up its red brilliancy with a mad cry of exultation even as the color bearer, gasping, lurched over in a final <u>throe</u> and, stiffening convulsively, turned his dead face to the ground. There was much blood upon the grass blades.

◀ What does the youth's friend do?

At the place of success there began more wild clamorings of cheers. The men gesticulated and bellowed in an ecstasy. When they spoke it was as if they considered their listener to be a mile away. What hats and caps were left to them they often slung[8] high in the air.

◀ What is the result of the battle?

At one part of the line four men had been swooped upon, and they now sat as prisoners. Some blue men were about them in an eager and curious circle. The soldiers had trapped strange birds, and there was an examination. A flurry of fast questions was in the air.

◀ How many men have been captured?

One of the prisoners was nursing a superficial wound in the foot. He cuddled it, baby-wise,[9] but he looked up from it often to curse with an astonishing <u>utter</u> abandon straight at the noses of his captors. He <u>consigned</u> them to red regions;[10] he called upon the <u>pestilential</u> wrath of strange gods. And with it all he was singularly free from recognition of the finer points of the conduct of prisoners of war. It was as if a

---

7. **ghouls.** Legendary evil being that robs graves and feeds on the dead
8. **slung.** Thrown
9. **cuddled it baby-wise.** Held it as one cradles a baby
10. **red regions.** Hell

Words For Everyday Use

throe (thrō) *n.*, pang, spasm

ut • ter (ə´tər) *adj.*, carried to the utmost point or highest degree; total

con • sign (kən sīn´) *vt.*, give, transfer, or deliver into the hands or control of another; commit to a final destination or fate

pes • ti • len • tial (pes tə len(t)´shəl) *adj.*, deadly

clumsy clod had trod upon his toe and he conceived it to be his privilege, his duty, to use deep, resentful oaths.

Another, who was a boy in years, took his plight with great calmness and apparent good nature. He conversed with the men in blue, studying their faces with his bright and keen eyes. They spoke of battles and conditions. There was an acute interest in all their faces during this exchange of view points. It seemed a great satisfaction to hear voices from where all had been darkness and speculation.

The third captive sat with a <u>morose</u> <u>countenance</u>. He preserved a stoical and cold attitude. To all advances he made one reply without variation, "Ah, go t' hell!"

The last of the four was always silent and, for the most part, kept his face turned in unmolested directions. From the views the youth received he seemed to be in a state of absolute <u>dejection</u>. Shame was upon him, and with it profound regret that he was, perhaps, no more to be counted in the ranks of his fellows. The youth could detect no expression that would allow him to believe that the other was giving a thought to his narrowed future, the pictured dungeons, perhaps, and starvations and brutalities, <u>liable</u> to the imagination. All to be seen was shame for captivity and regret for the right to <u>antagonize</u>.

After the men had celebrated sufficiently they settled down behind the old rail fence, on the opposite side to the one from which their foes had been driven. A few shot <u>perfunctorily</u> at distant marks.

There was some long grass. The youth nestled in it and rested, making a convenient rail support the flag. His friend, jubilant and glorified, holding his treasure with vanity, came to him there. They sat side by side and congratulated each other.

► What is one boy's manner toward his captors? What does the regiment find satisfying?

► What does the youth think the fourth prisoner is feeling?

Words For Everyday Use

mo • rose (mə rōs´) *adj.,* marked by or expressive of gloom
coun • te • nance (kaun´t'n ən(t)s) *n.,* look, expression
de • jec • tion (di jek´shən) *n.,* lowness of spirits

li • a • ble (lī´bəl) *adj.,* exposed or subject to some usually adverse possibility or action
an • tag • o • nize (an ta´gə nīz) *vt.,* act in opposition to; provoke the hostility of
per • func • to • ri • ly (pər fəŋ(k)´tə rə lē) *adv.,* without interest or enthusiasm

Chapter 24

The roarings that had stretched in a long line of sound across the face of the forest began to grow <u>intermittent</u> and weaker. The <u>stentorian</u> speeches of the artillery continued in some distant encounter, but the crashes of the musketry had almost ceased. The youth and his friend of a sudden looked up, feeling a <u>deadened</u> form of distress at the waning of these noises, which had become a part of life. They could see changes going on among the troops. There were marchings this way and that way. A battery wheeled leisurely. On the crest of a small hill was the thick gleam of many departing muskets.

◀ How does the regiment feel when the musket fire ends? Why do the men feel this way?

The youth arose. "Well, what now, I wonder?" he said. By his tone he seemed to be preparing to resent some new monstrosity in the way of dins and smashes.[1] He shaded his eyes with his grimy hand and gazed over the field.

His friend also arose and stared. "I bet we're goin' t' git along out of this an' back over th' river," said he.

"Well, I swan!"[2] said the youth.

◀ What new orders do the men receive? How do they feel about this order?

They waited, watching. Within a little while the regiment received orders to retrace its way. The men got up grunting from the grass, regretting the soft repose. They jerked their stiffened legs, and stretched their arms over their heads. One man swore as he rubbed his eyes. They all groaned "O Lord!" They had as many objections to this change as they would have had to a proposal for a new battle.

They tramped slowly back over the field across which they had run in a mad scamper.

The regiment marched until it had joined its fellows. The reformed brigade, in column, aimed through a wood at the road. Directly they were in a mass of dust-covered troops, and were trudging along in a way parallel to the enemy's lines as these had been defined by the previous turmoil.

They passed within view of a stolid white house, and saw in front of it groups of their comrades lying in wait behind a neat breastwork.[3] A row of guns were booming at a distant

---

1. **dins and smashes.** Loud sounds and violent attacks or blows
2. **swan.** Declare, swear
3. **breastwork.** Temporary fortification, or trench-like defense

---

Words For Everyday Use

in • ter • mit • tent (in tər mi´t'nt) *adj.*, coming and going at intervals; not continuous

sten • to • ri • an (sten tôr´ē ən) *adj.*, extremely loud

dead • ened (de´d'nd) *adj.*, impaired in vigor or sensation

enemy. Shells thrown in reply were raising clouds of dust and splinters. Horsemen dashed along the line of intrenchments.

At this point of its march the division curved away from the field and went winding off in the direction of the river. When the significance of this movement had impressed itself upon the youth he turned his head and looked over his shoulder toward the trampled and debris-strewed ground. He breathed a breath of new satisfaction. He finally nudged his friend. "Well, it's all over," he said to him.

His friend gazed backward. "B'Gawd, it is," he assented. They <u>mused</u>.

For a time the youth was obliged to reflect in a puzzled and uncertain way. His mind was undergoing a subtle change. It took moments for it to cast off its battleful ways and resume its accustomed course of thought. Gradually his brain emerged from the clogged clouds, and at last he was enabled to more closely comprehend himself and circumstance.

He understood then that the existence of shot and counter-shot was in the past. He had dwelt in a land of strange, squalling upheavals and had come forth. He had been where there was red of blood and black of passion, and he was escaped. His first thoughts were given to rejoicings at this fact.

Later he began to study his deeds, his failures, and his achievements. Thus, fresh from scenes where many of his usual machines of reflection had been idle, from where he had proceeded sheeplike, he struggled to <u>marshal</u> all his acts.

At last they marched before him clearly. From this present view point he was enabled to look upon them in spectator fashion and to criticize them with some correctness, for his new condition had already defeated certain sympathies.

Regarding his procession of memory he felt gleeful and unregretting, for in it his public deeds were paraded in great and shining <u>prominence</u>. Those performances which had been witnessed by his fellows marched now in wide purple and gold,[4] having various <u>deflections</u>. They went gayly with

---

4. **purple and gold.** Purple is a color traditionally associated with royalty, and the color gold is associated with wealth.

► Where does the regiment head? What does heading in this direction mean for the regiment?

► What transformation does the youth's mind undergo?

► About what does the youth begin to think?

► How does the youth feel about his memories of his public actions?

Words For Everyday Use

muse (myo͞oz) *vi.*, become absorbed in thought; turn something over in the mind meditatively
mar • shal (mär´shəl) *vt.*, place in proper rank or position

prom • i • nence (prä´mə nən(t)s) *n.*, greatness, distinction, importance
de • flec • tion (di flek´shən) *n.*, turning aside or off course

music. It was pleasure to watch these things. He spent delightful minutes viewing the <u>gilded</u> images of memory.

He saw that he was good. He recalled with a thrill of joy the respectful comments of his fellows upon his conduct.

Nevertheless, the ghost of his flight from the first engagement appeared to him and danced. There were small shoutings in his brain about these matters. For a moment he blushed, and the light of his soul flickered with shame.

◄ What shameful thing does the youth remember?

A <u>specter</u> of reproach came to him. There loomed the <u>dogging</u> memory of the tattered soldier—he who, gored by bullets and faint for blood, had fretted concerning an imagined wound in another; he who had loaned his last of strength and intellect for the tall soldier; he who, blind with weariness and pain, had been deserted in the field.

◄ What "specter of reproach" appears in the youth's mind? What good qualities does the youth see in this person? What does he realize about his actions toward this person?

For an instant a wretched chill of sweat was upon him at the thought that he might be detected in the thing. As he stood persistently before his vision, he gave vent to a cry of sharp irritation and agony.

His friend turned. "What's the matter, Henry?" he demanded. The youth's reply was an outburst of crimson oaths.

As he marched along the little branch-hung roadway among his prattling companions this vision of cruelty brooded over him. It clung near him always and darkened his view of these deeds in purple and gold. Whichever way his thoughts turned they were followed by the somber phantom of the desertion in the fields. He looked stealthily at his companions, feeling sure that they must <u>discern</u> in his face evidences of this pursuit. But they were plodding in ragged <u>array</u>, discussing with quick tongues the accomplishments of the late battle.

◄ What effect does the youth's memory of his cruelty to the tattered soldier have on his memories of the good deeds he performed?

"Oh, if a man should come up an' ask me, I'd say we got a dum good lickin'."

"Lickin'—in yer eye! We ain't licked, sonny. We're goin' down here aways, swing aroun', an' come in behint 'em."

"Oh, hush, with your comin' in behint 'em. I've seen all 'a that I wanta. Don't tell me about comin' in behint—"

"Bill Smithers, he ses he'd rather been in ten hundred battles than been in that heluva hospital. He ses they got

---

Words For Everyday Use

gild • ed (gil´dəd) *adj.*, overlaid with or as if with gold; given an attractive but sometimes deceptive appearance
spec • ter (spek´tər) *n.*, ghost; something that haunts the mind
dog • ging (dôg´iŋ) *adj.*, worrying, pursuing as a dog does prey
dis • cern (di sərn´) *vt.*, detect with the eyes
ar • ray (ə rā´) *n.*, grouping or arrangement

shootin' in th' night-time, an' shells dropped plum[5] among 'em in th' hospital. He ses sech hollerin' he never see."

"Hasbrouck? He's th' best off'cer in this here reg'ment. He's a whale."[6]

"Didn't I tell yeh we'd come aroun' in behint 'em? Didn't I tell yeh so? We—"

"Oh, shet yeh mouth!"

For a time this pursuing recollection of the tattered man took all elation from the youth's veins. He saw his vivid error, and he was afraid that it would stand before him all his life. He took no share in the chatter of his comrades, nor did he look at them or know them, save when he felt sudden suspicion that they were seeing his thoughts and scrutinizing each detail of the scene with the tattered soldier.

Yet gradually he <u>mustered</u> force to put the sin at a distance. And at last his eyes seemed to open to some new ways. He found that he could look back upon the <u>brass</u> and <u>bombast</u> of his earlier gospels and see them truly. He was gleeful when he discovered that he now despised them.

With this conviction came a store of assurance. He felt a quiet manhood, nonassertive but of sturdy and strong blood. He knew that he would no more <u>quail</u> before his guides wherever they should point. He had been to touch the great death, and found that, after all, it was but the great death. He was a man.

So it came to pass that as he trudged from the place of blood and <u>wrath</u> his soul changed. He came from hot plowshares[7] to <u>prospects</u> of clover[8] tranquility, and it was as if hot plowshares were not. Scars faded as flowers.

It rained. The procession of weary soldiers became a <u>bedraggled</u> train, despondent and muttering, marching with churning[9] effort in a trough of liquid brown mud under a low, wretched sky. Yet the youth smiled, for he saw that the world was a world for him, though many discovered it to be

► What does the youth gather force to do? What does he think about the beliefs he held before going into battle?

► What does the youth feel growing within him? What has the youth become?

---

5. **plum.** Plumb, directly, squarely
6. **whale.** Great fellow
7. **hot plowshares.** *Plowshare*—part of a plow that cuts a furrow or groove in the ground. Here, implies weapons and alludes to a line from the Bible: "They shall beat their swords into plowshares"
8. **prospects of clover.** A pleasant and peaceful place
9. **churning.** Difficult (like moving through a thick, heavy substance)

Words For Everyday Use

mus • ter (məs´tər) *vt.,* cause to gather
brass (bras) *n.,* bold self-assurance
bom • bast (bəm´bast) *n.,* pretentious inflated speech or writing
quail (kwā(ə)l) *vi.,* draw back in dread or terror; cower

wrath (rath) *n.,* strong vengeful anger
pros • pect (prä´spekt) *n.,* place that commands an extensive view; mental picture of something to come
be • drag • gled (bi dra´gəld) *adj.,* soiled and stained by or as if by trailing in mud

made of oaths and walking sticks. He had rid himself of the red sickness of battle. The <u>sultry</u> nightmare was in the past. He had been an animal blistered and sweating in the heat and pain of war. He turned now with a lover's thirst to images of tranquil skies, fresh meadows, cool brooks—an existence of soft and eternal peace.

Over the river a golden ray of sun came through the hosts of <u>leaden</u> rain clouds.

◄ What is in the past for the youth? For what is he eager now?

Words For Everyday Use	sul • try (səl´trē) *adj.*, hot with passion or anger lead • en (le´d'n) *adj.*, of the color of lead, or dull gray; heavy

Respond to the Selection

Describe a time when someone belittled you for some reason. How did you feel? How did you react? Did you accept the criticism, or did you struggle to prove the person who belittled you wrong?

Investigate, Inquire, and Imagine

Recall: GATHERING FACTS

1a. In Chapter 21, what do the veteran soldiers say when Henry's (the youth's) regiment returns from battle? What does Henry realize when he looks back from safety at the battleground? What does an officer say to criticize Henry's regiment? What happens to make Henry and Wilson (his friend) feel better about themselves at the end of Chapter 21?

2a. In Chapter 22, when Henry's regiment is engaged in battle again, what does he believe will be a "great and salt" reproach on the officer who called them mule drivers and mud diggers? What attitude does Henry have toward danger and death in the charge that takes place in Chapter 23? What does Wilson accomplish in this charge? What does Henry's regiment capture?

3a. In Chapter 24, when Henry has time to reflect on his actions, how does he feel about his public actions? What does he remember about his private actions? What thought haunts him? What does Henry "muster force" to do? How does he now feel about his earlier boasts about war? What does the narrator say has happened to Henry's soul?

Interpret: FINDING MEANING

1b. Look back to the end of Chapter 20, and explain whether you expected Henry's regiment to be treated this way on their return. What do you think the author might be indicating about heroism? To what extent is public recognition important in making someone feel heroic? Do you think public recognition is important in making someone a hero? Explain.

2b. How is Henry beginning to feel about himself as a soldier? Explain whether Henry has earned the right to think of himself in this way. Explain why this charge can be considered a victory, while the previous one could not.

3b. What does Henry now recognize about the character of the tattered man? In Chapter 20, Crane wrote of Henry's regiment, "And they were men." At the end of this novel, Crane repeats this ideas but focuses specifically on Henry, writing "He was a man." Why is Henry more of an adult now than he was at the end of Chapter 20?

Analyze: TAKING THINGS APART

4a. Identify some of the different ideas about what it means to be a hero presented not only in Chapters 21–24, but in the novel as a whole. What vision of heroism do you think was portrayed at the novel's end? What did you learn about what it means to be a hero, both publicly and privately?

Synthesize: BRINGING THINGS TOGETHER

4b. This novel is as much about growing up as it is about heroism. What do these two central ideas, heroism and growing up, have to do with each other? Explore how you think these ideas are related.

Evaluate: MAKING JUDGMENTS

5a. Which of Henry's experiences in the war would you say has had the most effect on shaping him as a person? Explain why this event had such a strong effect on Henry using evidence from the text to support your opinion.

Extend: CONNECTING IDEAS

5b. If you lived in Henry's time, would you want to get to know him? Summarize how your feelings about Henry have changed over the course of the novel. When did you like him the most? When did you like him the least? Do you respect him? In what ways are you like him and in what ways are you different from him?

Understanding Literature

Character. A **character** is a person or animal who takes part in the action of a literary work. A **one-dimensional character, flat character,** or **caricature** is one who exhibits a single quality. A **three-dimensional, full,** or **rounded character** is one who seems to have all the complexities of an actual human being. In what way would you classify Henry Fleming? In what way would you classify the tattered man? Explain your choices.

Symbol and Cliché. A **symbol** is a thing that stands for or represents both itself and something else. A **cliché** is an overused expression such as *happy as a lark* or *time is money*. A symbol that has now become so common it is considered a cliché closes this novel. What is this symbol and what does it represent? Did you find this line effective? Do you think Crane's original audience would have found it effective?

Metaphor. A **metaphor** is a figure of speech in which one thing is written about as if it were another. This figure of speech invites the reader or listener to make a comparison between the two things. Explain what is being compared in the following lines: "It appeared that the swift wings of their desires would have shattered against the iron gates of the impossible." In what way are the things being compared alike?

Plot Analysis of *The Red Badge of Courage*

The following diagram, known as Freytag's pyramid, illustrates the main plot of *The Red Badge of Courage*. For definitions and more information on the parts of a plot illustrated below, see the Handbook of Literary Terms on page 181.

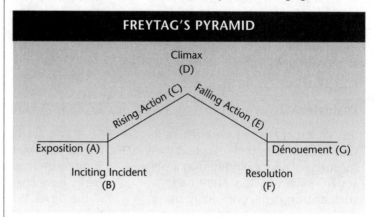

FREYTAG'S PYRAMID

Climax (D)

Rising Action (C)

Falling Action (E)

Exposition (A)

Inciting Incident (B)

Dénouement (G)

Resolution (F)

The parts of a plot are as follows:

The **exposition** is the part of a plot that provides background information about the characters, setting, or conflict.

The **inciting incident** is the event that introduces the central conflict.

The **rising action,** or complication, develops the conflict to a high point of intensity.

The **climax** is the high point of interest or suspense in the story.

The **falling action** is all the events that follow the climax.

The **resolution** is the point at which the central conflict is ended, or resolved.

The **dénouement** is any material that follows the resolution and that ties up loose ends.

Exposition (A)

The opening chapters of this novel introduce the main characters and the setting. The reader is introduced to Henry Fleming (also called "the youth") who is inexperienced in battle although he has always dreamed of war as a romantic struggle. The reader also meets some of his fellow soldiers in the 304th regiment, Jim Conklin (also called "the tall soldier") and Wilson ("the loud soldier"). In a flashback, Henry remembers how he enlisted in the war despite his mother's wishes. He also remembers her reaction to hearing that he had enlisted and her advice—not to think he can fight the whole rebel army but to do what is right, to send her his socks to be darned, and to steer clear of bad company. After he enlists, Henry marches through Washington, but then settles down into camp where he spends some boring months marching, drilling (training), and being reviewed.

Inciting Incident (B)

Jim Conklin spreads the news that the regiment will be moving and that the new recruits will soon take part in battle. This news fills Henry with self-doubt; he wonders whether he will have the courage to stand and fight or whether he will run. He asks his fellow soldiers, Jim Conklin and Wilson, if they share his fears but they seem mostly confident that they will perform well in battle, making Henry feel dejected and alone. Although the 304th regiment is not sent to battle the next day, Jim's gossip is not proved to be entirely baseless. Soon, the 304th regiment is marched to the field of battle. Just before the first fight, Henry's friend Wilson (the loud soldier) admits that he fears that he will die in the skirmish about to take place. The regiment sees their first corpse, and they witness a regiment of men fleeing in terror to the mockery of the veteran troops. Henry is filled with fear when he sees the soldiers fleeing, sensing that he too will surely follow their lead if the enemy is as terrifying as they seem to be. In the first skirmish, the soldiers of the 304th fight and Henry experiences the physical discomfort of the smoke, heat, and toil of battle. The 304th regiment drives back the enemy only to realize that this has been the first fight of many, and that the battle is unfolding all about them.

Rising Action (C)

Henry is exhausted and when the enemy charges again feels that they are unstoppable. Men from the 304th begin to flee. In a moment of panic, certain that they will all be killed, Henry, too, drops his rifle and runs from battle. He soon learns, however, that the Union forces were not defeated or killed. Instead, they have held and thrown back the enemy forces. Henry is filled with mixed emotions about what he has done. He feels shame and yet he tries to justify his actions to himself. Turning to a calm and beautiful spot in the wood for relief from the scenes of battle, Henry is horrified to discover the decaying corpse of a soldier in a chapel-like clearing in the woods. Once again, Henry flees in terror of death.

Climax (D)

Henry moves again toward the roar and clash of battle, fascinated as much as terrified by it. On a road, he meets up with a group of wounded soldiers; many of this group are maimed horribly, including a "spectral soldier" who appears to be about to die. Henry wishes that he too was wounded, that he had a "red badge of courage" which could help soothe his own shame. One of the wounded men, described as a "tattered soldier," tries to befriend Henry, but then asks him where he has been injured. The question fills Henry with shame and panic, and he wanders away from the tattered soldier. Henry then realizes that the "spectral soldier" who is so terribly injured is none other than his companion Jim Conklin, the tall soldier. Henry is filled with grief and rushes to take care of his friend. Henry is rejoined by the tattered soldier and the two move Jim into a field, away from the heavily-traveled road. Jim begins to behave strangely and takes off running through the field. He comes to a particular spot and then begins to convulse and die as Henry and the tattered soldier watch helpless and spellbound in horror. Henry is filled with the urge to make a speech expressing his emotion but can only shake his fist in helpless rage. Henry's new companion, the tattered man, announces that they should move on, saying that he himself isn't feeling well. Henry notices that the tattered soldier is beginning to look blue and wobbly. The tattered man says he cannot die yet because he has responsibilities—he is the father of two children. The tattered man again asks Henry about his own supposed injuries, expressing concern over them and reawakening Henry's feeling of shame. The tattered man begins to behave strangely, calling Henry by the name of one of his old friends. Henry bids the tattered soldier good-bye in a "hard" voice, and leaves the helpless, dying soldier alone wandering in the field.

Falling Action (E)

Henry witnesses a regiment of men fleeing in great panic from the enemy. Henry is granted his wish for a wound when he tries to stop one of the fleeing soldiers to ask him what happened. The terrified soldier bashes Henry over the head with his gun. Henry wanders injured and disoriented until he is helped by a soldier with a cheery voice who leads him back to his regiment. There, Henry is greeted by his friend Wilson (the loud soldier). Henry lies to his friend and to the corporal of the regiment, saying he was separated from the regiment, had fought with other regiments, and had been shot in the head. Wilson cares for Henry kindly and reveals that he has become less of a braggart and more of a friend.

Resolution (F)

The next morning, Henry and the 304th regiment return to the battlefield, where Henry surprises both himself and the other men by shooting at the enemy long after they have retreated. The regiment is then asked to perform a dangerous charge by officers who doubt their abilities, calling them mule drivers, and doubt that many of them will survive. Henry and Wilson behave courageously and heroically in the charge, and Henry carries the regiment's flag after the color-bearer is killed. Although the regiment's charge falls short of success and the regiment is labeled as mud diggers, an officer singles out Henry and Wilson for praise. In the next skirmish, Henry fights fiercely driven by the desire to avenge himself upon the officer who labeled them as mud diggers by proving his valor. Wilson captures the enemy's flag, and the regiment captures four enemy soldiers. The regiment celebrates their victory.

Dénouement (G)

Henry and the other soldiers march back to camp from the field of battle, and Henry has some time to think about his experiences and actions and to assess them. He remembers his "public actions" in battle with pride, but he thinks back on his hidden, secret actions—his running from battle and his desertion of the tattered soldier—with shame. The memory of abandoning the tattered soldier is particularly haunting. Henry tries to reconcile his conflicting feelings and put them into perspective. He realizes he must live with all his actions, both praiseworthy and blameworthy, and feels that he has grown. He looks back upon his earlier beliefs about war and death as pompous. He looks forward to a peaceful life outside of battle.

Creative Writing Activities

Creative Writing Activity A: Personal Essay about Growing Up

What experience in your own life do you see as most important on your road from childhood to adulthood? What have you done or what has happened to you to make you feel that you are growing up? What do you think about this event in your life? In what way has it changed you? Freewrite your responses to these questions. Then, work with the response that interests you most and expand it into an essay about an experience that helped you to grow up. Reflect on both sides of growing up—what you lose as well as what you gain.

Creative Writing Activity B: Exploring Other Points of View

The Red Badge of Courage focuses on Henry Fleming's point of view and his experiences. The novel also includes other characters with distinct personalities. How might some of these characters regard Henry's actions or the same events he witnesses? Choose a brief scene from the story and retell it from another character's point of view. You may choose a topic from the list that follows, or choose another scene and character that capture your imagination. Before writing, create a Venn diagram to compare and contrast Henry's point of view with the thoughts and feelings you imagine your chosen character must be experiencing. Remember to base your perceptions of the chosen character's thoughts and feelings on what Crane reveals about that character in the novel. For example, you probably wouldn't want to describe Henry's mother as being eager to see her son go off to battle. Use your Venn diagram as a source of ideas when rewriting a few paragraphs of a scene from another character's point of view.

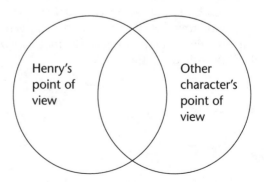

Henry's point of view

Other character's point of view

Possible Topics:

- Retell the scene when Wilson admits he fears that he will die in battle (in Chapter 3), from Wilson's point of view
- Retell the scene (from Chapter 10) in which Henry leaves the tattered man alone to die, from the tattered man's point of view
- Retell the scene (in Chapter 13) in which Henry returns to the camp, says he was shot in the head, and is cared for by Wilson, from Wilson's point of view

Creative Writing Activity C: Realistic Descriptions

Crane's writing is vivid and realistic. He is able to capture both beautiful and horrible images that seem true to life. Almost in the same breath, he describes a natural setting and a corpse:

> At length he reached a place where the high, arching boughs made a chapel. He softly pushed the green doors aside and entered. Pine needles were a gentle brown carpet. There was a religious half light. . . .
>
> . . . The corpse was dressed in a uniform that once had been blue, but was now faded to a melancholy shade of green. The eyes, staring at the youth, had changed to the dull hue to be seen on the side of a dead fish. The mouth was open. Its red had changed to an appalling yellow. Over the gray skin of the face ran little ants. One was trundling some sort of bundle along the upper lip.

Crane makes these scenes realistic by using sensory details—images of things that can be seen, heard, touched, tasted, or smelled. You can see and feel the gentle brown carpet of pine needles. You can see and feel the ant trundling a bundle across a lip. Write your own realistic descriptive paragraphs. One should describe something beautiful and one should describe something that is horrible, frightening, or ugly. After you decide on a topic for each paragraph, fill out two sensory detail charts, listing details that you can see, hear, feel, touch, or taste for each topic. Use the charts as a

Sensory Detail Chart				
Sight	Hearing	Touch	Taste	Smell

Critical Writing Activities

The following topics are suitable for short critical essays on *The Red Badge of Courage.* An essay written on one of these topics should begin with an introductory paragraph that states the thesis, or main idea, of the essay. The introductory paragraph should be followed by several paragraphs that support the thesis, using examples from the novel. The essay should conclude with a paragraph that summarizes the points made in the body of the essay and that reinforces the thesis.

Critical Writing Activity A: Growing Up—A Different Type of Battle

Think about what the phrase *growing up* means to you and freewrite your ideas about the following questions: What activities or events do you associate with growing up? Do you think of growing up as a gradual activity or a sudden one? Are there any situations in which a person is forced to grow up suddenly? What mental or emotional changes does growing up cause in a person?

Use the ideas you have gathered to help you develop a thesis in response to the following group of questions: In what way does Henry Fleming's character grow up over the course of the novel? How is he different at the novel's end than he was at its beginning? What has he left behind and what has he gained? What has inspired or forced Henry to grow up?

After you have developed an opinion about the topic of growing up in *The Red Badge of Courage,* state it in a thesis sentence, introduced in your first paragraph. Support your thesis with clearly organized paragraphs and evidence from the text. Form a conclusion in your final paragraph.

Critical Writing Activity B: Comparing and Contrasting War Literature

Compare and contrast the way Crane presents war in *The Red Badge of Courage* with the way another work of literature or a film presents war. The other work you choose does not have to be set in the Civil War. For example, you might choose to compare *The Red Badge of Courage* to a film you have seen about World War II or the Vietnam War. Remember, however, that you should choose the other work wisely; there should be a basis for comparison, or a reason why the reader would find the comparison and contrast interesting.

You might start by identifying the message, if any, each work conveys about war and the way in which war is described in each work. Organize your thoughts into a Venn diagram, where you include similarities in the place where the circles join and differences outside the intersection of circles (see the sample Venn diagram below). Use the ideas in the Venn diagram as inspiration for developing the thesis you will express in your introductory paragraph. Remember to support your thesis with evidence from both works in the body of your essay, and write a final paragraph concluding your comparison of the two.

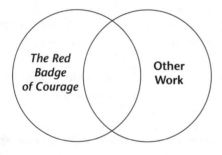

Projects

Project A: Examining History—The Civil War

Work in small groups of three to four students to prepare an oral report on some aspect of the American Civil War. Your group should research your topic in encyclopedias (either print or electronic versions), in online articles on the Internet, and in books or periodicals. Take notes on your findings, and gather any multimedia resources you wish to present, such as reproductions of photographs, maps, or recordings of songs. Your group should then prepare an outline of the information it plans to share with the rest of the class. Your presentation should be no more than five to seven minutes in length. Practice your presentation with your group so that it is as polished as possible. Remember to look at your audience when speaking and to vary your tone to keep the audience's interest. The key to success in this presentation is to choose a topic that is narrow enough for you to explore. Remember that whole books have been written on the Civil War so you cannot cover all of it. Here are some possible topics.

- Stephen Crane mentions Union soldiers wearing blue and Confederate soldiers wearing gray. Is this all there was to a soldier's uniform? What different types of uniforms did soldiers from both sides wear?
- Focus on life in camp instead of life during the battle. What was a day in the life of a typical soldier like? What did soldiers do at camp? What did they eat? What did they do for entertainment?
- Crane mentions maimed soldiers and amputation. What were medical conditions like in the Civil War? What problems did Civil War doctors face and how did they treat the wounded?
- Choose a major battle of the Civil War and explain what happened and its importance in the war as a whole. Possible choices include the First Battle of Bull Run, the Second Battle of Bull Run, the Battle of Chancellorsville, the Battle of Gettysburg, or the Battle of the Wilderness. You might also wish to explore Sherman's march to the sea.
- Crane makes no mention of the racial issues behind the Civil War. What role did African Americans play as soldiers in the war, either for Union forces or Confederate forces?

Project B: Portraying War in Art

The Civil War was one of the first wars to be documented in photographs. Photography was developed just before the Civil War was fought, and late nineteenth-century photographers captured powerful images of soldiers and battlefields, allowing the average person to see realistic images of war for the first time. Prepare a brief portfolio of images of war expressed visually in painting, sculpture, sketches, drawings, or photographs. Your portfolio should include at least one reproduction of a photograph taken during the Civil War. You can find such photos in your school or local library and photocopy them or you may print images you find on the Internet. As a comparison, find at least one image of war from an earlier period. You might, for example, try to find an image of war in ancient Greek or Roman art existing in sculptures or on vases to contrast the heroic images of war in Henry's imagination with the more realistic photographs. You might also wish to include your own artistic representations of war in a sketch, drawing, or painting. Write captions for each of your images explaining when and where your art came from, the artist, and the title. Your class might create a bulletin board showing images of war. Vote on which images to include. Try to capture many different types of images.

Project C: Role Playing a Scene from the Novel

Working in groups of two to three students, enact a scene from the novel for your classmates. Your group should choose a scene that you would like to dramatize, and determine who will play which part. As a group, discuss what each character will do and say. While you should restrict your actions to be realistic to the novel, you can add dialog as needed to convey the scene, because much of the novel focuses on what is going on in Henry's mind. For example, you might choose to enact the scene in which Henry and the tattered man helplessly watch Jim Conklin die. The scene you enact should be brief. Do not announce to your audience which scene you are performing. After each group performs their scene from the novel, the rest of the class should try to guess what scene the group has performed. After all groups have performed their scenes, vote on the top three groups you believe enacted scenes most vividly and realistically. You may want to videotape the performances.

Project D: Listening to the Voices of Wartime

While *The Red Badge of Courage* is a work of fiction, there are many nonfiction accounts of war written or told by the people who lived through it. Research the story of someone who lived through a war, and excerpt a paragraph or two that you find describes war in a particularly memorable way. The accounts of many Civil War veterans exist in letters and nonfiction excerpts. You can find such accounts in your school or local library. You might also turn to literature. The British soldiers Rupert Brooke and Wilfred Owen both wrote striking poetry about World War I. You might also choose to find a paragraph or two from Anne Frank's diary or Elie Wiesel's *Night;* both writers experienced the horrors of World War II. You might also choose to interview a family member or friend who has lived through or participated in a war to gather their firsthand experiences.

After you have selected the passage you would like to quote, prepare an oral interpretation of this person's account of war for your classmates. Remember that the effectiveness of your interpretation depends on how you use and vary verbal and nonverbal elements of communication to engage your audience's interest. Practice varying your tone of voice and your pitch aloud and experiment with maintaining eye contact and with making gestures in a mirror before you deliver your oral interpretation.

Glossary

PRONUNCIATION KEY

VOWEL SOUNDS

a	hat	ō	go	ʉ	burn
ā	play	ô	paw, born	ə	extra
ä	star	o͞o	book, put		under
e	then	o͞o	blue, stew		civil
ē	me	oi	boy		honor
i	sit	ou	wow		bogus
ī	my	u	up		

CONSONANT SOUNDS

		l	lip	th	with
b	but	m	money	v	valley
ch	watch	n	on	w	work
d	do	ŋ	song, sink	y	yell
f	fudge	p	pop	z	pleasure
g	go	r	rod		
h	hot	s	see		
j	jump	sh	she		
k	brick				
		t	sit		

abash (ə bash´) *vt.*, destroy the self-possession or self-confidence of

abide (ə bīd´) *vt.*, bear patiently; accept without objection

ab • ject (ab´jekt) *adj.*, cast down in spirit; sunk to or existing in a low state or condition

abom • i • na • ble (ə bəm´nə bəl) *adj.*, of or causing disgust or hatred

ac • cost (ə kôst´) *vt.*, approach and speak in a challenging or aggressive way

ac • cou • tre • ment *or* **ac • cou • ter • ment** (ə ko͞o´trə mənt) *n.*, equipment, trappings

ad • her • ent (ad hir´ənt) *n.*, believer in, especially of a particular idea or church; follower

adroit • ly (ə drôit´lē) *adv.*, skillfully, dexterously

af • fa • bly (a´fə blē) *adv.*, pleasantly; in a friendly manner

ag • gre • ga • tion (a gri gā´shən) *n.*, group, body, or mass composed of many distinct parts or individuals

aghast (ə gast´) *adj.,* struck with terror, amazement, or horror

ague (ā´gyōō) *n.,* fit of shivering

ail • ment (al´mənt) *n.,* bodily disorder or chronic disease

air • i • ly (ar´ə lē) *adv.,* in a light and graceful manner; proudly

al • leged (ə lejd´) *adj.,* asserted without proof or before proving

al • ter • ca • tion (äl tər kā´shən) *n.,* noisy heated angry dispute or quarrel

an • ec • dote (a´nik dōt) *n.,* short account of an interesting, amusing, or biographical incident

an • ni • hi • late (ə nī´ə lāt) *vt.,* cause to cease to exist; kill

an • tag • o • nist (an ta´gə nist) *n.,* one that contends with or opposes another

an • tag • o • nize (an ta´gə nīz) *vt.,* act in opposition to; provoke the hostility of

ap • pall • ing (ə pôl´iŋ) *adj.,* inspiring horror, dismay, or disgust

ar • dor (är´dər) *n.,* extreme vigor or energy; zeal

ar • ray (ə rā´) *n.,* grouping or arrangement

ash • en (a´shən) *adj.,* resembling ashes (as in color); deadly pale

as • sail (ə sāl´) *vt.,* attack violently with blows or words

as • sent (ə sent´) *n.,* agreement; consent

a • ver • sion (ə vər´zhən) *n.,* feeling of repulsion or distaste toward something with a desire to avoid or turn from it

ban • dy (ban´dē) *vt.,* toss from side to side carelessly

barb (bärb) *n.,* biting or pointedly critical remark or comment

bar • ri • cade (bar´ə kād) *n.,* barrier thrown up across a way or passage to check the advance of the enemy

bask (bask) *vi.,* take pleasure or obtain enjoyment

bat • ed (bāt´əd) *adj.,* restrained; reduced in force or intensity

bawl (bôl) *vi.,* cry out at the top of one's voice

bay (bā) *n.,* position of one unable to retreat and forced to face danger

be • drag • gled (bi dra´gəld) *adj.,* soiled and stained by or as if by trailing in mud

be • la • bor (bi lā´bər) *vt.,* attack verbally

be • rate (bi rāt´) *vt.,* scold or condemn strongly and at length

be • seech (bi sēch´) *vt.,* beg for urgently or anxiously

be • set (bi set´) *vi.,* set upon; attack

be • wil • der (bi wil´dər) *vt.,* perplex or confuse

bil • low • ing (bi´lō iŋ) *adj.,* rising or rolling in waves

blanch (blanch) *vi.,* become white or pale

blar • ing (blar´iŋ) *n.,* loud sound

bla • tant (blā´t'nt) *adj.,* completely obvious, conspicuous, or obtrusive especially in a crass or offensive manner

bleat (blēt) *vi.,* whimper; talk complainingly or with a whine

blithe (blīth) *adj.,* lighthearted; merry

blus • ter (blus´tər) *n.,* violent commotion

bom • bast (bəm´bast) *n.,* pretentious inflated speech or writing

brass (bras) *n.,* bold self-assurance

bra • zen (brā´z'n) *adj.,* marked by contemptuous boldness

bris • tle (bri´səl) *vi.,* take on an aggressive attitude or appearance

brood (bro͞od) *vi.,* dwell gloomily on a subject

ce • ler • i • ty (sə ler´ə tē) *n.,* quickness of motion or action

clam • or (kla´mər) *vi.,* become loudly insistent

clan • nish (kla´nish) *adj.,* of or relating to a close group

co • her • ent (cō hir´ənt) *adj.,* logically ordered; consistent

com • mis • er • a • tion (kə mi zə rā´shən) *n.,* sympathy; compassion

com • mon • place (kə´mən plās) *n.,* something commonly found

com • mo • tion (kə mō´shən) *n.,* excitement or confusion

com • pre • hen • sive • ly (kôm pri hen(t)´siv lē) *adv.,* completely or broadly

com • punc • tion (kəm pəŋ(k)´shən) *n.,* anxiety arising from awareness of guilt

con • ceit (kən sēt´) *n.,* fanciful idea

con • cil • i • ate (kən si´lē āt) *vt.,* gain (as goodwill) by pleasing acts

con • cil • i • at • ing (kən si´lē āt iŋ) *adj.,* compatible; reconciling; appeasing

con • de • scen • sion (kən di sen(t)´shən) *n.,* voluntary descent from one's rank or dignity in relations with an inferior

con • sign (kən sīn´) *vt.,* give, transfer, or deliver into the hands or control of another; commit to a final destination or fate

con • ster • na • tion (kôn stər nā´shən) *n.,* amazement or dismay that hinders or throws into confusion

con • tem • pla • tive (kən tem´plə tiv) *adj.,* marked by or given to thought or consideration

con • tor • tion (kən tôr´shən) *n.,* violent twist; twisted, strained shape

con • triv • ance (kən trī´vən(t)s) *n.,* artificial arrangement or development

con • ven • tion • al (kôn ven´shən əl) *adj.,* ordinary, commonplace

con • vul • sive (kən vəl´siv) *adj.,* violent, sudden, frantic, or spasmodic

coun • te • nance (kaun´t'n ən(t)s) *n.,* look, expression

co • vert • ly (kō´vərt lē) *adv.,* not openly; secretly

cra • ven (krā´vən) *adj.,* lacking the least bit of courage

creed (krēd) *n.,* set of fundamental beliefs; guiding principle

cre • scen • do (krə shen´dō) *n.,* a gradual increase, especially in reference to music

crone (krōn) *n.,* withered old woman

daunt • less (dônt´ləs) *adj.,* fearless

dead • ened (de´d'nd) *adj.,* impaired in vigor or sensation

de • bauch (di bôch´) *n.,* corrupt activity

dec • la • ma • tion (de klə mā´shən) *n.,* behavior toward others; outward manner

de • flec • tion (di flek´shən) *n.,* turning aside or off course

de • jec • tion (di jek´shən) *n.,* lowness of spirits

de • lib • er • a • tion (di li´bə rā´shən) *n.,* consideration, thought

de • lir • i • ous • ly (di lir´ē əs lē) *adv.,* in an irrational manner

de • lir • i • um (di lir´ē əm) *n.,* frenzied excitement

de • mure (di myur´) *adj.,* reserved, modest, serious

de • note (di nōt´) *vt.,* make known

de • nounce (di naun(t)s´) *vt.,* declare publicly to be blameworthy or evil

de • nun • ci • a • tion (di nən(t) sē ā´shən) *n.,* public condemnation

de • plet • ed (di plēt´əd) *adj.,* reduced in number

dep • re • cat • ing (de´pri kāt iŋ) *adj.,* playing down; making little of

de • ri • sion (di ri´zhən) *n.,* the use of ridicule or scorn to show contempt

de • ri • sive (di rī´siv) *adj.,* expressing or causing scorn or mockery

de • spi • ca • ble (di spi´kə bəl) *adj.,* so worthless or obnoxious as to rouse moral indignation

de • spon • dent (di spən´dənt) *adj.,* feeling or showing extreme discouragement, dejection, or depression

dev • o • tee (de vô tē´) *n.,* ardent follower, supporter, or enthusiast (as of a religion, art form, or sport)

dex • ter • ous • ly (dek´stə rəs lē) *adv.,* skillfully

din • gy (din´jē) *adj.,* dirty, shabby

dis • cern (di sərn´) *vt.,* detect with the eyes

dis • clos • ing (dis klōz´iŋ) *adj.,* exposing to view; revealing

dis • com • fit • ed (dis kum´fət əd), *n.,* the defeated in battle

dis • cre • tion (dis kre´shən) *n.,* ability to make responsible decisions

dis • dain (dis dān´) *vt.,* refuse or abstain from because of scorn; contempt, scorn

dis • may (dis mā´) *vt.,* deprive of courage or resolution through fear or anxiety

dis • sec • tion (di sek´shən) *n.,* act or process of analyzing and interpreting something in detail

di • ver • sion (də vər´zhən) *n.,* attack that draws the attention and force of an enemy from the point of the main operation

doc • ile (də´səl) *adj.,* easily led or managed; obedient

dog (dôg) *vt.,* hunt or track like a dog

dog • ged • ly (dô´gəd lē) *adv.,* in a manner marked by stubborn determination

dog • ger • el (dô´gə rəl) *n.,* verse styled for comic effect or to mock

dog • ging (dôg´iŋ) *adj.*, worrying, pursuing as a dog does prey

dole • ful (dōl´fəl) *adj.*, full of grief

drawn (drôn) *adj.*, showing the effects of tension, pain, or illness

drea • ry (drir´ē) *adj.*, feeling, displaying, or reflecting listlessness or discouragement

dumb • found *or* **dum • found** (dəm faund´) *vt.*, perplex; puzzle

dun (dun) *adj.*, having a dull grayish yellow color

ed • dy (e´dē) *vi.*, move in a circle, like a whirlpool

ed • i • fice (e´dəfəs) *n.*, building

ef • face (e fās´) *vt.*, cause to vanish

ela • tion (e lā´shən) *n.*, extreme joy

el • o • quent (e´lə kwənt) *adj.*, marked by forceful and fluent expression

e • nam • eled (e na´məld) *adj.*, covered with a glossy, hard surface

en • deav • or (en de´vər) *n.*, serious determined effort

en • dow (en dau´) *vt.*, provide with something freely or naturally

en • grossed (en grōsd´) *adj.*, completely occupied, engaged, or involved

en • gross • ing (en grō´siŋ) *adj.*, occupying the attention completely

en • light • ened (en lī´tend) *adj.*, freed from ignorance and misinformation

en • shrine (en shrīn´) *vt.*, preserve or cherish as sacred

ep • i • thet (e´pə thet) *n.*, disparaging or abusive word or phrase

ethe • re • al (e thir´ē əl) *adj.*, of or relating to the regions beyond the earth

ex • alt (eg zôlt´) *vt.*, raise in rank, power, or character

ex • as • per • at • ed (eg zas´pər āt əd) *adj.*, enraged, irritated, annoyed

ex • er • tion (eg zər´shən) *n.*, laborious or perceptible effort; fatiguing effort

ex • hor • ta • tion (ek sôr tā´shən) *n.*, language intended to incite and encourage

ex • pen • di • ture (ek spen´di chər) *n.*, act or process of expending; outlay

ex • ple • tive (ek´splə tiv) *n.*, exclamatory word or phrase, especially a swear or a curse

ex • tri • cate (ek´strə kāt) *vt.*, free or remove from an entaglement or difficulty

ex • ul • tant (eg zul´tənt) *adj.*, filled with or expressing great joy or triumph

fa • ce • tious (fə sē´shəs) *adj.*, joking or jesting often inappropriately

fal • ter • ing (fôl´tər iŋ) *n.*, weak or broken stammer or hesitation

fath • om (fa´thəm) *vt.*, penetrate and come to understand

feign (fān) *vi.*, pretend

fe • lic • i • tate (fi li´sə tāt) *vt.*, offer congratulations to

flinch (flinch) *vt.*, withdraw or shrink from or as if from pain

floun • der (floun´dər) *vi.*, struggle to move or obtain footing; thrash about wildly

flout (flout) *vt.*, treat with contemptuous disregard; scorn

flush (fləsh) *vi.*, blush

fo • liage (fō´lē ij) *n.*, cluster of leaves, flowers, and branches

for • mi • da • ble (fôr´mə də bəl) *adj.*, having qualities that discourage approach or attack; causing fear, dread, or apprehension

for • mu • la (fôr´myо̄о̄ lə) *n.*, conventionalized statement intended to express some fundamental truth or principle

for • ti • tude (fôr´tə tо̄о̄d) *n.*, strength of mind that enables a person to encounter danger or bear pain or adversity with courage

fra • cas (frā´kəs) *n.*, noisy quarrel; brawl

fren • zied • ly (fren´zēd lē) *adv.*, in a furious and wild manner

fret (fret) *vi.*, become vexed or worried

fringe (frinj) *n.*, edge

fume (fyо̄о̄m) *vi.*, be in a state of excited irritation or anger

fur • row (fər´ō) *n.*, trench in the earth, usually made by a plow

gab • ble (ga´bəl) *vt.*, say with incoherent rapidity; babble

gait (gāt) *n.*, manner of walking or moving on foot

gall • ing (gô´liŋ) *adj.*, especially irritating

gaunt (gônt) *adj.,* excessively thin and angular

ges • tic • u • late (je sti´kyo͞o lāt) *vi.,* make gestures especially when speaking

gild • ed (gil´dəd) *adj.,* overlaid with or as if with gold; given an attractive but sometimes deceptive appearance

gird (gərd) *vt.,* encircle; surround

glib • ness (glib´nəs) *n.,* ease and fluency in speaking or writing often to the point of being insincere or deceitful

glint • ing (glint´iŋ) *adj.,* reflecting in brilliant flashes; gleaming

gory (gōr´e) *adj.,* bloodstained

griev • ous (grē´vəs) *adj.,* serious; burdensome

grove (grōv) *n.,* small wood without underbrush

gy • rate (jī´rāt) *vi.,* swing with a circular or spiral motion

hag • gard (ha´gərd) *adj.,* having a worn or emaciated appearance

ha • rangue (hə raŋ´) *vi.,* make a ranting speech

ha • rass (hə ras´) *vt.,* annoy persistently

ha • ven (hā´vən) *n.,* place of safety

head • long (hed lôŋ´) *adv.,* headfirst

heave (hēv) *vi.,* rise and fall rhythmically

heed • less (hēd´ləs) *adj.,* inconsiderate, thoughtless

he • ral • dic (he ral´dik) *adj.,* of or relating to a bearer of news

here • to • fore (hir´tə fōr) *adv.,* up to this time

horde (hōrd) *n.,* crowd or throng

ilk (ilk) *n.,* sort, kind

im • ma • te • ri • al (i mə tir´ē əl) *adj.,* of no substantial consequence; unimportant

im • pel (im pel´) *vt.,* force

im • pend • ing (im pend´iŋ) *adj.,* about to occur

im • pe • ri • ous (im pir´ē əs) *adj.,* commanding; intensely compelling

im • pe • tus (im´pə təs) *n.,* driving force; stimulus

im • pre • ca • tion (im pri ka´shən) *n.,* curse

im • preg • na • ble (im preg´nə bəl) *adj.,* incapable of being taken by assault; unconquerable

in • dif • fer • ent (in di´fərnt) *adj.*, marked by a lack of interest, enthusiasm, or concern for something

in • dig • nant • ly (in dig´nənt lē) *adv.*, in a righteously angry, or displeased, manner

in • dig • na • tion (in dig nā´shən) *n.*, anger aroused by something unjust, unworthy, or mean

in • fan • tile (in´fən tīl) *adj.*, suitable to or characteristic of an infant; very immature

in • fer • nal (in fər´nəl) *adj.*, of or relating to a nether world of the dead

in • so • lent (in´sə lənt) *adj.*, insultingly contemptuous in speech or conduct

in • ter • mi • na • ble (in tərm´nə bəl) *adj.*, having or seeming to have no end

in • ter • mit • tent (in tər mi´t'nt) *adj.*, coming and going at intervals; not continuous

in • ter • po • si • tion (in tər pə zi´shən) *n.*, interruption; interjection

in • tri • cate (in´tri kət) *adj.*, having many complexly interrelating parts or elements

in • vin • ci • ble (in vin(t)´sə bəl) *adj.*, incapable of being conquered, overcome, or subdued

in • vul • ner • a • bil • I • ty (in vəl nə rə bi´lə tē) *n.*, quality of being immune to attack

iron • i • cal (ī rə´ni kəl) *adj.*, incompatibility between the actual result of a sequence of events and the normal or expected result

jab • ber (ja´bər) *vi.*, talk rapidly, indistinctly, or unintelligibly

jaded (jād´əd) *adj.*, fatigued by overwork; exhausted

jaun • ty (jôn´tē) *adj.*, lively in manner or appearance

jo • vial (jō´vē əl) *adj.*, good-humored; merry

lad • ened (lād´end) *vt.*, heavily loaded

lag (lag) *vi.*, stay or fall behind

lam • en • ta • tion (la mən tā´shən) *n.*, act or instance of mourning, grieving, sobbing

lan • guid (laŋ´gwəd) *adj.*, drooping or flagging from or as if from exhaustion; weak

lan • guor (laŋ´gər) *n.*, weakness or weariness of body or mind

lau • rel (lôr´əl) *n.*, crown of laurel, or the leaves of a plant; honor

lav • ish (la´vish) *adj.*, spending or giving generously

lead • en (le´d'n) *adj.*, of the color of lead, or dull gray; heavy

leer (lēr) *vi.*, glance at sidelong

li • a • ble (lī´bəl) *adj.*, exposed or subject to some usually adverse possibility or action

light (līt) *adj.*, of little importance

liv • id (li´vəd) *adj.*, very angry; enraged; ashen, pale

loi • ter (lôi´tər) *vi.*, remain in an area for no obvious reason

loon (lo͞on) *n.*, lout, idler, simpleton

low • er • ing • ly (lou´ər iŋ lē) *adv.*, in a dark and threatening manner

lu • cid (lo͞o´səd) *adj.*, clear to the understanding

lu • di • crous (lo͞o´də krəs) *adj.*, amusing or laughable through obvious absurdity, incongruity, exaggeration, or eccentricity

lu • gu • bri • ous (lu go͞o´brē əs) *adj.*, exaggeratedly or affectedly mournful or sad

lull (ləl) *n.*, temporary pause or decline in activity

lu • rid (lur´əd) *adj.*, shining with the red glow of fire seen through smoke or cloud; wan and ghastly pale in appearance

lus • ter (lus´tər) *n.*, glow of reflected light

mal • e • dic • tion (ma lə dik´shən) *n.*, curse

ma • ni • a • cal (mə nī´ə kəl) *adj.*, characterized by uncontrollable excitement or frenzy

ma • nip • u • late (mə ni´pyo͞o lāt) *vt.*, control or play upon by artful or unfair means especially to one's own advantage

mar • shal (mär´shəl) *vt.*, place in proper rank or position

me • lee (mā´lā) *n.*, confused struggle; hand-to-hand fight among several people

men • ace (me´nəs) *n.*, show of intention to inflict harm; threat, danger

men • ac • ing (me´nəs iŋ) *adj.*, threatening harm

mere (mēr) *adj.*, being nothing more than

me • thod • i • cal (mə thə´di kəl) *adj.*, habitually proceeding according to order

mire (mīr) *n.*, spongy earth (as of a bog or marsh)

mis • giv • ing (mis gi´viŋ) *n.*, feeling of doubt or suspicion especially concerning a future event

mono • logue (mon´ə log) *n.*, long speech monopolizing conversation

mo • not • o • nous (mə nä´t'n əs) *adj.*, tediously uniform or unvarying

mo • rose (mə rōs´) *adj.*, marked by or expressive of gloom

mor • sel (môr´səl) *n.*, small piece of food; bite

mor • ti • fi • ca • tion (môr tə fə kā´shən) *n.*, sense of humiliation and shame caused by something that wounds one's pride or self-respect

mud • dle (mə´d'l) *n.*, confused mess

muse (myo͞oz) *vi.*, become absorbed in thought; turn something over in the mind meditatively; become absorbed in thought

mus • ter (məs´tər) *vt.*, cause to gather

nip (nip) *vt.*, pinch, bite

non • cha • lant (nôn shə lənt´) *adj.*, having an air of easy unconcern or indifference

ob • du • rate (əb´də rət) *adj.*, stubbornly persistent in wrongdoing

o • blique (ō blēk´) *adj.*, neither perpendicular nor parallel

o • blit • er • ate (ô bli´tə rāt) *vt.*, remove from existence

o • bliv • i • ous (ə bli´vē əs) *adj.*, lacking active conscious knowledge or awareness

om • i • nous (ô´mə nəs) *adj.*, foreboding or foreshadowing something, usually evil

om • i • nous • ly (ə´mə nəs lē) *adv.*, in a manner that threatens evil

on • slaught (on´slot) *n.*, especially fierce attack

o • ra • tion (ô ra´shən) *n.*, elaborate, formal, and dignified speech

or • a • tor • i • cal (ôr ə tôr´i kəl) *adj.*, relating to, or characteristic of, a public speaker or speeches

orb (ôrb) *n.*, eye

o • ver • ture (ō və(r)´chur) *n.*, orchestral introduction to a musical dramatic work

pa • cif • ic (pə si´fik) *adj.*, tending to lessen conflict; peaceable

pae • an (pē´ən) *n.,* joyous song or hymn of praise, tribute, thanksgiving, or triumph

pa • gan (pā´gən) *n.,* follower of a religion that worships more than one god

pal • lor (pa´lər) *n.,* deficiency of color especially of the face

parched (pärcht) *adj.,* deprived of natural moisture; thirsty

par • ox • ysm (par´ək si zəm) *n.,* fit, attack, or sudden increase or recurrence of symptoms

pas • sive • ly (pa´siv lē) *adv.,* in a manner that lacks energy or will

pa • thos (pā´thôs) *n.,* element in experience or in artistic representation evoking pity or compassion

pa • tron • iz • ing (pā´trə nīz iŋ) *adj.,* treating haughtily or coolly

peal (pēl) *vt.,* chime, ring out

pee • vish (pē´vish) *adj.,* marked by ill-temper

pelt • ing (pelt´iŋ) *n.,* succession of blows or missiles

per • am • bu • late (pər am´byo͞o lāt) *vt.,* travel on foot; stroll

per • chance (pər chan(t)s´) *adv.,* perhaps, possibly

per • func • to • ri • ly (pər fəŋ(k)´tə rə lē) *adv.,* without interest or enthusiasm

per • func • to • ry (pər fəŋ(k) tə rē) *adj.,* characterized by routine or superficiality; mechanical

per • il • ous (per´ə ləs) *adj.,* dangerous

pert (pərt) *adj.,* rudely free and forward

per • tur • ba • tion (pər tər bā´shən) *n.,* disturbance, uneasiness

pes • ti • len • tial (pes tə len(t)´shəl) *adj.,* deadly

pet • u • lant • ly (pe´chə lənt lē) *adv.,* characterized by temporary ill humor

phi • lip • pic (fə li´pik) *n.,* discourse or declamation full of bitter condemnation; tirade

pic • tur • esque (pik chə resk´) *adj.,* resembling a picture; charming or quaint in appearance

pil • fer (pil´fər) *vt.,* steal

plain • tive • ly (plān´tiv lē) *adv.,* in a manner expressing woe or suffering

poi • gnant (pôi´nyənt) *adj.*, designed to make an impression

pomp • ous (pəm´pəs) *adj.*, having or exhibiting self-importance; arrogant

pomp • ous • ly (päm´pəs lē) *adv.*, arrogantly; in a self-important manner

por • tal (pōr´təl,) *n.*, door, entrance

por • ten • tous (pôr ten´təs) *adj.*, grave or serious

pos • ture (pôs´chər) *n.*, position or bearing of the body

preg • nant (preg´nənt) *adj.*, full, teeming

pre • sume (pri zo͞om´) *vt.*, expect or assume especially with confidence

prime (prīm) *vt.*, instruct beforehand; coach

probe (prōb) *vt.*, search into and explore with great thoroughness

pro • ces • sion (prə se´shən) *n.*, group of individuals moving along in an orderly often ceremonial way

prod • i • gal (prə´di gəl) *adj.*, recklessly extravagant

pro • di • gious (prə di´jəs) *adj.*, exciting amazement or wonder

pro • found (prə faund´) *adj.*, coming from, reaching to, or situated at a depth; having intellectual depth and insight

pro • fuse (prə fyo͞os´) *adj.*, exhibiting great abundance

prom • i • nence (prô´mə nən(t)s) *n.*, quality, state, or fact of being noticeable or conspicuous; greatness, distinction, importance

prom • i • nent (prô´mə nənt) *adj.*, readily noticeable

pro • phet • ic (prə fe´tik) *adj.*, foretelling events; predictive

pros • pect (prə´spekt) *n.*, place that commands an extensive view; mental picture of something to come

pro • spec • tive (prə spek´tiv) *adj.*, likely to come about; expected

pros • trate (prô´strāt) *adj.*, completely overcome and lacking vitality, will, or power to rise; *vt.*, put in a humble and submissive posture or state

prov • ince (pro´vints) *n.*, proper or appropriate function or scope; department of knowledge or activity

prow • ess (prau´əs) *n.*, distinguished bravery; especially military valor and skill

prox • im • i • ty (prək si´mə tē) *n.*, closeness

pulp (pulp) *n.,* soft mass of vegetable matter

purl (pərl) *vi.,* eddy, swirl

quail (kwā(ə)l) *vi.,* draw back in dread or terror; cower

qua • ver • ing (kwā´və riŋ) *adj.,* trembling

quer • u • lous (kwer´yo͞o ləs) *adj.,* habitually complaining; whining

rail (rāl) *vi.,* scold in harsh, insolent, or abusive language

ral • ly (ra´lē) *vt.,* arouse for action; rouse from depression or weakness

ral • ly • ing (ra´lē iŋ) *adj.,* arousing for action

re • con • noi • ter (rē kə nôi´tər) *vi.,* engage in observation or inspection

re • doubt • able (ri dau´tə bəl) *adj.,* illustrious; worthy of respect; causing fear or alarm

reel (rēl) *vi.,* waver; walk or move unsteadily

re • it • er • ate (rē i´tər āt) *vt.,* state or do over again or repeatedly sometimes with wearying effect

re • li • ance (ri lī´ən(t)s) *n.,* confidence

re • lin • quish (ri liŋ´kwish) *vt.,* give up

re • mon • strance (ri mən(t)´strən(t)s) *n.,* earnest presentation of reasons for opposition or protest

ren • dez • vous (rän´di vo͞o) *n.,* place appointed for assembling or meeting

rent (rent) *n.,* rip, tear

re • pose (ri pōz´) *n.,* state of resting after activity or strain

re • proach (ri prōch´) *n.,* expression of blame or disapproval

re • proof (ri pro͞of) *n.,* criticism for a fault

re • spite (res´pət) *n.,* period of rest or relief

re • splen • dent (ri splen´dənt) *adj.,* shining brilliantly; characterized by a glowing splendor

res • tive (res´tiv) *adj.,* stubbornly resisting control

re • sume (ri zo͞om´) *vt.,* return to or begin again after interruption

ret • ri • bu • tion (re trə byo͞o´shən) *n.,* dispensing or receiving of reward or punishment

rev • e • la • tion (re və la´shən) *n.,* act of revealing or communicating divine truth

re • ver • ber • a • tion (ri vər bə rā´shən) *n.,* act of echoing or resounding

rev • er • ie (re´və rē) *n.,* daydream

rid • dled (rid´ləd) *adj.,* pierced with many holes

ri • ot • ous (rī´ə təs) *adj.,* violent, disorderly

ri • vet (ri´vət) *vt.,* fasten firmly

ro • bust (rō bəst´) *adj.,* having or showing power, strength, or firmness; healthy

rue • ful • ly (roo´fə lē) *adv.,* mournfully, regretfully

sa • ga • cious (sə gā´shəs) *adj.,* of keen and farsighted penetration and judgment

salve (sav) *n.,* healing or soothing influence or instrument

sar • don • ic (sär də´nik) *adj.,* disdainfully or skeptically humorous

scoff (skôf) *vt.,* show contempt; mock

scrim • mage (skri´mij) *n.,* minor battle; confused fight

scru • ti • nize (skroo´t'n īz) *vt.,* examine closely and minutely

scru • ti • ny (skroo´tə nē) *n.,* searching study, inquiry, or inspection

sec • u • lar (se´kyə lər) *adj.,* not overtly or specifically religious

seeth • ing (sēth´iŋ) *adj.,* be in a state of rapid agitated movement

sem • blance (sem´blən(t)s) *n.,* outward appearance or show

sham (sham) *n.,* cheap falseness

shirk (shʉrk) *vi.,* evade the performance of an obligation

si • dle (sī´d'l) *vi.,* go or move with one side foremost, especially in a furtive advance

sin • is • ter (si´nəs tər) *adj.,* accompanied by or leading to disaster

sin • u • ous (sin´yə wəs) *adj.,* of a snakelike or wavy form

slink (sliŋk) *vi.,* move stealthily or furtively (as in fear or shame)

so • ber (sō´bər) *adj.,* subdued in tone or color

souse (sous) *vt.,* plunge in liquid; immerse

spare (spār) *adj.,* healthily lean

spas • mod • ic (spaz mô´dik) *adj.,* affected or characterized by involuntary muscular contractions

spec • ter (spek´tər) *n.*, ghost; something that haunts or perturbs the mind

sprint • er (sprint´ər) *n.*, person who runs a fast race for a short distance

sten • to • ri • an (sten tōr´ē ən) *adj.*, extremely loud

sto • ic (stō´ik) *n.*, one apparently or professedly indifferent to pleasure or pain

stol • id (stô´ləd) *adj.*, having or expressing little or no sensibility; unemotional

stout • ly (stout´lē) *adv.*, bravely, boldly

stow (stō) *vt.*, put away for future use; store

stu • pen • dous (stu pen´dəs) *adj.*, causing astonishment or wonder

stu • por (stoo´pər) *n.*, state of extreme dullness or inactivity resulting often from stress or shock

sub • dued (səb dood´) *adj.*, lacking in vitality, intensity, or strength

sub • ject (səb jekt´) *vt.*, bring under control or dominion

sub • lime (sə blīm´) *adj.*, lofty, grand, or exalted in thought, expression, or manner

suc • cor (sə´kər) *n.*, relief, help, aid

suf • fuse (sə fyooz´) *vt.*, spread over or through in the manner of fluid or light

sul • len (sə´lən) *adj.*, gloomily or resentfully silent or repressed

sul • try (səl´trē) *adj.*, hot with passion or anger

surge (sərj) *n.*, swelling, rolling, or sweeping forward like that of a wave

sur • ly (sər´lē) *adj.*, menacing or threatening in appearance

sur • mount (sər maunt´) *vt.*, stand or lie at the top of

swash • buck • ler (swəsh´bə klər) *n.*, daring soldier or adventurer

tab • leau (ta´blō) *n.*, graphic description or representation; picture

tan • ta • lize (tan´t'l īz) *vt.*, tease or torment

te • mer • i • ty (tə mer´ə tē) *n.*, unreasonable or foolhardy contempt of danger or opposition

tem • pest (tem´pəst) *n.,* violent storm

thor • ough • fare (thər´ō far) *n.,* way or place for passage

throe (thrō) *n.,* pang, spasm

throng (thrôn) *n.,* large number of assembled persons; crowd together in great numbers

tid • ing (tī´din) *n.,* piece of news

tot • ter • ing (tô´tər in) *adj.,* being in an unstable condition

tou • sled (tau´zəld) *adj.,* disheveled; rumpled

tran • quil (tran´kwəl) *adj.,* free from agitation of mind or spirit

treach • ery (tre´chə rē) *n.,* violation of allegiance or of faith and confidence; treason

trep • i • da • tion (tre pə dā´shən) *n.,* fearful uncertain agitation

trough (trôf) *n.,* conduit, drain, or channel for water

trudge (trəj) *vi.,* walk or march steadily on

trun • dle (trən´d'l) *vt.,* roll; transport in or as if in a wheeled vehicle

tur • bu • lent (tər´byo͞o lənt) *adj.,* causing unrest, violence, or disturbance

un • daunt • ed (ən dôn´təd) *adj.,* courageous and determined in the face of danger or difficulty

un • fal • ter • ing (ən fôl´tə rin) *adj.,* firm; not weakening

un • gain • ly (ən gān´lē) *adj.,* clumsy, awkward

un • scathed (ən skāt͟hd´) *adj.,* wholly unharmed; not injured

un • scru • pu • lous (un skro͞o´pyə ləs) *adj.,* unethical, dishonest

ut • ter (ə´tər) *adj.,* carried to the utmost point or highest degree; total

val • iant (val´yənt) *adj.,* possessing or acting with bravery or boldness; courageous

van • i • ty (va nə´tē) *n.,* something that is vain, empty, or valueless

veil (vā(ə)l) *vt.,* cover, provide, obscure, or conceal with or as if with a veil

vex • a • tion (vek sā´shən) *n.,* irritation

vi • and (vī´ənd) *n.,* item of food, especially a choice or tasty dish

vig • i • lance (vi´jə lən(t)s) *n.,* quality or state of being alertly watchful, especially to avoid danger

vin • di • ca • tion (vin də kā´shən) *n.*, justification against denial or censure

vis • age (vi´zij) *n.*, face, countenance, or appearance of a person

vi • tal • ly (vī´t'l ē) *adv.*, in a manner that is destructive to life; mortally; fatally

vo • cif • er • ous (vō si´fər us) *adj.*, noisy, loud

wal • low (wô´lō) *vi.*, roll oneself about in an lazy or clumsy manner

wane (wān) *vi.*, decrease in size, extent, or degree

well (wel) *vi.*, rise like a flood of liquid

wend (wend) *vi.*, travel

wheel (wēl) *vt.*, cause to change direction as in a circle

with • al (wi thôl´) *adv.*, together with this; besides

wood • en • ly (wu´d'n lē) *adv.*, in an awkwardly stiff manner

wrath (rath) *n.*, strong vengeful anger

Handbook of Literary Terms

Character. A **character** is a person or animal who takes part in the action of a literary work. The main character is called the protagonist. A character who struggles against the main character is called an antagonist. Characters can also be classified as major characters or minor characters. Major characters are ones who play important roles in a work. Minor characters are ones who play less important roles. A *one-dimensional character, flat character*, or *caricature* is one who exhibits a single quality, or character trait. A *three-dimensional, full*, or *rounded character* is one who seems to have all the complexities of an actual human being.

Characterization. **Characterization** is the act of creating or describing a character. Writers use three major techniques to create a character: direct description, portraying the character's behavior, and presenting the thoughts and emotions of the character. Direct description allows the reader to learn about such matters as the character's appearance, habits, dress, background, personality, and motivations through the comments of a speaker, a narrator, or another character. The writer might present the actions and speech of the character, allowing the reader to draw his or her own conclusions from what the character says or does. The writer might also reveal the character's private thoughts and emotions. See *character*.

Cliché. A **cliché** is an overused expression such as *happy as a lark* or *time is money*. Most clichés begin as vivid, colorful expressions but become uninteresting because of overuse.

Conflict. A **conflict** is a struggle between two people or things in a literary work. A plot is formed around conflict. A conflict can be internal or external. A struggle that takes place between a character and some outside force such as another character, society, or nature is called an *external conflict*. A struggle that takes place within a character is called an *internal conflict*.

Crisis. The **crisis**, or turning point, is the point in a plot when something happens to determine the future course of events and the eventual fate of the main character.

Description. A **description** gives a picture in words of a character, object, or scene. Descriptions make use of sensory details—words and phrases that describe how things look, sound, smell, taste, or feel.

Foreshadowing. **Foreshadowing** is the act of hinting at events that will happen later in a poem, story, or play.

Irony. **Irony** is a difference between appearance and reality.

Metaphor. A **metaphor** is a figure of speech in which one thing is spoken or written about as if it were another. This figure of speech invites the reader to make a comparison between the two things.

Narrator. A **narrator** is a person or character who tells a story. Works of fiction almost always have a narrator. The narrator in a work of fiction may be a major or minor character or simply someone who witnessed or heard about the events being related.

Plot. The parts of a plot are as follows: The *exposition* is the part of a plot that provides background information about the characters, setting, or conflict. The *inciting incident* is the event that introduces the central conflict. The *rising action*, or complication, develops the conflict to a high point of intensity. The *climax* is the high point of interest or suspense in the story. The *falling action* is all the events that follow the climax. The *resolution* is the point at which the central conflict is ended, or resolved. The *dénouement* is any material that follows the resolution and that ties up loose ends.

Point of view. **Point of view** is the vantage point from which a story is told. If a story is told from the first-person point of view, the narrator uses the pronouns *I* and *we* and is a part of or a witness to the action. When a story is told from a third-person point of view, the narrator is outside the action; uses words such *as he, she, it,* and *they*; and avoids the use of *I* and *we.* In some stories, the narrator's point of view is *limited.* In such stories the narrator can reveal his or her own private, internal thoughts or those of a single character. In other stories, the narrator's point of view is *omniscient,* or all-knowing, meaning that the narrator can reveal the private, internal thoughts of any character.

Protagonist. A **protagonist** is the main character in a story. The protagonist faces a struggle or conflict.

Realism. **Realism** is the attempt to present in art or literature an accurate picture of reality.

Suspense. Suspense is a feeling of anxiousness or curiosity. Writers create suspense by raising questions in the reader's mind and by using details that create strong emotions.

Symbol. A **symbol** is a thing that stands for or represents both itself and something else. Some traditional symbols include doves for peace; the color green for jealousy; the color purple for royalty; winter, evening, or night for old age; roses for beauty; roads or paths for the journey through life; and owls for wisdom.